The Advocate's Homicides

Teresa Burrell

Silent Thunder Publishing
San Diego

This book is a work of fiction. References to real people, events, establishments, organizations, or locales are intended only to provide a sense of authenticity and are used fictitiously. All other characters and all incidents and dialogue are drawn from the author's imagination and are not to be construed as real.

Cover Art by Madeline Settle
Edited by Marilee Wood

Library of Congress Number: 2016912589
ISBN: 978-1-938680-21-2

Silent Thunder Publishing
San Diego

Dedication

To my brother Don Johnson,
who will always remain a giant of a man
and a phenomenal brother
in my mind and in my heart.
We miss you every day.

Acknowledgements

A special thanks to those who helped make this book possible.

Chris Broesel
Apollo Madrigal
Brian Settle
Corey Thomas
Robin Thomas

My Wonderful Beta Readers
You are all so amazing!

Beth Sisel Agejew
Linda Arterberry
Linda Athridge-Langille
Vickie Barrier
Nancy Barth
Susan Intermoia
Marilyn LaFiura
Joy Lorton
John McCoy
Jill Parseghian
Rodger Peabody
Lily Qualls Morales
Colleen Scott
Heather Siani
Loretta Simons
Jodi Thomas
Sandy Thompson
Nikki Tomlin
Brad Williams
Denise Zendel

THE ADVOCATE SERIES

THE ADVOCATE (Book 1)

THE ADVOCATE'S BETRAYAL (Book 2)

THE ADVOCATE'S CONVICTION (Book 3)

THE ADVOCATE'S DILEMMA (Book 4)

THE ADVOCATE'S EX PARTE (Book5)

THE ADVOCATE'S FELONY (Book 6)

THE ADVOCATE'S GEOCACHE (Book 7)

THE ADVOCATE'S HOMICIDES (Book 8)

THE ADVOCATE'S ILLUSION (Book 9)

THE ADVOCATE'S JUSTICE (Book 10)

THE TUPER MYSTERY SERIES

THE ADVOCATE'S FELONY
(Book 6 of The Advocate Series)

MASON'S MISSING (Book 1)

FINDING FRANKIE (Book 2)

Part I:

Tray Copley's Case

Chapter 1

Three Years Ago...

Homicide Detective Greg Nelson leaned over the dead body in the shallow grave and touched the arm with his gloved hand. The male corpse was greenish in color. "Looks like he's been here awhile, at least a few days. Rigor has come and gone. I'd say he's been dead about a week but definitely less than a month."

"How do you know that?" Detective Smothers asked.

"His color points to about a week. He still has his hair, nails, and teeth, so I'm guessing less than a month. But it depends on how long he's been buried here. He could've been preserved somewhere before he was buried. The coroner will be able to determine the time."

Smothers wrinkled his nose. "He's in pretty bad shape, and he sure doesn't smell very good."

"Is this your first body, Detective?"

"My first in the field. I've seen some in the morgue."

Nelson wiggled his tie to loosen it. "Where's the man who found him?"

"Over there." Smothers pointed to an unshaven, scruffy-looking man standing near a tree with a boy who looked to be ten or eleven years old. They stood just beyond the yellow tape that had been tied to the trees encircling the grave.

"Was the kid with him?"

"Afraid so."

Nelson glanced around at the cops walking the premises. "Has anyone found anything else?"

"Nothing earth shaking—a couple of animal bones and a lot of trash. The dogs are on their way."

Nelson pulled his gloves off and walked over to the man and the young boy. "I'm Detective Greg Nelson." Nelson reached out his hand and the man shook it but didn't respond. "What are your names?"

"Sorry." He exhaled. "I'm Jerry Bartlett and this is my son Joey."

"Which one of you found the body?"

"We were together, but I saw it first," Jerry said.

Joey looked terrified. "Perhaps I should talk to you alone," Nelson said, nodding toward the boy.

Jerry looked at his frightened son, "Good idea."

Nelson signaled for an officer standing about ten feet away. She walked over to them. "Officer Barnes, will you please take young Joey here for a little walk outside the perimeter while I talk to his father. He's had a rough morning."

When they left, Nelson said, "Please tell me what happened."

"My son and I were camping about a mile from here. We were hiking, as we often do, and Joey had to take a whizz. There was no one around, so he went right there." He pointed to the gravesite. "And when he did, it washed away some of the dirt on the hand. I saw what looked like a finger sticking out of the ground."

"There was more than a finger exposed when we got here. Did you dig around it?"

"I always carry a small hand shovel in my backpack. I kept thinking it was some kind of a joke and the hand would be plastic or rubber or something. I used the shovel to remove some of the dirt around it, but then I realized it was real so I stopped and called 9-1-1."

Nelson collected Bartlett's personal information and questioned him a while longer. They both watched as the canine unit drove up and Kruegster, a mahogany-colored malinois with a black face and black ears, jumped out of the car.

"What's the dog for?" Bartlett asked.

"He's trained to look for evidence."

"Do you always use the dogs?"

"No, but it's easier in this kind of setting because there's so much ground to cover."

Nelson asked him a few more questions about his camping trip, such as how often he went to Coyote Ridge and how long he had been there this time. Then he spoke briefly with his son, who corroborated the information.

Nelson was walking back towards the body when the K-9 officer yelled from about sixty feet away. "We have another one!"

Chapter 2

Fourteen-year-old Tray Copley looked up at his attorney, Sabre Brown, who stood about three inches taller than him at five-foot-six. "What if I did something really, really bad?" he asked, and then quickly looked down at his feet.

"Come, sit," Sabre said, as she sat down on the bench in the backyard outside Tray's foster home. He sat down next to her. Tray could have easily passed for ten years old. His dark, curly hair glistened in the sunlight. "Anything you tell me is confidential, so no matter how bad the thing is you did, I still can't tell anyone if you don't want me to."

"Even if it was against the law? I mean, what if I robbed a bank or something? Wouldn't you call the cops?"

"No. I'm bound by what they call 'attorney-client privilege.' As your attorney, I can't tell anyone."

"Really?"

"Yes. Really. When people are charged with a crime, they can tell their attorneys everything without worrying about getting in trouble. Attorneys can provide the best defense when they know everything that has happened."

"So, if I was going to," he paused, "rob a bank or something, I could tell you about it?" He sounded so serious.

Sabre smiled, trying to lighten the mood, quite certain that he wasn't planning to rob a bank. She spoke softly. "Tray, do you plan to rob a bank?"

He smiled uncomfortably and shifted in his seat. "No, of course not."

"Good. The rules are different for things you

haven't already done. If you plan to commit a crime in the future, I can't be any part of that. But if you've already done something bad and it's not ongoing, it will remain confidential."

"What do you mean by 'ongoing'?"

"Like if you robbed that bank and then took a hostage and you were hiding him. I couldn't help you keep him hidden because he would still be at risk." Tray grimaced. She looked directly into his sad eyes. "Tray, have you done something I should know about?"

He shook his head and then turned away. "It's not important." His head turned back toward Sabre. "Do you think the judge will let me and my sister go home tomorrow?"

"Maybe, but it depends on how well your mother is doing. I haven't seen the recommendations from the social worker yet, but the last I heard, your mom was testing clean and going to her twelve-step program. Is that what you want? To go home?"

"Yes. It would be nice—as long as Mom isn't using drugs. She's a good mom when she's not high."

"Your mom is determined to stay clean. Hopefully she can, but if she's not quite ready, then you'll continue to stay at this home with your sister." She hoped that his mother was still clean. She had seen parents fail many times and seen so many disappointed children who couldn't go home because their parents couldn't stop using drugs. "You like it here, don't you?"

His shoulders slumped. "Mr. and Mrs. Longe are nice people, and it's better now that my sister is here, but I still want to go home."

"I know. We'll see how it goes tomorrow at the hearing."

"Thanks for getting my sister here."

"Of course. I know how important it is for you two

to be together."

"Sissy really likes it here and I know June and George—I mean Mr. and Mrs. Longe— really like her too."

"I'm sure they do, but they took her because they wanted to make you happy. They care a lot about you."

The edges of Tray's lips turned up for just a second, but then the sad face set in once again.

Sabre had gotten to know Tray well over the past eight months, even though he hadn't talked a lot at first. Over time, he had started to open up to her. His case had come into the San Diego juvenile dependency system because his mother's boyfriend had molested Tray. He refused to talk about the molestation, but his little sister had seen enough for the court to find dependency jurisdiction in the case. Unfortunately, the standard in criminal court was much higher than dependency court, so the sister's testimony wasn't enough to convict the mother's boyfriend of a crime. All this court could do was try to protect the children.

Upon investigation, it was discovered that the mother was a drug addict and the kids were parenting themselves. Tray was far more than a big brother to his half sister. He made sure she was fed, brushed her teeth, went to school, and did her homework. He acted as her parent when their mother was strung out. Even when she wasn't high Tray took care of his sister, probably out of habit. The social worker thought it would be healthier for Tray not to have so much responsibility, so when they were removed from their home, the worker placed them in separate foster homes. Tray ran away from three different foster homes and ended up in Mary Ellen Wilson Group Home for a while. After about a month in the group home, Tray became very complacent and did whatever he was told to do. Sabre noticed a real change in his personality, and the social worker recommended another foster home placement. The therapist, Dr. Bell, was concerned that Tray's therapy would be interrupted but agreed to the change as long as Tray continued with him in therapy. That's when he went to the Longes' home.

"Where's Shanisha?" Sabre asked.

"She's inside. I'll go get her."

Sabre waited outside. She wondered what Tray was worried about—or worse, what he might be planning. He was a very quiet, polite, and sweet boy, but Sabre knew he carried a lot of sadness within him. She had hoped therapy would bring it out, but sometimes she got the feeling that Tray confided in her more than he did his therapist and that wasn't very much.

Tray returned with his six-year-old sister, holding her hand all the way. In Shanisha's other hand was a drawing on an 8-1/2 by 11 sheet of paper. Cornrows covering the front half of her head led to tight ringlets across the back. She was very shy and stood close to Tray, half hidden by his leg, her dark brown eyes wide.

"Hi, Shanisha. Do you remember me?"

She nodded.

"Your hair is so pretty. Did Mrs. Longe do that for you?"

She nodded again, but this time she smiled. June and George Longe were good foster parents, and their being a bi-racial couple made for a perfect fit with Tray and Shanisha. The children's mother was white and both their fathers were African-American, just like June and George. Neither of the fathers was around at the present time. Shanisha's father was serving time in Donovan State Prison, and Tray hadn't seen his father for over three years.

"That's a beautiful smile you have."

That brought an even bigger grin.

"What do you have in your hand?"

Shanisha handed the drawing to Sabre.

"She made it for you," Tray said.

"Oh my, that's really special." Sabre looked at the drawing with four stick people standing on the left with the sun shining overhead. To the right was a bed with another person lying in it. "Are you in the picture?"

Shanisha pointed to the smallest stick figure standing.

"And is that Tray?" Sabre asked.

"Uh huh," Shanisha murmured.

"And who are those people?"

"June," she said, pointing to the shorter of the two adults. "George." She pointed at the other one.

"And who is this in the bed?"

"Mommy. She's sick."

Tray reached his arm around Shanisha and pulled her a little closer to him.

As they visited, Shanisha began to open up, but she said nothing more about her mother. After a while, Sabre said, "Shanisha, you can go back to your house and play if you'd like."

"I'll take her," Tray said, as he took Shanisha's hand. "Come on, Pooh Bear."

"Thanks, and then I'd like to talk to you a bit more if you don't mind." Sabre watched as they walked away, holding hands until they neared the door, and then Shanisha let go and bolted forward.

Every time Sabre saw the two siblings together, she observed how close they were. Although Sabre agreed that Tray shouldn't be parenting his sister, she had fought to get them back together because she felt the sibling bond was so strong that it was better for both of them. After Tray spent a few months in the

Longe home, the therapist agreed it was healthier to have them together.

Sabre knew Tray was damaged from the molestation. She wondered if he was shaming himself and if that was what he meant by doing something "really bad." Sexual abuse victims often blamed themselves and she feared he had not really dealt with it in therapy. He refused to admit that anything had even happened to him.

When Tray came back and sat down, Sabre said, "I'm ready to listen if you want to tell me the 'really bad' thing you were talking about earlier."

"It was nothin'."

"I hope you're not blaming yourself for what happened to you with that horrible man."

"It's not about that," Tray snapped, his voice low. "It's something else, but nothin' to worry about. Can I go now? I have a new video game I'd like to play."

"Sure."

Sabre watched him as he walked to his back door with his head slumped over.

I wish I could help him, she thought.

Chapter 3

"Dang! That stupid woman!" Sabre spouted just as her best friend, Attorney Bob Clark, approached her in front of Department Four at the San Diego Superior Court, Juvenile Division.

"What's the matter, Sobs?" Bob asked, using his favorite nickname for her. It came from Sabre Orin Brown's initials.

"Your client, that's 'what's the matter.' She's an idiot!"

Bob smirked as Sabre flung her brown, shoulder-length hair off her face. "You'll have to be a little more specific; I have a lot of clients who are idiots. In fact, most of them are idiots. That's why they're here in the first place. So, who is it this time?"

"Jeannine Copley."

"Is she here?"

"I haven't seen her, but I just read the social worker's report."

"I read that a couple of days ago. Jeannine was doing fine. The recommendation was to return the kids."

"There's a supplemental report this morning. It appears your client started using again."

"Mr. Clark," a woman screamed as she stomped down the hallway toward Sabre and Bob.

"And there she is—my lovely, effervescent, sardonic, delusional, narcissistic mother of the year," Bob said before the loud woman reached his side. When she was in earshot, he said, "Good morning, Ms. Copley. Are you looking for me?"

"That social worker is trying to keep my kids from me. I want them back. Today."

"Now, Ms. Copley, you know I'm going to do everything I can for you. We'll march right in there and set this for trial," he said in a tone similar to hers. "Don't you worry; you'll get your day in court."

"I don't want a trial. I want the kids now. She told me they'd be returned today."

"It seems we have a bit of a snag, but as soon as we can get our hands on those drug test results and show you are clean, we'll get those kids home for you."

"They wouldn't test my pee. They said it wasn't mine," Jeannine yelled.

Bob moved his hands in a downward motion gesturing that she speak a little more quietly.

She lowered her voice. "They said it couldn't be mine because it was too cold. But it was."

Bob cocked his head to one side, looked into her dilated eyes, and listened to every word she said as if he believed her. Sabre chuckled. He was so good with his clients and he would fight for them as if he believed them, but he seldom ever bought what they tried selling him.

Bob put his arm around his client's shoulder and led her down the hallway far enough so no one else could hear them.

"So why was the urine cold?"

"Because I brought it from home."

"Why?"

"I have trouble peeing in their stupid little cups, so I did it ahead of time."

"I'll make an argument to the court for your kids to go home today. Probably not the one you just gave me, however. We'll save that one for trial. I don't expect the judge will send your children home today, so you need to be ready for that when we go in there. For now, you need to keep calm. Getting out of control isn't going to help your case, especially in front of the judge.

Understand?"

"Yeah, but I get so tired of her butting into our lives."

"I know, but you have to trust me." He smiled at her. "I know you're having some problems today. I can see it in your eyes."

She started to object, but Bob raised his hand to stop her. "You must let me do all the talking in there. Any outburst in court will go against you."

The bailiff, Michael McCormick, stepped into the hallway and called for the Copley case.

"That's a trial set," Bob said to McCormick.

"Okay, let's just have the attorneys."

Sabre, Bob, and Mike Powers, the attorney for Shanisha's father, all entered the courtroom, took their seats at the table, and waited for the court clerk to find a trial date. When all three attorneys finally agreed on the date, the clerk summoned the judge. Bob stepped outside and came back with his client. The court clerk called the case.

The county counsel sitting at the far left of the table said, "Deputy County Counsel Dave Casey on behalf of the Department of Social Services."

Sabre stood. "Sabre Brown for the minors, Tray and Shanisha Copley, who are not present in court."

Mike Powers, a tall, heavy-set man with curly, salt-and-pepper hair stood up next. "Michael Powers appearing for Shanisha's father, James Darden, who is not present in court."

"Robert Clark, for the mother who is present," Bob said as he rose to his feet. "This is a request for a trial set, Your Honor."

Judge Hekman, a gray-haired woman in her late sixties, stared at Bob and then asked the clerk for the date.

"I'm joining in that request on behalf of the father,"

Mr. Powers said.

Bob remained standing.

"Is there something else, Mr. Clark?" the judge asked.

"There is some concern about the drug testing, Your Honor."

"I know *I'm* concerned about it, Mr. Clark," Judge Hekman said.

Bob ignored her sarcasm, and continued, "My client is asking that the children be returned to her pending the trial. She has been involved in all her programs and her recent unsupervised visits went very well."

"She only had unsupervised visitations under the condition that she test clean—which she is not, Counselor. I'm amending my previous order. There will be no unsupervised visits until the trial. We'll revisit the issue then. You know I'm not going to give her unsupervised visits if she tests dirty," the judge said. "Please explain that to your client."

"What?" Jeannine blurted as she rose to her feet. "That's insane!"

Bob took her arm and tried to ease her back into her seat. The bailiff stepped forward, taking a stance between the mother and the judge. Jeannine yanked her arm away from her attorney.

"You stupid...." Her arms started flailing as she moved toward the judge.

"Sit down," the bailiff shouted, but she pushed him. McCormick dodged to his right, getting only a light blow to his shoulder. He grabbed her by the arm, swung her around, and cuffed her. Three more deputy sheriffs poured into the courtroom and escorted her out.

Bob turned to Sabre. "That went well," he said.

Chapter 4

Sabre entered the juvenile court attorneys' lounge, which was once a storage closet. At the end of the room, opposite the door, stood a large, wooden structure. It had fifty cubbyholes, each of which was approximately ten inches wide, fifteen inches deep, and eight inches high, just large enough to hold file folders or reports. Every cubbyhole was marked with the panel attorney's name and served as their mailbox. On the right side adjacent to the mailboxes were two small padded chairs with an end table between them. The table had two wire baskets. One held the new detention reports in it; the other contained social studies and review reports from the Department of Social Services.

A few minutes later, Bob walked in. "Good morning, Sobs."

"Hey. Are you on detentions today?"

"Yes, are you?"

"No. The public defender has the minors, and I saw Richard Arroyo outside and he said he was on, so it's just you and the silverback."

"That's an interesting nickname."

"He probably got it from you. You're the one who comes up with most of the nicknames around here."

"Not this one. Arroyo got it from that little clerk upstairs in records who had the hots for him—something to do with his animal magnetism."

Sabre chuckled. "This place is so 'middle school.'"

Bob picked up the blue detention petitions and shuffled through them. "There are four new filings this morning. That's the most we've had since the funding cutbacks started."

"I know. The State cut funding at Child Protective Services, leaving the department short of social workers. Then the government claims child abuse is down because there're no petitions filed, when in actuality there is no one there to file the petitions. The ones who are there are so overworked it's ridiculous."

"Uh, huh," Bob said, and continued through his petitions. "A tox baby case. Too routine." He placed the petition at the bottom of his stack and read the next one. "Molest of a four-year-old. Disgusting!" Bob shuffled that one to the bottom. "Aha! Something a little more interesting."

"What is it?" Sabre asked, trying to read the petition over his shoulder.

"The mother is accused of negligence for taking her six-year-old son to work with her."

"What? That's ridiculous. What is she? A drug dealer or something?" She reached for the blue paper in his hand. "Let me see that."

"Better." Bob chuckled as he handed her the petition. "She's a hooker."

Sabre read the attached report. "It says she works at a brothel."

"There's a brothel here in San Diego? How do I not know about that?"

Sabre smacked him lightly on the arm. "You dork." Then she went on reading. "And the other women kept him busy while she was with a client."

"Lucky six-year-old," Bob muttered.

"They let him play video games and would read to him sometimes."

"Can you imagine how they'll keep him occupied when he's a teenager?" He reached for the report Sabre was reading. "And where is this brothel, anyway?"

"It was in East County, not that far from where you live, but it's been shut down. Apparently, four working women lived in the house."

"I want the mom on this case. I'll bet I could win it."

An announcement came over the loudspeaker. "Attorney Sabre Brown, please come to Department Three."

"Department Three? That's Judge Trapnell's courtroom. I don't have a delinquency case this morning."

"Or maybe you do. A rerun perhaps?"

"It's possible." She gathered up her files. "Have fun with your hooker mom. I'll see you later."

When Sabre walked into Department Three, Judge Trapnell was on the bench, the clerk and the bailiff sat at their desks, the Deputy DA was in her seat, and panel attorney Chris Firmstone was standing behind the counsel table. Everyone stopped talking when she walked in, giving her an uncomfortable feeling.

"Ms. Brown, thanks for coming," Judge Trapnell said.

"No problem. What can I do for you?"

"I understand you represent Tray Copley in the dependency matter. Is that correct?"

"Yes, he's a good kid. Has something happened to him?"

"A petition was just filed on him. Mr. Firmstone was appointed to represent him, but when Mr. Firmstone went to see the minor, Tray wouldn't talk to him. I can't imagine some kid not relating to 'curly-haired, surfer-boy' Firmstone, can you?" In typical Judge Trapnell fashion, he didn't wait for an answer. "When Tray came into court, he said he wanted his 'old' attorney. *His* words, not mine. That would be you, Ms. Brown. He says he'll only talk to *you*."

"I'll gladly speak with him. Where is he?"

"He's in the hall. Can you go see him now so we can resolve this matter?"

"I have a couple of cases in Department Four. Let me tell them I'll be a little late and I'll go see Tray."

The bailiff stood up, and said, "I'll tell McCormick in Department Four."

Sabre couldn't imagine what Tray might've been charged with. He was such a sweet kid, a little troubled from his past but very well behaved.

"Thanks," she said to the bailiff. Then she turned back to the judge, and asked, "What are the charges?"

"He's charged with PC 187."

"Murder?" Sabre gasped. *Something is wrong here.* She took a deep breath.

The judge said, "Mr. Firmstone has the petition and the reports. You two can sort out who's going to represent him and report back to me. Sometime before noon, please."

"I'll go see him right now, Your Honor."

Chapter 5

Sabre walked through the tunnel that led from the courthouse to juvenile hall. The tunnel had been built so the delinquents didn't have to go outside in order to get to court. It cut down on the escape attempts and made life easier for the deputy sheriffs and the probation officers. Sabre hated that walk. The tunnel was gloomy and depressing and reminded her of something that might've been used to move prisoners on a chain gang. It was silly when she thought about it logically because there wasn't anything unusual about the hallway. It was just a lot of concrete, but it gave her that feeling nevertheless.

While Sabre waited outside the interview room, she read through the report. What she read didn't seem real to her. This was not the Tray she knew. There had never been any sign of violent behavior from him, but it wasn't the first time she was surprised by a client's reaction to a terrifying situation. Tray was in C Block where the more violent offenders were housed. That bothered Sabre because he was so small and so vulnerable. She would see what she could do about that.

Tray, accompanied by a probation officer, rounded the corner and walked toward her, Tray's face etched in desperation. *He must be so scared.* A glimmer of hope seemed to appear on his sweet face when he spotted Sabre, followed soon afterwards by that same desperate look.

"Hello, Tray," Sabre said.

"Hello." His voice was weak.

"Are you his attorney?" the officer asked.

"Yes."

"I'll put him in the interview room so you can speak to him," the PO said, as he led Tray to a small room with two chairs and a small table. He opened the door, led Tray inside, and then held the door open for Sabre. "Would you like me to stay with you?" It seemed to be a service they offered whenever she saw a client in C Block, and on occasion Sabre had allowed the PO to stay right outside the door.

"No, thank you. I'll be fine."

"Suit yourself." He nodded toward a young man standing behind a podium. "Tell that guy at the desk when you're ready and someone will come get him."

Tray's height and his small frame suddenly concerned Sabre. *How would he survive with boys twice his size? And he's not streetwise like the gang members are. Tray had seen way more than he should have for a child his age, but his experience was different from most street kids. He didn't know how to defend himself.*

"I'm so sorry you are in here. Are you okay?"

He shrugged and his eyes glistened, but no tears fell.

"I just got the paperwork from the court. Do you understand what you've been charged with?"

"The cops said I killed Glen." He wrinkled his face in disgust when he said his name.

"Can you tell me what happened?"

He shrugged. "I don't know."

"You don't know if you want to tell me, or you don't know what happened?"

"I don't know what they're talking about. I didn't kill anybody. That's stupid."

"Did the cops question you?"

"Some old cop asked me a bunch of questions, but I didn't have any of the answers 'cause I don't know nothin' about that creep."

"When was the last time you saw Irving?" Sabre asked.

"When the social worker took us away."

"From your mom?"

"Yes. I never saw him after that."

"It says in the police report that you were seen with Glen Irving the day he disappeared."

"That's what that old cop kept saying. But I never saw him."

"Did you ever talk to him after you left your mom's?"

"No," he said sternly.

"Have you had any contact with him of any kind? On the Internet? Anything?"

"No. That's sick." His whole body shuddered, and his mouth turned down in disgust. "Why would they think I was with him?"

"I don't know, but it says that they have an eyewitness."

"I wouldn't be with that creep. He's disgusting. I hate him."

"I know, and I'll try to find out what's going on."

"Can I go home?"

"We'll go to court this morning and your attorney will ask the judge to release you, but to be honest, I don't think he will. These are really serious charges and they have some reason to believe it was you. I know your attorney will do everything he can to help you."

"But *you* are my attorney."

"I'm your attorney on the dependency case, but this is a whole different kind of case. Mr. Firmstone was assigned to represent you and he's a really good attorney."

"He came in to see me, but I want you to do it." He paused. His eyes were wet and his voice trembled as he said, "Please. I'm scared."

"I know you are. Juvenile hall is a scary place to be. I'll do everything I can to get you out whether I represent you or not."

"Please," Tray begged.

"I'll talk to Mr. Firmstone and we'll tell the judge that you want me to represent you, but he's more experienced at this kind of case than I am."

Tray seemed to relax a little with that news. The tension lifted from his face. "Okay."

Sabre looked at his sweet face and couldn't imagine he had committed this heinous crime.

"Tray, remember last time we talked, you said something to me about 'doing something really bad'. Do you remember that?"

"Yes, but…." He stopped talking.

"Does that have anything to do with this?"

"No."

"You're sure? Because it's like I told you before, I can't tell anyone. But if you've done something wrong, I need to know, so I can figure out how to help you."

"It's nothing like that."

Chapter 6

Attorney Firmstone and Sabre sat outside of Department Three waiting for Tray's case to be called.

"I just don't believe Tray murdered someone," Sabre said.

"The petition says Irving died from a blow to the head. Could it have been self-defense or an accident?"

"If Tray did kill Irving, which I'm sure he didn't, then it would have to be self-defense." She shook her head. "Why would he even be with this guy? He can hardly stand to say his name."

Chris raised his eyebrow.

"I know," Sabre said. 'That doesn't bode well for his defense. It just shows that Tray hates him." Sabre sighed.

"I take it he wasn't kidnapped or anything?"

"No. He's never been reported missing. His foster parents would've surely let me know if he'd been missing." She looked at the report. "Irving's been dead, what...a week?"

"He was seen on Saturday, if we can believe the witness, so nine days at the most."

Sabre knew the answer, but she still asked, "There's no chance that Tray will be able to go back to his foster home today, is there?"

"No." Chris glanced around the room. "Are his foster parents here?"

"They are." Sabre raised her chin as if pointing at a couple sitting in the front row of seats about fifteen feet away. "They're over there—the mixed-race couple in the front. I spoke to them briefly. They don't believe he did anything either, and they're willing to take him home."

"That says a lot. They must really like this kid."

"He's a good kid."

"I looked for his parents," Chris said, "but they weren't checked in and they didn't answer when I called their names. What's their story?"

"Mom is a druggie and she just relapsed. He hasn't seen his dad in about three years. The department hasn't located him either, so he's probably not in prison, at least not in California. I'm sure he won't be showing up any time soon."

Firmstone glanced at the police report. "The murder is definitely connected to some sexual abuse because the body had the word GOOF written in black marker across his forehead."

"I saw that in the report. I'm not familiar with that term, but apparently you are."

"It's prison slang for a pedophile, usually one who likes young boys. It was used in the prisons in the 1940s, more in Canada than here."

"Apparently, the kids have started using it too," Sabre said. "Recently, one of my other clients referred to the guy who molested him as a goof. I thought at the time that was a strange way to describe him. Now I know why."

"It's becoming more common, I guess."

"Anyway, I'm sure Tray isn't the only one Irving had molested, so it doesn't necessarily mean Tray murdered him. There's never just one molest victim with these guys." Sabre shivered with repulsion and changed the subject. "What do you want to do about representing him? He wants me to do it, but you are so much more experienced than I am with this kind of case."

"I'd love to try to help this kid. Since we don't get that many murder cases, I'd hate to lose it, but I'm good either way."

"I just want him to have the best representation."

"If he won't talk to me, I can't represent him very well, but I expect he'll come around with a little time."

The bailiff from Department Three approached them. "Are you two ready on Copley?"

"Sure," Sabre said. They both stood up and followed the bailiff.

"So, what's the plan?" Firmstone asked.

"How about if we leave the attorney appointment up to the judge?"

***

Judge Trapnell was on the bench when Sabre and Chris walked in. He waited until they were at the table and then asked, "Who's going to represent this child?"

Chris and Sabre looked at each other as if to ask, 'Who's going to talk first?'. Chris raised his eyebrows.

Sabre said, "Your Honor, Tray has asked that I represent him. He's comfortable with me and I believe he will be more forthcoming. Hopefully that will give him the best defense. However, I'm not nearly as experienced in this type of case as Mr. Firmstone and I want what is best for this young man."

"How many P.C. 187 cases have you handled, Ms. Brown?"

"Only one, Your Honor, and that was not a juvenile. I have represented two juveniles where someone was killed, both P.C. 192 cases. One was a vehicular manslaughter and the other an accidental shooting."

"And you, Mr. Firmstone?"

"I have handled six P.C. 187 cases and eight P.C. 192s, Your Honor. All of them were initially filed in juvenile court, although in four of the murder cases, the cases were sent downtown and the minors were tried as adults."

"Clearly, you are more experienced, Mr. Firmstone. However, I've seen this young man and he doesn't appear to be a hardened criminal. I can see where he would benefit from counsel who already has a relationship with him." Judge Trapnell looked from one attorney to the other. "Therefore, I'm going to appoint you both as co-counsel on this case."

"Really, Your Honor?" the prosecutor, Marge Benson, said. "He needs two attorneys?"

"You have a whole department behind you, Ms. Benson, but if you are intimidated by this team, maybe you can get one of your esteemed colleagues to help you."

"I'm not intimidated, Your Honor," the prosecutor said indignantly. "I'm just trying to save the taxpayers a little money."

"That's very thoughtful of you, Ms. Benson, but my concern at this moment is that this young man has effective counsel. Look at it as a compliment to you, that it takes two defense attorneys to match one of you."

Sabre did all she could to keep from smiling at Judge Charlie Bozo's sarcastic, yet smooth, remarks. He received his nickname from his father when he was a child, but he made the mistake of telling someone in an interview years ago and it had followed him to juvenile court. It seemed to fit him since he "clowned around" unlike most of the stuffed shirts who sat on the bench. The majority of attorneys, both defense and prosecutors, respected Judge Trapnell. He was smart, knew the law, and wasn't afraid to make decisions even when they went against public policy, but he did it all with a sense of humor. He had been on the bench for nearly thirty years and had long since quit trying to walk the political tightrope that was expected of him.

The judge looked at the bailiff. "Bring the child in, please."

Sabre appreciated that he referred to her client as a child, instead of "the defendant." Judge Trapnell had a way of not dehumanizing the defendants as so many judges and prosecutors seemed to do. But, she also knew that if the facts were such that he found the "child" guilty, he seemed to have no trouble issuing a harsh sentence for him or her.

The bailiff returned with Tray who, when he spotted Sabre, had a pleading look on his face. The bailiff brought Tray to the table and the boy sat next to Sabre. "Are you going to be my attorney?" he asked softly.

She whispered to him, "The judge is going to let you keep both Mr. Firmstone and me on the case." She thought she heard a slight sigh of relief emanate from her young client. He looked so scared and innocent sitting there next to her. Sabre was relieved too. Tray had the best of both worlds. So many unanswered questions ran through Sabre's mind. *How did this happen? How could Tray have gotten caught up in this mess? Could he have actually killed Irving?*

Chapter 7

Bob and Sabre sat across from each other at the small table with the pink tablecloth at Pho Pasteur, where they dined almost daily. The waiter brought them each a #124, the only meal Bob ever ordered.

"Tell me about Tray. I can't believe he killed Irving. He's such a well-behaved kid."

"I don't believe he did. There has to be more to this. I'm hoping JP can figure it out."

"He's your man. Or at least he should be. Speaking of which, are you ever going to give that guy a chance?"

"What are you talking about?"

"You have to know JP's smitten with you."

"He's never asked me out."

"Because he's afraid of you."

"Yeah, 'cuz I'm so scary." Sabre turned her head to the side, opened her mouth real wide, stuck her tongue out, and shook her head like a wild woman.

"See. You *are* scary. You should ask *him*."

"I'm not going to ask him out. We have a great working relationship. When you start crossing those lines, things get messy." She took a drink of her water. "I think the vodka's getting to your brain," Sabre said.

Bob picked up his water glass. "This isn't vodka; it's water."

"I know that's water, but tell me you didn't have a glass of vodka last night."

"Of course I had my vodka last night. I had to toast the goddess Brodinia."

Sabre shook her head. "They've charged Tray with murder. They have a witness who says she saw him at a grocery store with Irving on Saturday, and no one saw Irving after that. He was killed sometime between then and when they found his body on Sunday, a week later."

"What does Tray say?"

"He claims he was at his therapist's office during that time frame, but I can't verify that right now because his therapist is in Africa."

"Then the witness must be wrong."

"Oh yeah. By the way, she's a nun."

"Well, there you go. You can't trust those church people. Too much religion. It's worse than the vodka."

The waiter brought their meals and they began to eat.

"I think you should try a new dish next time we come here," Sabre said.

"Why?"

"Because there are a lot of good things on the menu."

"Nope, I like this."

The banter continued throughout the meal. Sabre checked the time on her phone. "We need to get going. I'm meeting JP at 1:30."

***

Elaine, Sabre's red-haired receptionist, buzzed Sabre.

"Yes, Elaine?"

"Your cowboy is here."

"Please send him in."

Before Sabre let go of the button, she heard JP say, "I have a name, you know."

She was still smiling when JP walked into her office. "Elaine can't get past your Stetson hat and your boots. She doesn't see them often. Mostly we get attorneys dressed in tailored suits."

"I'm just a country boy. It comes with a uniform."

He seated himself in front of her desk.

Sabre reached across her desk and handed JP a blue document.

"Isn't Tray Copley that cute little black kid you were telling me about who made the dollhouse for his sister?" JP asked as he looked up from the petition charging Tray with murder.

"That's the one."

"I can't believe he killed anyone," JP said, "even that creep Irving." He narrowed his eyes and shook his head. "A guy like that was so low he had to look up to see hell."

Sabre smiled at his comment. "I don't believe it, either. And you get to prove that he didn't."

"Where do you want me to start?"

"The police report says there's an eyewitness who puts Tray with Irving the day he disappeared. We don't know for certain if that was the same day he was killed."

"So we don't know *when* he was killed?"

"Not exactly. We know it was about a week ago," Sabre said. "But if Tray was with him, then he lied to me because he said he hadn't seen Irving since he was removed from his home by CPS. It makes more sense that the eyewitness is wrong, that she didn't see Tray." Sabre smiled. "Oh, and by the way, the eyewitness is a nun."

JP raised his eyebrows. "A nun?"

"Nuns make mistakes too."

"Okay, I'll see if I can break her down." He smirked. "Or would you suggest I try to charm her?"

"Whatever works, baby," Sabre said jokingly. She regretted the comment as soon as she said it. She sounded too flirtatious. She really liked JP, but the last thing she wanted right now was to get involved and have her heart broken again. "And talk to the foster parents and see if Tray was missing for any length of time or if he could've even been where the nun says he was."

"Will do." JP made another note. "What other evidence do they have on Tray?"

"The DSS record showing that Tray had been a victim of Irving's sexual abuse."

"That might give him a motive, but I'm sure there are a lot of people who wanted to kill that man. The murder obviously has something to do with Irving being a pedophile or they wouldn't have gone to the trouble to write GOOF on his forehead with a black marker."

"Agreed."

"Do we know of any other molest victims?"

"Irving's not in the criminal system. At least nothing was turned up by DSS when Tray's case was filed."

"I'll see if I can find anything. It's most likely the perp is someone close to one of the children who was violated. So, we need to find out who else has been affected by Irving. I'll question his friends and family—if he has any." JP jotted a few notes down in his notebook. "Do you want me to talk with Tray?"

"Not yet; he's too gun-shy. Attorney Firmstone tried to question him this morning and he just clammed up. I'm hoping he'll open up to me, but he's pretty scared."

"So far you haven't given me enough for the DA to charge him. What else do they have?"

"They have Tray's notebook with the word GOOF written all over the cover with a black marker. GOOF was also written on the inside of his school locker in several places. The style matches what was written on Irving's forehead. They have a handwriting analyst who says the words on the body, in the locker, and on the notebook were all written by the same person."

"And that person is Tray?"

"Yes. They compared the writing to other things Tray has written and according to the analyst, the handwriting is a match. And here's another thing: according to the news, when they found Irving, they found a second body."

"But they haven't charged Tray with that murder, have they?"

"No. There's been no mention of that body at all. See what you can find out about the other victim."

"I'll get right on it." JP rose from his chair. "How about if we get some dinner first? I'm starving."

Sabre hesitated.

"Never mind," JP said. "On second thought, I don't really have the time. I'll catch something on the run."

Sabre wondered if he was asking her out. They had eaten together many times, but lately the tension had begun to grow between them. Sometimes he appeared to be interested in her and other times he seemed so distant.

That's the last thing I need right now.

"Let me know what you find out," she said.

Chapter 8

JP read through the police report one more time. He was looking for anything that might help with his investigation, but the report was sparse. Everything they had on Tray was circumstantial. They didn't even have a murder weapon. JP made a list on his whiteboard of the facts in the case, a technique he had become proficient at while he was with the sheriff's department, and it still came in handy. In the center of the board he wrote the name *Glen Irving*. He drew a line to the left and wrote *Tray Copley*. Then he added another line and wrote *Nun*. He added the facts he knew about each, which were very few so far.

Another line ended with the word GOOF, all in capitals just like on the victim. This was the most damaging evidence they had.

JP sat back and looked at the board. He thought about Sabre and how certain she was that this young man couldn't have committed such a crime. But then, she always approached a case as if her clients weren't guilty until it was proved otherwise. Even then, she'd give them the best defense she could. He could hear her saying, "Every defendant deserves the best our Constitution can give him or her. I don't have to agree with my clients or like what they did, but if their rights aren't protected, then neither are ours. I'm defending their *rights*, not their actions."

JP, on the other hand, saw most criminals as a bunch of scumbags, although when it came to minors, he was a little more open. Working cases with Sabre created a good balance.

He suddenly found himself thinking more about Sabre than the case. He hated that he was so attracted to her. He knew a relationship with her wouldn't work. She was beautiful, smart, educated, and classy. He was just a cowboy who was eighteen years older than she was. She could have any man she wanted. *Why would she ever want him?*

He shook off further thoughts of Sabre, picked up the phone, and called the foster parents to see if he could meet with them.

***

An hour later, JP pulled up in front of the home of June and George Longe, Tray's foster parents. The home was in an older neighborhood, and based on the well-kept yards, he surmised that it was primarily owner-occupied. A motor home was parked on a concrete slab that ran along the side of the house.

An attractive, petite woman in her early sixties with platinum, shoulder-length hair greeted him at the door. She introduced herself as June Longe and explained that her husband was working. June was soft-spoken and her eyes were kind. June offered JP something to drink, which he declined. They sat down at the dining room table to chat.

"How long has Tray lived with you?" JP asked.

"About four months," June said.

"Have you had any problems with him?"

"Not really. He does what he's told to do. He cleans up after himself. He keeps his room cleaner than any child I've ever had. He likes to help around the house, especially if we're doing a chore together. I expect he just likes to be with someone who cares for him. And he's great with his sister. I have to remind him sometimes that I'm the parent and he doesn't have to do so much for her. He's getting better about letting me take over that role. I think it's just that he had to take care of her at home and he's used to it." She paused. "I'm sorry. I'm rattling on. But he's such a sweet kid. I can't imagine he committed any crime, let alone killing someone."

"You're fine, ma'am," JP said. "How well does he do in school?"

"He's a very bright boy, but he has fallen behind because he missed so much when he was at home. But he always does his homework and I work with him every night. He reads to me and his sister, now that she's here with us. The teachers say he's showing a lot of improvement."

"Does he have many friends?"

"There's one boy he hangs around with sometimes. His name is Drew and he lives a couple of doors away. Tray doesn't have a lot of friends at school. It's not like he has enemies or anything and he hasn't had any trouble at school. I think when he's there he stays to himself a lot. He's not real social."

"He doesn't hang out with Drew at school?"

"Drew is a year older than Tray and started high school this year. Tray is still in middle school."

"I'll need Drew's last name and his address."

June walked to the desk and got a sticky notepad. She wrote “Drew Fletcher” on the paper along with his address, and handed it to JP.

"Thank you." JP stuck it on a page in his notebook. "Between a week ago Saturday and today, has Tray been anywhere by himself?"

"No. He goes to school, to see his therapist, and he had one visit with his mother."

"Has he spent any time at Drew's house? Even a couple of hours?"

"A couple of times, but never for more than a few hours."

"Do you know if he was there last Saturday?"

"Yes, he was. That was a bad day for me. My father had a heart attack and was rushed to the hospital. Drew's mother agreed to watch Tray, so he was at Drew's house most of the morning. He had a therapy session late morning and Maggie, Drew's mom, volunteered to take him there because I was still at the hospital. Tray ended up staying with the Fletchers until after dinner. That's when I finally got home."

"Is your father okay?" JP asked with genuine concern.

"Yes, thanks for asking. He's home and as spry as any eighty-five-year-old can be."

"I'm glad to hear that." JP smiled. "You said Tray had one visit with his mother. When was that?"

She looked at her calendar again. "It was Friday, the third."

"Did you take him to the visit?"

"No, a worker from DSS picked him up and took him."

"Was the visit with his mother supervised?"

"Technically, no. Tray was having unsupervised visits with his mother until she relapsed a few days ago."

"Did he have overnights?"

"He had supervised visits for a long time, but his mother was in rehab and she was doing real well. After a few months, she was able to have unsupervised visits and then overnights, but she was still at the rehab center so most of the time she was supervised. She could take him out of the center for short periods." June clamped her teeth. "He could not have done this. I know him."

"I know Tray is a good kid, and Sabre and I want to help him. Hopefully, we'll learn that someone else killed Irving. But we need to find out everything we can, even if it isn't what we want to hear."

"I know, but I believe in him and I know he didn't do it."

"His friend, Drew, isn't in foster care, is he?"

"No. He lives there with his mother. His father passed away two years ago. I've known the family for years; otherwise I wouldn't let Tray go there. Drew's mother is one of my best friends."

"Do you think Drew's mother would let me talk to him? Maybe I can find out if the boys went anywhere or if Tray went somewhere by himself. Or it may be that Tray has said something to his friend that would help us."

"I can call Drew's mom and pave the way for you."

"That would likely help. Does she know that Tray has been arrested?"

"Yes. She was here when the cops came." June picked up her cell phone and placed a call to Maggie, Drew's mother, who gave JP permission to come over right away.

Chapter 9

JP walked up the street and knocked on the Fletchers' door. Maggie answered.

"Howdy, ma'am," JP said. "I'm JP Torn."

"Nice to meet you," Maggie said, as she unlocked the security screen. "Please come in."

Maggie showed JP to a seat and handed him a glass of iced tea. He graciously accepted the tea, even though he didn't really want it.

"How can I help?"

"There is a witness who supposedly saw Tray with the victim on a day when he would've been here with you. We think that person is mistaken, so we're trying to track Tray's movements. We're also not exactly sure when the victim was killed. Do you know if the foster parents ever let Tray go out alone?"

"Not that I've ever seen. June is pretty strict with her kids."

JP sensed the defensiveness in her voice. "I know Mrs. Longe is an excellent foster parent and I'm not suggesting otherwise. I also know that teenage boys have a way of doing things that parents don't know about. I can't tell you the number of times I did things as a kid."

"Teenagers are a different breed. Don't get me wrong, Drew and Tray are the best, but they are struggling with acceptance and 'fitting in' like every other kid their age."

"Such as?"

"Pushing the curfew limits; keeping their rooms clean, although that one is more Drew than Tray; using some bad language. Stuff like that, but nothing big."

"Have Drew and Tray come home late any time in

the past week?"

"Not that I recall. They don't walk home by themselves. June and I take turns picking them up from school. Sometimes Tray stays and works with a tutor or meets with the therapist. Drew often waits for him and gets his homework done while he's waiting."

JP made a note to check with the school. "I just need to account for all of Tray's time so we can prove it wasn't him with Irving. I understand that on Saturday, May 4, you were watching Tray while Mrs. Longe went to the hospital with her father. Is that correct?"

"Yes."

"Were you with the boys the whole time?"

Maggie thought for a moment. "Tray came over a little before nine that morning. June's father had been taken to the emergency room. She called and asked me if I would watch Tray. He had an appointment with his therapist at 11:00, so I dropped the boys off there and I went to show a house." She quickly added, "I'm a real estate agent."

"Drew went with him to therapy?"

"Not to the actual therapy session. There's a skateboard park near the therapist's office and the boys took their skateboards. Drew hung out at the park until Tray was done, and then they stayed at the park until I picked them up."

"How long would you say you were gone?"

"It was a little after one when I finished the first showing, but I called Drew several times to check on them. It took longer than I intended, but they were having a good time and were glad to stay there. I'm a single parent and I have to make a living. It's been a struggle ever since Drew's father passed away."

"I'm sorry to hear that, ma'am."

"Thank you. It's been over two years now, so we've learned to cope."

"You said it was a little after one when you finished the first showing. Did you have another one?"

"Yes. I'm sorry; I got off track. I intended to pick the boys up and take them home, but by the time I finished the first one, it was time for the second one. That one was even worse. The house has a retaining wall that was recently replaced and it was leaning. The buyer is concerned that there is something wrong with the wall, so now we have to bring in another engineer, even though it's been inspected three times and it's structurally okay. The issues are all cosmetic."

JP tried once again to get this woman back on subject. "I'm sorry to hear that, ma'am. Do you know what time you picked up the boys?"

"Yes. I believe it was around five."

"And you picked them up at the skatepark?"

"Yes." Maggie continued to tell another story about the problems she had had that day, none of which pertained to the task at hand.

JP waited politely and when she finished, he asked, "Would you mind if I speak with Drew?"

"Not at all."

"I need to find out if Tray was ever by himself during that time period, or any other time in the past few weeks, that Drew might be aware of. And I want to know if Tray has confided in his friend."

"Of course."

"It's entirely up to you, ma'am, but if I could talk to Drew alone, he might be more forthcoming. I have found teenagers are far less willing to talk in front of their parents."

"Sure. Let me get him."

Before she could walk away, JP asked, "Does he know about Tray's arrest?"

"Yes. He saw them take him away. He was devastated."

"Does he know what he was arrested for?"

"Yes. I told him." Then, as if she felt she should explain, she added, "I didn't want Drew to see the arrest on the Internet or hear about the murder allegations somewhere else."

Maggie went upstairs and returned with a thin, gangly kid with bushy hair and the first stages of acne on his face. The young man smiled when he was introduced to JP. Then he flopped himself down in an easy chair, throwing one leg over the arm.

His mother scowled at him, but didn't say anything. "I'll be in the kitchen if you need me," Maggie said.

"You know Tray Copley, right?"

"He's my best friend," Drew said.

"I expect you'd like to help him if you could, right?"

"Yes."

"Then I need you to be totally honest with me."

Drew didn't wait for a question. "Tray didn't kill anyone."

"How can you be so certain?"

"Because I just know."

"Tell me about a week ago last Saturday."

"What about it?"

"You and Tray spent the day together, right?"

"Yes. Mrs. Longe's father had a heart attack, and my mom took us to the skatepark."

"Was Tray at the skatepark the whole time?"

"Except when he was with the therapist."

"What did you do while he was there?" JP asked.

"I hung out at the park. There're other kids there on their skateboards all the time. We were mostly carving the bowl and jumping the stairs."

"Carving the bowl? What is that?"

"You know how the bowls at the skateboard parks go up on the sides?" He put his hands palms down in front of him and made a swooping motion outward with hands going in opposite directions. "You skate up the side and back down, or around, but the park was pretty busy that day so we had a small spot so we couldn't make a very big loop."

"How long was Tray gone?"

Drew shrugged his shoulders. "About an hour, I guess. I didn't really pay attention to the time, but it wasn't that long."

"Did your mother call and check on you?"

"Probably. I don't really remember, but I'm sure she did. She always does."

"Did the two of you go anywhere besides the park?"

"Nope."

"Drew, has Tray ever told you anything about Irving?"

Drew cupped his left hand inside his right and popped his knuckles. Then he switched hands and popped the other ones.

JP waited for an answer.

"He said he was a creep who tried to touch him and that's why he is in foster care."

"Did Tray ever threaten to hurt Irving or anything like that?"

Drew removed his leg from the arm of the easy chair and sat up a little straighter. "You mean, like, kill him?"

"Yes. Did he ever threaten to kill him? I know that sometimes people say things when they're angry that they really don't mean."

"Tray's not like that," Drew said. "He hardly ever gets mad. But I would've killed that creep if he ever tried anything like that on me."

"Did you tell Tray that?"

Drew shrugged his shoulders again. "Probably. Goofs don't deserve to live."

"Why did you call him a goof?"

"Because that's what he is."

"What do you mean?"

"He's a child molester. They call them goofs."

"Who are *they*?"

"Lots of people."

"Did Tray ever call him that?"

He shrugged.

JP waited for an answer.

"I don't think so. My uncle used to call them that."

"Did you ever use that term in front of Tray?"

"I don't know. Maybe." He shook his head. "I don't think so, 'cuz we only talked about it that one time and I don't think I said anything like that."

"Was anyone else at the park that day?"

"Lots of people. It was real crowded."

"Was there anyone else you knew?"

"There were several guys there that I recognized, but I don't know most of their names. I did some tricks with Anthony for a while."

"Who is Anthony?"

"Just some guy we've hung out with before."

"Do you know his last name?"

"No."

"How old is he?"

"I dunno. About my age, I guess."

"Does he go to your school?"

"No, I don't think so. I've never seen him anywhere else, just a couple of times at the park."

"Can you describe him for me?"

"He's taller than Tray but shorter than me."

"So, about five-foot-five maybe?" JP asked.

"I guess," Drew said. "He has dark hair. I think he might be Indian or something. He has a little bit of an accent."

"Is there anything else you can tell me about that

day? Anything unusual happen?"

"No."

JP wasn't totally satisfied that Drew was telling the truth, or at least not all of it, but he didn't get the impression that Drew had been involved in a murder.

Chapter 10

JP entered the Harbinger House Rehab Center on Texas Street. After several attempts to gather information on Tray's mother, Jeannine Copley, he gave up on learning anything from the administration. They all spouted "privacy laws."

There were two sections in the Harbinger House. Phase I was where new inhabitants stayed. This area was highly supervised and the residents weren't allowed to come and go freely. Each room had four beds and a bathroom. The timing for meals was very strict, curfews were tight, and visitors were limited or not permitted in most cases. There was only one community room that was used for dining and socializing. The residents called Phase I the "lock-up."

Residents in Phase II had a lot more freedom but required at least thirty days sobriety. There could be no write-ups for bad behavior in Phase I before the individual was considered for placement in Phase II. Each room had a bathroom and only two beds instead of four. Two "community rooms" were provided for residents' use. One was for dining and doubled as an activity room for card games, board games, and crafts. The second room was set up like a living room with two sofas, three stuffed chairs, a bookcase, and a large-screen television. Phase II allowed visitors between 10:00 a.m. and 8:00 p.m. Children were allowed to stay overnight with their mothers with permission. Lights had to be off in the community rooms by 11:30 p.m.

JP left the administration office and walked into Phase II. He had been there before to see other clients for Sabre, so he knew his way around. His last visit there was a week ago to see Maribel Vargas, who had just qualified as an "assistant" at the front desk. He knew that one paid receptionist worked the front desk with help from resident assistants. It was a privilege for residents to work the desk, and it took a long period of sobriety as well as other responsible behaviors. The assistants didn't usually last long because they were often released shortly after they reached the level that qualified them for the position.

JP spotted Maribel helping another resident. He hung back and didn't make eye contact with the other workers. When Maribel was free, he stepped forward.

"Good morning, Maribel," JP said.

"Nice to see you again." She paused. "Is something wrong with my case?"

"No, not at all. Everything is good."

"So what do you need?"

"I'm here about someone else. Do you have a minute?"

"Sure. Who's the resident?"

"Jeannine Copley."

"She's not here any longer."

"I know. Do you know why?"

Maribel looked around and then lowered her voice. "I don't know, but come with me." She turned to another clerk and said, "I'll be right back."

She walked with JP toward the recreation room. "There are always rumors when someone here fails their program. I believe about half of them."

"What are the rumors about Jeannine?"

"You need to talk to Tanika, Jeannine's roommate. She always knows what's going on around here and in the streets. She's a tough woman who has seen it all."

They stepped into the rec room and Maribel glanced around until her eyes lit on a large woman sitting at a table in the back of the room. "There she is, over there near the window."

JP followed Maribel across the room toward an African American woman with her hair pulled straight back into a short ponytail. JP knew by her size that her drug of choice was not methamphetamine—the most common in this facility. *Marijuana, alcohol, heroin maybe,* he thought. She was far too heavy to be a meth freak.

"Tanika, this is JP. He'd like to talk to you for a minute."

"Is he a cop?" Tanika asked, looking him over from head to toe.

"No. And he's a good guy."

"Okay." Tanika looked directly at JP. "Sit," she commanded.

JP did as he was told. He suspected he would get more out of her if he didn't tower over her, and he was pretty certain she was used to being the boss.

"What you need to know?"

"I need some information about Jeannine Copley. You know her, right?"

"She was my roomie 'til she done gone and screwed up."

"What did she do?"

"She started seeing her ol' man and he got her tweakin' again. I told her to dump his skinny butt before he tripped her up, but she wouldn't listen." She shook her head. "She was so close to gettin' her kids back and then she go'd and screwed up. The fool."

"When did she start using?"

She thought for a second. "It was weekend before last. Saturday, I think. She went out for somethin', and when she come back, she was high. I kept her hid and covered for her, but the next night her ol' man came by and gave her some stuff."

"Did she leave then?"

"No, she didn't leave until Friday. She hadn't had

nothin' all day that day 'cuz her son was comin' by for a visit. He's just the cutest thang, real polite and sweet."

"Did you see Tray when he came?"

"Not that time, but I seen him before a couple of times. I don't think he ever made it here that day."

"Why do you say that?"

"'Cuz I talked to Sondra later, and she said she just seen Jeannine leavin' alone with her bag."

"And Jeannine never came back after that?"

"No."

"Was she kicked out of the program for using?"

"No. She just bounced on her own." Tanika looked up and then called out to a thin woman who had just walked into the room. "Hey, Sondra. Come here."

The woman sauntered over. "What?"

"Remember when Jeannine left last week? Was her kid with her?"

Sandra looked at JP from head to toe. "You a cop?"

"No. I'm not. I'm trying to help Tray."

"Yeah, I heard he was in some big trouble. Good for him. One less chomo in the world. What do you wanna know?"

"Was Tray here for a visit with his mother last week?" JP asked.

"He was here, but I didn't actually see him with Jeannine. But she might've gone out with him for a while, 'cuz she was gone somewhere. But then an hour or so later, I saw her leave the building carryin' her bag. Tray was not with her."

"You're certain of that?"

"Yeah, I'm sure. I went outside for a cigarette and I saw Tray and his little sister sittin' on the sidewalk. Before I could get to them, someone from DSS picked them up."

"How do you know it was someone from DSS?"

"'Cuz I've seen her here before. She drives the kids here and back all the time."

"You've both been very helpful. Thank you."

"That kid don't deserve to go to jail for killin' no molester. He should be gettin' a freaken' reward or somethin'."

***

"Thanks for coming by," Sabre said to JP as they walked back to her office. As she passed the receptionist, Elaine, she saw her mouth the word, "hot." Sabre smiled and shook her head.

"My pleasure, ma'am."

"Really? *Ma'am*?"

"Sorry. It's an old habit."

Sabre accidentally brushed against JP as she walked around to the back of her desk. A tingle shot through her body. Elaine was right, she thought; he *is* hot. JP took the seat across from her.

"Do you really think this kid is innocent?" JP asked.

"I do. I just can't believe that he would do anything like this."

"So, how do you explain the evidence?"

"What do we have really? It's all circumstantial."

"They have a witness. Not just any witness, but a nun who saw Tray with Irving just before he was killed."

"Even if Tray was with him, which he says he wasn't, it doesn't mean he killed him."

"Look what this guy did to him. I'd probably kill him too. And I sure as hell would if he molested someone I loved."

"I'm thinking that too," Sabre said. "A parent, or someone very close to the victim, is more apt to have done this than the victim himself."

"So maybe Irving did something to Tray's sister. That would rile Tray up. He's mighty protective of her."

"That's true, but there's absolutely no evidence of anything happening to her."

"Perhaps Tray's mother or father?"

"Yes, but why would his mother all of a sudden decide to kill Irving? She has known about this for months. What would have provoked her?"

"The right drugs, maybe?"

"That's possible, but she seems to get pretty out of it when she uses, and then she hits the streets to make some money to get more drugs."

"Did the father know?" JP asked.

"We don't know. The social worker hasn't been able to locate him."

"Maybe he just found out and went after the guy."

"That's possible, so I guess you better find him. At the very least, we need to have someone to point the finger at."

"What about the other evidence against Tray? Like the word *GOOF* in black marker across his forehead."

"Who even uses that term for a pedophile?" Sabre asked.

"It's used a lot in some prisons."

"Exactly. So how does Tray know it?"

"C'mon, Sabre, you're stretching here. Street kids know those terms because so many of them have parents who are convicts. The slang in the prisons is also on the streets."

"But that's just it. Tray isn't really a street kid. He's had a rough life with his mother's addiction, but at the same time, he has been way more sheltered than most of the kids in his situation."

"Well, his best friend, Drew Fletcher, used the word *goof* when I talked to him. Perhaps Tray learned it from him. Maybe the term has become common among teenagers. You never know what slang they're using. There are slang changes all the time. It's hard to keep up."

"Or maybe Drew had more to do with this than we've figured so far."

"I considered that, but from what I can tell, he never even met the guy," JP said.

"But Drew was with Tray around the same time that the nun said she saw Tray with Irving."

"But Tray was seeing his therapist then, so he couldn't have been in Albertsons. The nun has to be wrong unless Tray wasn't at his appointment after all. I have an appointment to meet with Sister Maria Luisa Hilasco next week. I figure finding Tray's mother is top priority, unless you feel differently."

"You're right. The nun isn't likely to go anywhere," Sabre said.

"By the way, I checked on the second body. They don't know who he is yet, but they don't think he's linked to Irving. It was a totally different M.O. Apparently, he was shot several months ago, maybe as many as six. They're still working on the time of death."

“So, that likely won’t be of any help to us.” Sabre paused. "When will Dr. Bell be back from his trip to Africa?"

"According to his office, he's due back in about a week."

"That should clear up a few things."

“Maybe, but I’m not sure you’re going to like what you hear.”

“Why is that?”

“Dr. Bell’s office assistant said the doctor left on Friday for Africa, so he couldn’t have met with Tray on Saturday.”

“And she was certain?”

"She made the reservation and she took him to the airport. I checked with my friend at Homeland Security. Dr. Bell's flight was scheduled for Friday, May 3, and he was on the flight. There's no way he could have kept that appointment."

Chapter 11

Sabre sat down in front of Tray in the interview room. The room was so small it felt like a cage to Sabre, and she felt a bit claustrophobic. Tray didn't fidget as much or look as scared as he had in court. *Perhaps he was getting used to his surroundings.*

"I'm so sorry you're stuck here, Tray, but we're doing everything we can to help you. In order to give you the best defense, I need you to be completely honest with me. Can you do that?"

He nodded.

"When did you last see your mother?" Sabre asked.

"Last week."

"Do you remember what day it was?"

Tray wrinkled his brow. "I think it was Friday. Yeah, it was Friday because we got out of school early that day."

"About what time was it?"

"A driver from CPS picked me and Shanisha up right after I got home from school."

"And you went straight to Harbinger?"

"Yes."

"Did you stay there with your mother?"

"No. We went to McDonald's and got some hamburgers and fries, and then we went to the park."

"Was anyone else with you or your mom?"

"Just Shanisha."

"How did you get to McDonald's?"

"We took the bus."

Tray's answers were almost robotic. She wondered how much he had thought about all this. She expected it was constantly on his mind.

"And your mom paid for the bus?"

"She had bus passes. I think the social worker gave them to her."

"Did you take the bus to the park too?"

"No, we walked. It wasn't that far."

"What did you do at the park?"

"What does this have to do with anything?"

Sabre was a little surprised by his question. He didn't sound angry or sarcastic, but the question surprised her. She wondered if something happened at the park that he didn't want to talk about. "I'm trying to establish where you were when Irving was killed, so I need all the details."

"Is that when it happened? When I was with my mom?"

"We don't know exactly. So, what did you do at the park?"

"We sat on the park bench and ate."

"I thought you went to McDonald's."

"We did, but we took our food to go."

"Was anyone else with you?"

He hesitated. "Just my sister. I already told you." His voice rose as he spoke.

"What did you do after you ate?"

"We played on the bars and I pushed Shanisha on the swings. She loves to swing."

"I loved to swing when I was little," Sabre said. "I still do. It feels like you're flying. Did you swing too?"

"A little, but I had to keep getting off because Shanisha kept wanting me to push her."

"Did your mom talk to anyone at the park?"

"No," he said quickly.

"Did you or Shanisha talk to anyone?"

"There was another little girl that Shanisha played with on the bars. They were crawling through that clubhouse thing and sliding down the slide."

"Were there other adults there?"

"I think so."

"Did you see a nun there?" Sabre knew this was not where the nun said she saw Tray, but if she saw him at the park, she may have been confused about Irving.

"A what?"

"A nun."

He wrinkled his forehead and scrunched his mouth in a look of complete confusion. "None what?"

Sabre furrowed her brow at his response, then realized his confusion and chuckled. "Tray, do you know what a *nun* is?"

He shook his head.

Sabre Googled *nun* on her phone and showed Tray a picture of a nun in a habit, although she wasn't sure if the nun was wearing her habit when she supposedly saw Tray. She made a note to check on what she was wearing.

"Oh yeah, I've seen pictures of those before, but I never saw a real one."

Sabre found his earlier comment funny but didn't say anything. This was a difficult conversation for Tray.

"And you never saw Irving anywhere that day?"

"No." He shuddered.

"What did you do after you went to the park?"

"We went back to the rehab center and then someone picked me and my sister up."

"Who picked you up?"

"I don't remember her name, but the social worker sent her. She's taken me places before."

"Tray, you seem to be hiding something. Did your mom meet up with someone at the park? You can tell me. I'm not going to bust her."

"She was trying so hard." His voice shook as he spoke and Sabre waited for him to finish. "When we were at the swings, she was talking to some guy."

"Did you know him?"

"I don't know his name. I've seen him before, but I'm not sure where. I saw him give her something. She was ready to go right after that. On the way home, I begged her to not start using. She said she wasn't, but I knew she was lying."

"What happened when you got back to the center?"

"She gave us a hug and went inside. We waited outside for the driver to come. That's when I knew for sure 'cuz she never leaves us alone when she's clean."

"I'm so sorry, Tray."

He shrugged his shoulders. "It's no different than before."

Only this time it was different. This young man was sitting in custody for a crime he likely didn't commit, or if he did, it's because his mother put him in harm's way. Sabre grew angrier at his parents. She took a deep breath.

"Tray, let's talk about the Saturday before your visit with your mother. Where were you?"

"I was at my friend Drew's house."

"All day?"

"His mom dropped me off at the therapist's office and then we went to Kennedy Skateboard Park."

"What time was your appointment?"

"Eleven. It's always the same."

"Did you go to Albertsons supermarket either with your therapist or on your own?"

"No."

"And you never saw Irving that day?"

"No. I told you I've never seen him since the social worker took us away from our house." Sabre could hear the irritation in his voice. This was unusual for Tray. "Why do you keep asking me?"

"There's a witness who says she saw you with him at Albertsons."

"That's stupid. I wouldn't be with him." He shuddered again.

"I know. That's why I need to know everything, so I can prove that you couldn't have killed him."

Tray sighed. "I don't get it. Why would she say I was with him? That doesn't make sense. Ask Dr. Bell. I was with him, and then I went to the skatepark with Drew."

Chapter 12

Leonard Cohen belted out the first line of "Hallelujah" as a ringtone on Sabre's phone.

"Hello, Bob," Sabre said when she answered.

"Hi, honey. What's up?"

"Why aren't you here at the courthouse?"

"I am. I'm driving around the parking lot trying to find a parking spot. Is there some high profile case going on here today?"

"Not that I know of, so say your parking-spot chant and get in here."

"I can't just waste the chant. What if there are only so many parking spots in the chant? I need to save them for special occasions."

"Such as?"

"Such as a spot at the grocery store when I need some vodka. Or if I need a pack of cigarettes."

"But you don't smoke anymore."

"Actually, I'm just on a smoking break. I'm going to take it up again when I'm eighty-five. I figure if I'm still alive, then I deserve to do whatever I want. Besides, that way I don't have to feel like I'll never have another cigarette."

"That's quite a plan."

"I'm pretty sure I won't make it to the ripe old age of eighty-five, though."

"I hope you do. But by then, you'll have handicapped license plates and you'll be able to find spots easier, so you still don't need to save your chant for those parking spots."

"I found one, but I'm out by the fence, almost to Children's Hospital."

"I'll see you out there."

Sabre walked out of the courthouse to meet Bob. At first she couldn't see him because he was hidden by the multitude of cars. When she saw him appear from behind a Toyota pickup, she walked toward him until they met.

"You *are* in the back forty," she said.

"I told you. I used to not mind because I could leisurely enjoy a cigarette as I walked toward the courthouse, but now there's nothing to enjoy. I may have to take up smoking again before I reach eighty-five."

"Never mind. I need to talk to your client, Tray's mother. She may be his only alibi for the time when Irving was murdered."

"That's frightening."

"I take it she isn't back in rehab."

"Nope. She's on the streets. I'm not even sure if I can find her, and if she's using, she won't be of much use to Tray."

"I need to try. Can you let me know if she turns up?"

"Sure, snookums," Bob said. "Are we lunching today?"

"I can't. As soon as court is done, I'm going over to the Hall to see Tray. Maybe he has some idea where his mother might be."

***

"How are you holding up in here?" Sabre asked, as she sat down across from Tray in the tiny interview room.

Tray shivered, but he didn't respond.

"Tray, what happened?"

"It just gets uncomfortable sometimes."

"Did someone do something to you?"

"Not really."

"Tray, I need to know if someone is hurting or threatening you. Maybe I can stop it before it gets worse."

"I try to keep to myself, but they call me names."

"What names?"

"Mostly Zebra. Sometimes Skunk or Domino."

"Because you're mixed race?"

"I guess. I don't talk or walk like them. They cuss all the time and sometimes, they're just plain mean. I don't get it."

"Who are these boys?"

He shrugged his shoulders. "I think the nicknames were started by a guy named Malcolm, but once you get tagged with a nickname everyone calls you that."

"I can report the harassment if you want me to," Sabre said.

"No. That'll just make it worse. I just want to go back to June's house. And I want to see my sister." Before Sabre could answer, Tray said, "But she can't come here. This place is awful. I'll see her when I get out, I guess. And what about my mom? She's back on the streets again, isn't she?"

"Why do you think that?"

"Because I know she would've come to see me if she wasn't. She's a good mother when she isn't using."

"We don't know where she is. We've been looking, but we haven't been able to locate her. We need to talk to her about the time you spent with her at that last visit. Do you have any idea where she might be?"

"Remember the guy in the park who was with Mom?"

"Yes. What about him?"

"I think I remember where I know him from. There's a house a few blocks from where we used to live. I followed her there once. They make drugs in that house."

"How do you know that?"

"I saw them cooking 'em. And when some dude started to light up a cigarette, two other guys freaked out. They said the house could blow up."

"Where was your mom?"

"She was passed out on the sofa by the time I went inside. I couldn't even get her awake."

"Did you hear any of the names of the people in the house?"

"No, they just kept calling the guy with the cigarette, 'dumb nigga.' That's all I heard."

"What did the men look like?"

"The guy with the cigarette was short, skinny, and real fidgety, like he was high on something. The other two guys were taller, and one was a big, fat, ugly guy with a bald head."

"Do you remember where the house is?"

"Yes. I've been back there a couple of times. Mom always goes there when she gets real bad. One time when I was watching Shanisha, she fell and bumped her head and it started bleeding. I didn't know what to do, so I ran and got Mom."

"Did she come home?"

"Yes, but she went back the next day."

"Do you know the address of this house?"

"No, but I can tell you how to get there. If you start at my house and walk to the right until you get to the stop sign, you turn right. Go a couple more blocks until you get to the house with a bright pink garage door, and turn left. It's the fourth house on the right side of the street."

"Thanks, Tray. We'll try to find her."

"If you do, will you ask her to come see me? Maybe I can get her to go back to rehab." His eyes were filled with pain as he spoke.

Sabre was sad that this poor boy felt the need to

get his mother into a drug program. She was the parent, not him. Yet, he was sitting in juvenile hall, and instead of worrying about his own situation, he was trying to help his mother. Sabre's feelings went from sadness to anger toward that woman.

When Sabre left juvenile hall, she immediately called JP and left a message for him to call her back. She needed him to find Tray's mother.

Chapter 13

JP walked down El Cajon Boulevard, stopping at every bar along the way. At each one, he showed the bartender and some patrons the photo of Jeannine Copley, Tray's mother. Some knew her, but no one had seen her in several weeks. He was almost to the end of El Cajon Boulevard when he spoke to two women standing on the street corner. One was dressed in a tight, short, black skirt, a bright pink tube top, and stiletto heels. The other was dressed in what appeared to be a cat-woman costume.

"Hello, cowboy," the woman in the tube top said. "Are you looking for a little action?"

"Actually, I'm looking for a missing person." He handed her the photo of Jeannine Copley. "Do you know this woman?"

She shook her head. "No, sorry."

Cat woman spoke up. "That's Jeannine. She hasn't been working for months. Last I heard, she was in rehab. Unless Jolly got his hooks in her again."

"Who's Jolly?"

"He keeps his girls high on crack. Makes 'em work for the fix."

"Do you know where I can find Jolly?"

"I ain't never been there, but I heard it's just off Chase somewhere."

"Here in El Cajon?"

"Uh huh."

"What does Jolly look like?"

"He's real big, over 300 pounds, not quite as tall as you. And not nearly as good-looking."

"Thanks for your help."

Cat woman slinked up closer to JP and rubbed her body against his, making a purring sound. JP pulled a twenty-dollar bill out of his pocket, handed it to her, and stepped away.

"Sure you don't want your money's worth?" she asked.

"You told me what I needed to know. We're good. Thanks."

"Meow," she said in a long purring tone.

JP tipped his hat and walked away. He checked his phone and saw he had a message from Sabre, so he called her back.

Sabre gave him the information she had obtained from Tray about the crack house.

"He didn't happen to mention a guy named Jolly, did he?" JP asked.

"No. He didn't seem to know anyone's name. Who's Jolly?"

"He's a pimp who seems to have a hold on Jeannine. Did he tell you what any of the guys look like?"

"He said two are real skinny and one is a 'big, fat, ugly guy with a bald head.'"

"That sounds like Jolly. I'll call Ernie and see what he knows about him, and then I'll go check out the house."

"Are you any closer to finding Tray's father?" Sabre asked.

"To tell you the truth, I've spent so much time looking for his mother that I haven't had a chance to do much else, but I did run a background check on him and Ernie got some inside information for me. Horatio Whisenant served five years in Centinela State Prison for armed robbery. And get this, he would've been out sooner, but he beat up a goof a few months before his release."

"He beat up a pedophile?"

"Yup. Can you imagine what he would do to someone who molested his own kid?"

"He just rose up the suspect list," Sabre said.

"Do you have a current address for him?"

"No, but Ernie's checking for me. I'll get right on it after I check out the info you just gave me."

"JP, please be careful."

"Always."

Chapter 14

As soon as JP got in his car, he called Ernie, his friend at the sheriff's department, and asked him about Jolly.

"I know Jolly. He's been busted a few times and served a few years, but we haven't been able to get him lately. He's a small fish who brags a lot and acts real tough. He usually rolls over on someone bigger when he's caught and walks away with a slap on the wrist. I'd like to see him off the streets before he blows up a meth lab and innocent people get killed. What's Jolly to you?"

"He appears to be the pimp for the mother of our juvenile client, Tray Copley."

"The teen charged with killing the pedophile?"

"Yup. I'm trying to find the mother because she may be his alibi if they ever establish a time of death. Or she may even be the killer."

"That's right. You asked me to see what else I could find on Tray's father, Horatio Whisenant. I didn't come up with much. The last address I have for him is the house he lived in with Jeannine and Tray three years ago. He was there for approximately five years with Tray. Prior to that, as you know, he was at Centinela State Prison. I haven't found anything new on him."

"Apparently he hasn't been in any trouble since his prison bout."

"Or he hasn't been caught. Where are you headed now?"

"I'm going to the crack house. Want to come along?"

"Can you get a beer afterwards?"

"Sure, if it doesn't take too long. I thought I would stake the house out for a while."

"What the heck. I'm just getting off duty. Who knows, maybe we'll find Jolly."

"I don't have an address, but I'll meet you at Tray's house. I have directions from there, but no street names. We can go together from Tray's." JP gave him the address to the house where Tray normally lived with his mother and sister.

***

Ernie was waiting for JP when he pulled up in front of Tray's house. Ernie got out of his car and slid into JP's. They followed Tray's directions and pulled up in front of a house in need of serious repair. The front yard needed mowing, and trash had built up on the side of the house.

Ernie pulled a photo out of a folder he had been holding. "Here's a picture of Jolly in case he comes out."

JP took a good look at the photo and then handed it back to Ernie. "I'll be back," he said, and exited the car.

"Where are you going?"

"I'm going to see if I can see inside."

"Want me to go with you?"

"You better stay here. I have enough trouble with people thinking I'm a cop, but they'll smell you coming."

JP walked up to the side of the house, accidentally kicking a beer can as he neared the wall. He stopped and stood still, even though the noise was drowned out by the rap music that bellowed from the house. He moved along the side of the house until he reached a window that was uncovered. An open window was nearby, and the smell of cat urine filled his nostrils.

He heard a loud, booming male voice say, "Shut that off. I'm sick of that noise."

The rap stopped and JP stood still. Just then he heard the sound of the window opening next to him. He pushed his body against the wall and remained still, except to remove his pistol from his shoulder strap. The urine smell grew stronger as the window opened.

JP heard a sigh, and a female voice mumbled, "That's better." The voice sounded familiar. It may have been Jeannine, but he couldn't be certain.

"What the hell are you doing, you stupid bag bride?" the loud, booming voice said.

"I need some air. I'm getting sick."

"Too bad. Get the hell out if you can't take the smell."

The window slammed shut.

JP waited and then moved slowly up to the window to see if he could see in, but just as he did, the lights went out in the room and he couldn't see anything. He moved around the house but found no other uncovered windows. When he heard the front door open, he worked his way back to the front of the house and hid behind some bushes. He watched as a thin, scruffy-looking man about five-foot-ten came out of the house. He twitched as he walked toward an older model Chevy, and then he got in and drove off.

Shortly thereafter, a young couple in their twenties, both with backpacks, walked up to the door and knocked. This time JP saw Jolly open the door and invite them inside. They stayed in the house for about three or four minutes and then left.

JP decided it was time for him to make his way back to the car. He reached the sidewalk just as a car drove up and parked in front of the house. JP walked in the opposite direction and past his car where Ernie was sitting and observing. He kept going until he reached the end of the block, where he turned left and kept out of sight until the car left. Then he returned to his car.

"I thought you were leaving me," Ernie said. "Did you see anything?"

"Not much more than you could see from the car, but I got a strong whiff of what smelled like cat urine. Either that house is full of cats, or they're brewing up some crack as we speak."

"I know. I can smell it from here, and I'm betting they're not animal lovers. With the traffic I observed just in the short time we've been here, they seem to have a pretty good business going," Ernie said. "Did you see the kid's mom?"

"I heard a woman in there who some guy referred to as a 'bag bride,' which you and I both know is a crack-smoking prostitute. That fits Jeannine's description when she's off track, but I can't be sure it was her."

"Yeah, it could be a thousand other women as well." Ernie twirled the pen he was holding between his fingers.

"Did you get photos?" JP asked.

"Does Grizzly Adams have a beard?" Ernie repeated a phrase he had heard JP say before.

"I guess that's a 'yes.'"

"Sure did. I even got one of Jolly when he came to the door."

"You want to bust them, don't you?"

"You bet."

"Can you get a warrant?"

"I'm sure we've seen and smelled plenty. Besides, there's already a warrant out for Jolly for some traffic infraction, but we didn't want to use it until we had more. So, at the very least, we can nab him. But with the photos I took and your statement, the judge will sign one. It shouldn't take more than a half hour or so."

"So, do it."

"What about the kid's mom?"

"If she's in there, she'll get arrested and it'll be easier to talk to her. Besides, maybe if she gets busted she'll get back in rehab."

Ernie called Vice and explained the situation. He and JP waited and watched for the next forty-five minutes. Only one other man went to the door and left a few minutes later. Two scantily dressed women went inside and were still there when two vice detectives arrived. Ernie got out and spoke to the detectives briefly and then returned to the car.

"Let's go," Ernie said. "We need to get out of here in case Jeannine is in there. You'll never get the information you want if she thinks you busted her."

Before they drove away, two other detectives arrived in a dark sedan and both ends of the block had squad cars deterring the exit or entrance onto the street. Ernie showed an officer his badge and briefly explained the situation.

"Want to get that beer?" Ernie asked.

"Does a one-legged duck swim in circles?"

"I take it that's a 'yes,' cowboy."

Chapter 15

The bell rang just as JP exited his car at St. Kieran Catholic School. JP walked onto the campus while school was letting out. He headed toward the office through a sea of girls in blue plaid skirts, white shirts, and navy sweaters, while the boys wore white shirts and navy blue pants. For a fleeting second, JP wondered if the uniforms added a more disciplined mindset or if dressing alike just squelched their individuality.

JP walked into the office. Samples of children's work peppered the walls. A young woman stood at the front desk.

"I'm here to see Sister Maria Luisa Hilasco," JP said.

"Your name?"

"JP Torn. We have an appointment." He looked at his watch. "It appears I'm about ten minutes early."

"That's okay. I'll tell her you're here." She turned away and walked out the back entrance of the office.

JP looked around, but there was no place to sit, so he stood near the counter and waited. The young woman returned about three minutes later.

"Please follow me." She led him out the back door and across a little square to a classroom marked 6B. The door was open and after signaling for JP to enter, she left.

At first glance, JP didn't see the nun. Suddenly, a head in a nun's habit popped up from behind her desk. She was an attractive woman who appeared to be in her late thirties. "Sorry, I dropped my pen." She stood up and said, "Are you JP?"

"Yes."

"Good. I'm Sister Maria. Please have a seat." She pointed to a student desk in front of her. When JP looked inquisitively at the desk, the sister said, "Better yet, grab one of those folding chairs over there. It'll be more comfortable."

JP picked up a folding chair, opened it up, and sat down directly across from her.

"What can I do for you?"

"I'm the investigator for Attorney Sabre Brown. She represents a minor who is being charged with murder. She doesn't believe he committed this crime. You're listed as a witness." JP found himself over-explaining the situation and felt a little uncomfortable in the nun's presence. He realized he had an unusual feeling of intimidation. He thought of a time when he was about seven years old and went to catechism with his friend, Tom, with whom he was spending the night. Tom's mother made them go to catechism after school. Tom was teasing the girl sitting in front of him, which JP found comical. The nun saw them, walked over to Tom, and smacked him on the hand with a ruler. She reached over to give JP similar discipline, but he saw the ruler coming and jumped up and ran out, knocking the chair over as he did. He never went back.

"The body they found on Coyote Ridge?" Sister Maria asked, bringing him back to present day.

"Yes, ma'am," JP said. He wondered how many murder investigations she was involved in, but he realized she was just making sure they were talking about the same thing. "How did the police happen to question you?"

"I saw a photo of the dead man in the newspaper and I recognized him. I called the police and told them I had seen him with a child on Saturday at Albertsons supermarket."

"Did they ask you to identify the child?"

"Yes, they showed me photos of children and I picked him out."

"How many photos?"

"About twenty."

"Really?"

"Yes."

"Can you be sure it was the same boy?" JP wanted to show her the photo of Tray for clarification, but he didn't want to implant Tray's image in her mind any more than the police had already done. Perhaps in court she wouldn't be able to identify him. "Yes, I'm positive. I was very close to him. They were standing in the checkout line right in front of me. I even spoke to the young man."

"Why was that?" JP asked.

Sister Maria looked down at her clasped hands and then back at JP. "The man had his hand on the boy's shoulder. The boy put the sodas, a bag of donuts, and a Hershey bar on the belt. As he did, the man kept his hand on the boy's shoulder. It made me very uncomfortable."

"Like creepy uncomfortable?"

"I'm afraid so. He seemed way too possessive."

"Did it occur to you that they might be father and son?"

"It wasn't that kind of touching. Besides, the boy called him Glen."

"Did the boy appear to be there against his will?" JP asked.

"No, not really."

"So, how did the young man act?"

"Pretty normal, I guess, except when he talked."

"What did he say?"

"It wasn't so much what he said, but how he said it. When I commented to him on his choice of groceries, he said something about a special occasion or treat or something. But he sounded kind of robotic. Since I didn't know him, I thought perhaps it was his normal speech pattern. But maybe he was scared." She paused and fiddled with the pen she was holding.

"What else bothered you?"

"I had seen this man a couple of times before."

JP looked up in surprise. "Where? And when?"

"A couple of weeks ago, he was hanging around near the school grounds. One of the other teachers spotted him first. She thought he was there to pick up one of the kids, but no student approached him. Then he walked away."

"But he came back?"

"Yes, on two other occasions. The teacher on duty always stays with the children until they are all picked up, so we're certain nothing ever happened. But the third time I saw him, I called the police and they drove by for a couple of days right around dismissal time. He stopped coming after that."

"How long ago was that?"

"The last time he came to the school was a little over a week before I saw him with that young man at Albertsons. That was on a Saturday, so it must have been Wednesday when I last saw him at the school because the cops drove by for two days and then school was out for the weekend. The cops came by at least one day the following week, but I didn't see the man again until we were at the supermarket."

JP started to stand and then stopped. "Do you remember the name of the clerk who checked you out?"

"I'm sorry, I don't."

"Was it a man or a woman?"

"A woman."

"Young or old?"

She thought for a minute. "It's hard to say because

she had so much makeup on. If I had to guess, I'd say she was about fifty."

"Was there anything unusual about the makeup, or was there just a lot of it?"

"Mostly she just had heavy face makeup and bright red lips. Oh, and her eyelashes weren't real." She suddenly squinted her eyes and looked very pensive.

"Was there something else?"

"I'm not sure it will help, but there was someone else who saw them."

"Who?"

"There was a man standing at the end of the aisle just behind where we were checking out. He seemed to be watching the man and the kid. I thought maybe he was a store manager or something."

"Was he wearing a badge or store uniform of any kind?"

"Not that I saw. He was dressed in a nice dress shirt and slacks, I think. I know he wasn't wearing jeans."

"What did he look like?"

"A little older, I think. That's another reason why I thought he might be a store manager."

"Tall or short?"

"Not too tall."

"Was he fat or thin?"

"He couldn't have been too fat or too thin because I think I would've remembered that. I'm just not sure since I only glanced at him for a second. I'm not certain how long he was there or if he was even looking at them. After the man and kid checked out I looked back, but he wasn't there.

Chapter 16

Tracking Tray's father, Horatio Whisenant, was more difficult than JP expected. It had been three years since Tray had seen him, and for all JP knew he could be in another state or even another country. He read through the family history portion of the social studies and other reports the social workers had written on Tray's dependency case. Horatio's mother lived in Alabama and his father was listed as *whereabouts unknown*. There was a sister named Cynthia listed, but no last name or address were provided. JP called Sabre to ask if she knew anything more about her.

"No, and Tray has never mentioned her," Sabre said.

"Could you ask him the next time you see him?"

"Sure. I'll probably go by there after court today. Do you have any other leads on the father?"

"No, but I'm going to see Jeannine in Las Colinas this morning, if she'll see me. Maybe she'll have more information."

"Don't forget," Sabre said, "she is represented, albeit not for the criminal charges, but she'll have another attorney appointed soon."

"I already spoke with Bob. He's going with me. In fact, he should be here any minute. And there's no need to talk to her about what happened last night. I just want to see what she has to say about the visit she and Tray had on the seventh. That's the only time we haven't accounted for when Tray wasn't with his foster parents or in school, unless he skipped."

"I spoke with the school office and they have no record of Tray missing school, or even a class, for nearly a month prior to his arrest."

"That's good, but we still need to sort out the events that took place on that Saturday—the day Tray was supposedly seen with Irving at the supermarket. His friend, Drew, seems credible, although I still think he's holding something back, and Tray claims he was with his therapist the remainder of the time period."

"Have you talked to his therapist yet? Maybe his office assistant got the dates wrong."

"He's still on vacation, but he's due back soon. I've left messages with his answering service and his office saying it's paramount I meet with him right away," JP said. "Have they determined the time of death yet?"

"The DA said they expect to have a report later today. I'll let you know. In the meantime, just try to find another suspect. Even if we can account for Tray's time, we can create more reasonable doubt if we can point the finger at someone else."

"I'm sure there are plenty of victims out there whose parents would fit the profile, but finding them isn't going to be easy. I think the best way to do that is to get to know Irving."

***

Bob and JP waited in the interview room at Las Colinas for Jeannine.

"Thanks for doing this," JP said.

"No problem. I needed to meet with my client anyway. Why don't you ask your questions, and then I'll meet with her alone for a bit. Maybe I can talk some sense into her—although I don't know why I think that'll work; I haven't been very effective so far."

"Sounds like a plan."

"Jeannine was probably high as a kite when they picked her up from that crackhouse, so she might not be in very good shape this morning."

The door opened in the back of the interview room, and a female officer led Jeannine Copley inside. "I'll be right outside when you're through," the officer said. She nodded toward the chair, and Jeannine sat down across the table from JP and Bob. The door closed when the guard left.

Jeannine put her right elbow on the table and the palm of her hand under her chin to hold her head up. Her fingers wrapped around her mouth and nose. Her eyes were droopy and JP wondered if she would stay awake for the interview.

"Hello, Jeannine," Bob said. "Pretty rough night?"

"Uh-huh," she said, without moving her hand.

"This is JP Torn. You may remember him. He was the investigator for Tray on the dependency case and is now working on his criminal case."

"I remember him."

"He has some questions for you—not about your arrest last night, but about Tray. Are you up to answering a few things? It may help keep Tray out of prison."

She raised her head from her hand. "Why would Tray go to prison?"

"He's in juvenile hall right now. He's been charged with murder."

"That's just crazy," she said in a louder voice. "My boy wouldn't kill anyone. Who'd he supposedly kill?"

"Glen Irving."

Jeannine wrinkled her forehead. "I shoulda killed him myself." She shook her head. "I know Tray wouldn't have done that. He's too good a boy. Did that creep attack him again or something?"

Bob explained that Irving's body was found and a lot of the evidence was pointing toward Tray.

"We're not sure exactly when he was killed," JP said. "But we're trying to account for Tray's time. When was the last time you saw your son?"

She frowned as if it hurt to think. "A couple of weeks ago, I guess."

"You didn't see him on Friday, the third of May?"

She shrugged her shoulders. "I don't know. Maybe."

"It was the Friday before the review hearing a little over two weeks ago."

She rubbed her head with her right hand. "I can't remember."

"Please think. It's really important for Tray's sake that you tell me the truth," JP said. "He and Shanisha were supposed to spend the afternoon with you. Tray said he saw you."

"If Tray says I saw him, then I saw him. That kid don't lie."

"I need to know what you remember. It would've been the same day that you left Harbinger House. He said that you took him and his sister to McDonald's. Was he lying?"

"Look, I did see him that day, but...."

"But what?"

Jeannine looked at Bob. "I don't want to say any more. I just want to get my kids back."

Bob turned to JP. "Maybe you should step out for a few minutes. Let me see if what she knows will help Tray."

"Fair enough."

JP left the room.

"So, Jeannine, what is it you're not telling?"

After some discussion with his client, Bob brought JP back into the room.

"Jeannine understands it's important that you know where Tray was on Friday afternoon." He looked at his client. "Tell him what you told me."

"I did see Tray that afternoon. A driver from DSS

brought both of my kids to me. She gave me some bus passes and we used them to go to McDonald's. Then we went to the park and that's where I met up with Jolly. I didn't stay at the park."

"So you left the kids alone at the park?"

"Yes, and if the social workers knew that, they wouldn't let me have my kids back. That's why I didn't want to say anything."

"How did you expect them to not notice that you weren't there when they came to pick up your kids?"

"I told Tray I had to leave. That it was real important. Tray said they would walk back to the rehab center and wait for the driver. Apparently they did because no one seems to know I wasn't there."

"How long were you with Tray and Shanisha?" JP asked.

"About forty-five minutes. They only had an hour and a half scheduled with me, so Tray didn't have time to go anywhere else."

"Where did you go?"

Jeannine fidgeted with her hair. "Jolly and I went straight to the house where I was last night. I've been there ever since, except for when I went to the review hearing."

"And you didn't see Irving in the park the day you left Harbinger House?"

"No," she said loudly, and grimaced.

"When was the last time you saw him?"

"I haven't seen him since I kicked him out."

JP remembered that Irving left on his own, but he felt no need to call her out on that one. "What can you tell me about Irving's family?"

"Not much. His mother has Alzheimer's and is probably in a nursing home by now. He took me by her house once, but we didn't go inside." JP jotted down the information that Jeannine could remember about

Irving's mother's house, but it wasn't enough to find it.

"Does he have any siblings here in San Diego?"

"He has four or five sisters, but I don't think any of them live here. One of them was here for a while, but she left." Jeannine squirmed in her chair as she spoke.

"Did you ever meet her?"

"No, Glen and her didn't get along. They had some kind of fight a long time ago, and I don't think they were even on speaking terms."

"I need to ask you a few questions about Tray's father."

"He dumped us a long time ago. Who cares about him?"

"Do you know where he is?"

"No idea. The social worker tried to find him when this all started, but she wasn't able to. The last I heard anything was a couple of years ago."

"What was that?" JP asked.

"That he started a new family. He was working, but I don't know where."

"Do you know anything about his sister, Cynthia?"

"She used to spend time with the kids once in a while, but after Horatio left us, she stopped coming around too."

"Do you have an address for her?"

"No, but she lived on Date in La Mesa. It was a really tiny, old house with one tall palm tree in the front yard."

"I'm familiar with that neighborhood. Is the house closer to the top of the hill or the town?"

Jeannine thought for a second. "I think it's more toward the top, but I don't know. I remember she had a sweet view from the porch."

"Do you remember the color of the house?"

"I think it was white, but I'm not sure. I was only there a couple of times."

“Thanks. You've been a big help."

Jeannine sat up a little straighter and took a deep breath. "Have you seen Tray?" she asked.

"Yes, he's staying strong, but it would help if you could get out of here, clean up, and go visit him. He needs you. More importantly, he needs to know that you are clean."

Chapter 17

JP liked this part of town—old, historic La Mesa. Many of the houses were over one hundred years old. The neighborhood was quiet, and it was a quick walk to Jitters, the neighborhood coffee shop. His friend, Augustine, lived here for a while just after his divorce so his son could attend Helix High. JP and Augustine hung out together a lot during that time, so he became pretty familiar with the area, but finding Cynthia's house wouldn't be easy since almost every house on the street had palm trees. JP started up the short street where palm trees forty or fifty feet high lined the narrow road. He eliminated each house that had more than one palm tree, focusing on the right side of the street because he knew the left wouldn't have a view from the front of the house. About halfway up, he saw a house with one tall palm tree and a porch, but the house was too large to fit the description Jeannine had given him.

He kept driving, eliminating house after house, until he was about three-quarters of the way up the hill and there it sat on the right side of the road—a tiny, old, white house in need of paint with one huge palm tree and seven steps that led up to a porch with an old wicker rocker. JP drove the rest of the way up the hill to see if there were any others that fit the description, but there were not, so he returned.

JP walked up the steps, confident he had the right house but not really expecting Cynthia to still be the tenant. He knocked. A woman in a wheelchair opened the door.

Through the screen, JP said, "Hi, my name is JP Torn. I'm looking for Tray Copley's Aunt Cynthia."

"That's me. Is Tray all right?"

"Not exactly."

Cynthia turned her wheelchair around, and called out, "Derrick, come here, please."

A tall kid about thirteen or fourteen years old meandered into the living room, eating an apple.

"Open the door and let me out onto the porch. I need to talk to this gentleman."

The young man opened the door and wheeled her out, and then went back inside.

"Have a seat," she said to JP.

JP parked himself on the edge of the porch railing. Jeannine hadn't said anything about Cynthia being in a wheelchair. He wondered if there had been an accident. Then he noticed she didn't have a lot of control over her hands, either.

"Isn't this a great view?" Cynthia asked.

JP looked out over the valley. He could see for miles. All the houses on the hillsides and in the valley were peppered with trees of all sorts. The blue sky seemed to go on forever. "I can see why you like it here."

"So what's the story on Tray?"

There was no way to sugarcoat the situation, so JP summarized it. "He's in juvenile hall and been charged with murder. I'm the investigator for his attorney, Sabre Brown. She doesn't believe he's guilty."

Her head shook from side to side. JP wasn't sure if the movement was voluntary or not.

"Who's the victim?"

"A man named Glen Irving."

"I know I haven't seen Tray in a long time, but that doesn't sound like the little boy I knew. Is he involved in a gang?"

"No, nothing like that. He's a good kid and a good

student." JP paused. "What I need from you is information on his father. Tray hasn't seen him in about three years. I was hoping you could help."

"I don't see much of my brother either. Don't even know where he lives." Her head twitched again. "I should've kept in touch with those kids. It got harder after Horatio left them. And then I was diagnosed with MS, and my illness took over most of my life. I hate that my brother didn't stay in touch with his kids. That's just not right."

"I'm sorry about your illness, ma'am."

"That's okay. I'm learning to live with it." She quickly changed the subject. "How can I help?"

"When was the last time you saw your brother?"

"Over a year ago."

"Do you know what part of the city he was in? Or was he living with someone?"

"He was in National City somewhere, or at least that's what he told me. He was living with some skank named Allison, but I don't know if he's still with her or not. They had a new baby, but that doesn't seem to mean anything to him."

"Was he working?"

"I don't know," she said. "Wait. Yes, he was. He was working at a tire place because he told me that if I needed tires to let him know and he would get me a deal."

"Did you?"

"No, I was afraid of how he was getting the deal. My brother doesn't always follow the rules in life, as you can see by the way he dumped his kid." Cynthia gazed out through the palm trees at the valley. "Do you think it would be okay for me to visit Tray?"

"I think he'd like that, ma'am." He removed two cards from his wallet and handed them to her. "The first card is Tray's attorney. Call her to see if she can get you on the list for a visit. The other one is mine. Please call me if you hear from your brother or if you think of anything else that might help us find him."

"How can he help Tray?" she asked.

"I don't know, ma'am, but we need to reach him just the same."

JP thanked her for her help and as he walked to his car, his phone rang. It was Sabre.

JP told her, "I'm just leaving Cynthia's house. I have a lead on Tray's father, but I need to go back to my house and do a little research. I also need to check on my pup."

"Good. This should help you when you try to pin Horatio down. I just got the ME's report. Their best guess is that Irving died most likely on Saturday, but Sunday at the latest. They know it wasn't before Saturday because the nun saw him that day. Have you spoken to the checker at Albertsons yet?"

"I'm going back there today to meet with a woman named Jodi Ellis. She's working the late shift today, and she's agreed to see me on her break."

"Have you had any luck finding the other man Sister Maria saw in the store, the one at the end of the aisle who she thought might be a store employee?"

"No. I've talked to the store manager and all the assistant managers in Albertsons, as well as security to determine if it was any of them. Several of those employees fit the limited description she gave us. I've eliminated a couple of them who weren't there that day, and the others don't remember seeing anything. It could've just been a customer, and there's no way we could find him if that's the case."

"I was just hoping we could find someone who would say it wasn't Tray."

"What about the security videos?"

"I've filed a discovery motion to acquire access to

them. We should have them in a few days."

"If we see Tray on the video, then we know he was there. If he's not on the video, we still don't know for sure."

"I know," Sabre said. "The videos have a greater chance of hurting us than helping us."

"I did track a guy who was getting signatures on a political petition outside the store that day. He's going to be at the Target near there tonight. I'll let you know if he saw or remembers anything."

Chapter 18

Jodi Ellis, a clerk at Albertsons, sat across from JP at McDonald's, the closest fast food restaurant to Albertsons. She had already purchased a small hamburger, fries, and a Coke, and was ready to eat her lunch. He guessed her age to be about forty. He thought her makeup aged her, but he had to assume she thought otherwise. JP was not a fan of heavy makeup. He preferred the more natural look, and looking at her features, he thought she might be quite attractive without the paint.

"Thanks for meeting me today," JP said. "I know you have limited time on your break, so I'll try not to take up too much of it."

"It's fine," Jodi said. "Aren't you going to eat?"

"I'm not hungry, but I think I'll get a cup of coffee. Would you like anything else?"

"No thanks."

JP walked to the counter, paid for a cup of coffee, and returned with a steaming hot beverage. Jodi was picking at her fries.

Opening his phone, JP showed her a photo of the nun, which Sister Maria had so graciously let him take. "Do you recognize this woman?"

"I've seen her in the store before. She comes in once a week or so."

"Have you ever talked to her?"

"Just the usual while I'm checking, never anything really personal. I know she's a nun at St. Kieran's School. She told me that some time ago when she was buying something for the school. I mean, I could see that she was a nun by the way she was dressed, but I didn't know she was a teacher until that day."

"Do you remember the last time you saw her in the store?"

"She was there about two days ago."

"And before that?"

Jodi thought for a minute, and then said, "She was there a couple of weeks ago. I don't remember exactly when, but I do remember she seemed uncomfortable."

"How do you mean?"

"She kept staring at the man in front of her. Then she would look at me and back at him, like maybe she was trying to tell me something. I finished checking him out and he left."

"Did you ask her if something was wrong?"

"I did, but she said there wasn't."

"What did the man look like?"

"I couldn't really describe him. He was wearing a baseball cap and sunglasses, so I didn't really see his face."

"Was he alone?"

"No, he had a young boy with him."

"Could you describe the boy?"

"Not really. He was a light-skinned, black kid. That's about all I remember. If that's important, I really can't help you. I honestly didn't pay much attention to the kid."

With further questioning, all JP established was that she didn't know anything more. She couldn't tell him what the kid was wearing, how tall he was, how old he was, or anything else that might help eliminate Tray as a suspect. JP showed her about eight pictures of African-American boys about Tray's age; Tray's picture was included. She said it could be any one of them with the exception of one who looked older and much darker than Tray.

***

Later that day, JP walked out of Target and spotted the man with the petition. He appeared to be about forty-five and needed a shave, but was a nice-looking man. When he smiled, he revealed a missing tooth that detracted from his looks. JP walked closer to him and was approached, as he knew he would be, by the solicitor.

"Sir, are you interested in lowering your taxes?" the man asked.

"Always," JP responded.

The man handed him a copy of the petition. JP took it, looked closer at the man, and said, "Weren't you at Albertsons a couple of weeks ago?"

He sniffed. "Yes, I was. Did you already sign this?"

"Were you there on a Saturday?"

"I think so." He sniffed. "Yeah, I'm pretty sure I worked there on a Saturday and Sunday."

"That would've been the first weekend of May?"

"Sounds right."

"I'm a PI and I'm looking for a missing child. He may have been at that Albertsons." JP thought that would be the easiest way to obtain information. It would take a lot less explaining and may provoke some sympathy. "Would you mind answering a few questions for me?"

"Sure. I'll do that."

JP took out his phone and showed him a photo of Irving. "Do you recognize this man?"

He looked it over carefully, sniffed, and shook his head. "I don't know that I do. Did that man take the kid?"

"We don't know. He would've been with a small, teenage, African-American boy. And the man was wearing a cap and sunglasses."

He shook his head again. "Man, I wish I could help, but I don't remember seeing that guy, but I see so many people. Like you, for instance; I don't remember seeing you."

JP didn't have the heart to tell him that his story was a ploy since the man hadn't figured that out.

Chapter 19

JP spent nearly two hours attempting to call the 142 listings for tire stores in the San Diego area. He started in National City and worked his way outward. Each time he asked to speak to Horatio. Finally, he reached Big O Tires in San Marcos.

"May I speak to Horatio Whisenant, please?" JP asked.

"Just a sec," the young man said. JP heard him ask someone if there was anyone there named Horatio. "Sorry, I'm new here. Horatio doesn't work here anymore. He left about six months ago."

"Do you know if he went to another store?" JP asked.

The guy on the phone repeated the question and then said, "No idea."

JP was discouraged. If Whisenant left the tire company, he could've gone anywhere or nowhere. Since JP had called over half his list, he decided to keep trying in hopes that the man got another job for which he had experience.

Another eighteen calls were made with no success until a man said, "Stanley Tire, how can I help you?"

"May I speak to Horatio, please?"

"He's on his lunch and won't be back until one o'clock. I'm the manager on duty right now. Is there something I can help you with?"

"Actually, you're who I should talk to. My wife was in there not long ago, and I just want to let you know what great service she received. She talked to a couple of workers there, but the only name she could remember was Horatio. She said he was very friendly and explained everything to her. She felt very safe in her car when she left."

"Well, thank you for taking the time to call. We don't get to hear that sort of thing very often. I'll pass the word on."

JP jotted down the address of the store and stuck the paper in his pocket.

"Come, Louie," JP called to his beagle pup. "You need to go outside."

Louie ran across the living room floor and followed JP out the door. JP left him there, and went to his kitchen to make a turkey sandwich that he wrapped in a paper towel. Then he returned to the back door and let Louie inside.

"Be a good boy. I won't be long."

JP grabbed the sandwich and a bottle of water from the refrigerator and drove to Stanley Tire, eating his food as he drove. He arrived about 12:40, hoping to catch Whisenant before he started his shift. When he pulled into the parking lot, he saw a small, Mexican fast-food restaurant next door. He parked his car and walked to the restaurant. There was an African-American man sitting alone at a table out front. He was wearing a black shirt with a "Stanley Tire" insignia on it. As JP approached the table, he could read the name patch. It read, "Horatio." The man appeared to be almost done with his food and was sipping on a large soft drink.

"Mind if I sit here?" JP asked.

Horatio glanced around suspiciously at the empty tables. "No. I'm nearly done," he said in a deep baritone voice.

"You're Horatio Whisenant, right?"

Horatio set his drink on the table. "Yes, do I know you?"

"No. My name is JP Torn. I'm a private investigator for your son, Tray Copley."

"What do you want?" His tone was a little harsh.

"Your son is in juvenile hall. He's been charged with murder."

"Murder? What the hell has happened to that kid? He was such a good boy."

"He's still a good boy, but a lot has happened since you've been gone. When was the last time you saw him?"

"Two or three years ago. I couldn't live with that skeezer anymore."

"Jeannine?"

"Yes. She just couldn't stop the drugs, and then she'd go whoring around. I don't do drugs. I tried some stuff when I was a teenager, but then I figured out how stupid it was. But Jeannine, she'd go along for a year or two doing just fine, and then a little pressure and she'd be out lookin' for some cookies for her dumb self. So I left her ass."

"I'm not judging or anything, but why didn't you take Tray with you?"

"I thought about it, but I figured I'd come back for him when I got my life straightened out. I didn't have a job and I had no place to live, but I knew I couldn't stay there or I would've killed that ho. Besides, Tray's little sister needed him. He always took care of her and since she wasn't mine, I couldn't take her. Jeannine got pregnant with her when I was in prison. Can't blame her for that. I was gone five years, but I don't think she even knows who the daddy is."

JP watched carefully for any change of expression when he asked the next question. "Do you know a guy named Glen Irving?"

"No. Don't think so. Why?"

JP saw no flicker of recognition from Horatio. He was either a good liar, or he didn't know anything about Irving.

"Did you hear about that body they found last week in El Cajon in Coyote Ridge?"

"Yeah, was that him? I saw something on the news, but they didn't give his name."

"Yes. About a year ago, Jeannine hooked up with Irving and he moved in with her and the kids. About six months ago it was discovered that Irving had sexually molested your son."

Horatio's face tightened and his eyes widened. JP could see the anger in his face as both of his hands formed fists. He said nothing.

JP continued. "The Department of Social Services filed a petition and removed the children from her care. Since they couldn't find you, the children went to foster care."

"What the hell? They couldn't find me? *You* found me." He spit out the words.

"I guess I looked a little harder, but in all fairness, you haven't left much of a trail. Tray's alibi is a little flimsy for the day Irving was killed."

"When was he killed?"

"Two weeks ago on Saturday or Sunday. That's as close as they can get since the body was found about a week later. He was in the care of his foster parents all day Sunday, but he spent some time with his best friend on Saturday. I don't know how credible his friend will sound on the stand."

Horatio rubbed his head as if he were thinking. "So the concern is Saturday. I wasn't hustlin' that day. I was home most of the time with the old lady and the kids and my old lady's sister from Hemet. But I could be his alibi. Would that work?"

"No," JP said. "His attorney is not going to put you on the stand to perjure yourself."

"So, what do you want from me?"

JP decided to be straight with him. "If that

happened to someone I cared about, I'd want to kill him."

"And you thought maybe I did it."

"I'm just doing my job."

"If I'd known about it, I probably would've, but I didn't. I know I haven't been much of a father, but I'll tell you this: I'd like to meet the motha who ganked that goof, so I can thank him."

The word *goof* caught JP's attention. "Do you know if you ever used the word *goof* around Tray?"

"I don't know. Maybe. That's what the inmates called kid diddlers in prison. Why?"

"Just curious." JP handed his card and Sabre's card to Horatio. "If you want to see your son, call this number," he said. "You may have to be cleared by Social Services, and I'm sure Sabre, his attorney, will ask Tray if he wants to see you, but a visit may be good for both of you." JP wasn't certain if seeing his father would be good for Tray or not, but it might be nice if Tray had a choice. And at least his father was working and attempting to stay out of prison... unless Horatio had just fed him a bunch of bull.

Chapter 20

JP walked up to the small house in an older neighborhood where Glen Irving's mother and sister lived. The lawns on the block were well maintained. No fences and none of the old homes seemed to need a paint job. JP had researched the neighborhood and knew it had the distinction of being mostly owner occupied. That was rare in an older area like this.

Irving's sister, Suzanne Prado, answered the door when he knocked.

"I'm JP Torn. Thanks for seeing me."

"I'll help if I can," Suzanne said, as she escorted JP into the living room. "This is my mother, Charlotte Irving. Mother, this is JP Torn."

"Hello," Charlotte said.

"As I explained on the phone, Mother has Alzheimer's, but she's having a good morning so far today."

"Good," JP said. "Nice to meet you, ma'am."

"You're a southern boy like Elvis. I was born in the south, you know. Just outside of Memphis over eighty years ago. Not too far from Graceland. Course Graceland didn't belong to Elvis then. I went to Humes High School with him, you know."

"With Elvis?"

"Yes. Nice young man." Then she stared toward the window in silence.

Suzanne added, "That's true. She did go to high school with Elvis. She's told us many stories about him. She said he was kind of shy and always very polite to teachers, addressing them as 'ma'am' and 'sir.' Elvis was different from the rest of the boys. He went to school in dress pants, while the others wore jeans, and he often wore flamboyant clothes. She has some great tales to tell." Suzanne paused. "But you're not here about that. What can I tell you about my brother Glen?"

"Glen," his mother said. "Nice young man. When's he coming to see me?" She seemed to direct her question at JP.

He didn't know how to respond, so he looked at Suzanne.

"Mom, remember what I told you? Glen isn't with us any longer."

"Maybe he'll come over later," Charlotte said.

Suzanne picked up the remote control. "Mom, it's time for your TV shows." She turned on the television and then said to JP, "Let's go into the dining room. Would you like some coffee or tea?"

"No, I'm fine. Thanks." He followed her into the room just a few steps away, and taking Suzanne's cue, sat down at the little table.

"She forgets that he's dead. I suppose it's just as well."

"I'm so sorry about your mother. It's hard to know what to do sometimes."

"Yes it is," she said. "So you're representing the kid who killed him?"

"Yes, the boy who is charged with his murder, but I'm not certain he did it. He claims he's innocent. That's why I'm investigating."

"The police haven't told us that much. Why do they think he killed Glen?"

"A few months ago Glen was living with our client's mother."

Suzanne shook her head, and for a second, she closed her eyes. A look of pain flashed across her face. "What did he do?"

She knows, JP thought. "He molested the young man." JP paused. "Did you know about that?"

"No. I haven't seen my brother in years. We weren't on speaking terms."

"Why is that?"

"I have a son, Rory. I never trusted Glen around him because he would touch him in a way that made Rory uncomfortable."

"You mean sexually?"

"No, but he would caress his back or try to hold his hand. Glen was living in Anaheim, not far from Disneyland, at the time. He wanted Rory to stay a weekend with him, and he promised to take him to Disneyland. When I said no, he kept trying to see Rory alone to convince him. I finally told him to get out and that he wasn't ever taking my son anywhere."

"How did your brother respond to that?"

"He left. He knew exactly why. He never even tried to reach me again."

"How long ago was that?"

"About eight years ago."

"Are you aware of any other children who may have fallen victim to your brother?"

She thought for a few seconds. "Not for certain, but once I was in Orange County and I stopped at his house to see him. He didn't invite me inside because he said the house was just too messy. We talked outside for a little while and then a kid, about eleven or twelve years old, came out and said he had to get home. Glen tried to coax him into staying, but he left. I watched as he walked to an apartment just a few doors away. That was before the incident with Rory, but it made me very uneasy. That's probably why I was so careful with him around my son."

Suzanne gave JP her brother's address when he had lived in Anaheim and the location of the apartment that the child had entered, but he knew finding the boy was a long shot. The chances of him still living there were almost nonexistent.

After more conversation, JP learned that Irving had five sisters and no brothers. "My father died when I was only three years old. Glen was five. My mom remarried and our stepdad Bill, who, although he was good to all of us, favored Glen. He took Glen everywhere he went—fishing, hunting, sometimes even to work—right from the start. We didn't think much of it because he was the only boy. Bill was around for about four years, and then one day he just left. At least that's what I thought happened. Mom never talked about it, but my older sister told me once that Mom kicked Bill out when she found him messing around with Glen. But I think the damage had already been done."

"Can you think of anyone else who might have a grudge against your brother?"

"I know how these things work. I'm sure he has molested many kids besides your client, so I'm sure there are a lot of angry mothers and fathers who would like to kill him. I know my husband would've if I had told him what I suspected about Glen and the way he was talking to Rory."

"So your husband still doesn't know?"

"No. He passed away two years ago, so I'm pretty sure he didn't kill him."

JP thought this woman was pretty sharp. She picked right up on his suspicions. "So I have to ask: where is your son?"

"He's in New York in film school. He's in his third year at the university. I doubt if he even remembers his Uncle Glen. I asked Rory at the time if Glen had done anything to him and he said no, but he made it clear that he didn't like him or the way he looked at him."

"And where were you a week ago Saturday?" JP didn't really see her as a suspect, but he was getting desperate.

"It was my mother's eightieth birthday. We had a big party for her at the recreation center. It started at two in the afternoon, and it was nine-thirty before we returned home. She had a wonderful time, by the way."

"I had to ask," JP said.

"If I were going to kill Glen, I would've done it a long time ago. Besides, I don't think he ever got the chance to hurt Rory—although I can't bear the thought of how many children he probably hurt over the years."

"Did the Orange County incident make you suspicious for the first time of his behavior?"

"Yes, but in all fairness, I wasn't around my brother much after he became an adult. We were only two years apart in age and we were really close until our stepdad came into the picture, but by the time we were teenagers, Glen was...how should I put this...different, and we were never close again."

"Different how?"

"He didn't seem too interested in girls. He had very few friends. He would stay up all night and then not want to go to school the next day."

"What did he do all night?"

"Watched TV or read comics." She paused. "And he would play with his old Lego sets. He was actually pretty smart, but sometimes he would act very childish."

"Can you think of anyone else he may have harmed or anyone who might have a grudge against him?"

"No. Like I said, I didn't see that much of him."

"Do you know where he was living?"

"After he left Orange County, he lived here with Mom until about three or four years ago. When her illness got too bad, he couldn't handle being around her. That's when I came back from northern California. He moved out and I moved in. I only saw him once or twice, but Mom would talk about him a lot. On some level, I think she knew what he was doing."

"Why?"

"Because she told me not to bring my little boys here when he was here. I explained that I only had one child, Rory, and he was away at college. She said, 'That's good. That's good.' I once tried to ask her what she knew, but she didn't explain. Now she just seems to remember him as a child, which is just as well for her sake."

"Did Glen work?"

"He didn't keep a job too long, but when he did, it was mostly janitorial work. He worked at Walmart for a while. That may have been his longest job. It lasted about three years, I think, but it was quite a while back. Mom might be able to tell us if you think it will help."

"It might."

They walked into the living room. Suzanne picked up the remote and paused her mother's show.

"Mom, do you know where Glen works?"

"Dale."

"No, Mom. I'm asking about Glen."

"Dale," she said again. "That's probably not a good place for him. Too much temptation."

Charlotte stared off into space and Suzanne hit the *Play* button on the remote and she turned toward the TV.

"Sorry. It was worth a try."

"Thanks," JP said. He gave her his card and asked her to call if she thought of anything else.

Chapter 21

JP talked to the manager at Walmart where Irving had worked for a couple of years but found nothing that was helpful. Most of the employees he had worked with were no longer at that store. The two who knew him maintained that he was quiet and kept to himself. No one had anything significant to add.

JP sat at his computer and Googled the word *Dale,* hoping it had something to do with Glen Irving's workplace—although he realized it could just as easily be the name of someone Charlotte Irving once knew. His search turned up a lot of information about Dale Earnhardt, Jr., which JP found interesting but unhelpful. The Urban Dictionary defined *Dale* as a "kind and loving person," but JP was pretty certain that Charlotte wasn't using that word to describe her son.

He Googled *Dale San Diego* and found a medical doctor and an insurance company, but neither had ever had an employee named Glen Irving. He Googled *Dale El Cajon*, the community where Irving's mother was living, and found two law offices with *Dale* in their names. It took a little longer to establish that Irving had not worked at either firm.

He tried *Dale La Mesa*, a neighboring community, and discovered Dale Elementary School. He picked up the phone and called his friend Detective Greg Nelson.

"Hey, Greg, how's it going?"

"It's all good. Just busy. What's up?"

"You know I'm investigating the Irving case. Tray Copley is Sabre Brown's client."

"I saw that."

"I'm trying to track Irving's work history. I'm sure Sabre will get the information you have when she receives the discovery from the DA, but it would be helpful if you could check on one thing for me."

"What is it?"

"Can you tell me if Irving ever worked at Dale Elementary School in La Mesa?"

"Yes, he did. I can't imagine what damage he may have done there," Greg said. "Why? Do you know something I don't?"

"No, I'm just trying to sort out the timeline right now. When did he work there?"

JP heard papers shuffling.

"He was hired about a week before school ended last June, worked through the summer, and left shortly after school started."

"Did he quit or was he fired?"

"The paperwork read, "Didn't meet probationary standards," so it's hard to tell if it was his work skills or his charming personality."

"Thanks for the info," JP said.

"Sure, let's get together for a drink sometime. It's been a while."

"I'm in, but I suppose we should wait until this case is over."

"That's probably best."

JP dialed Sabre. As soon as the phone rang, he realized his call was just an excuse to talk with her. After all, there wasn't anything she could do with the information he had found, at least not right now. He wanted to hang up, but it was too late.

"Hello," Sabre said.

"Hey, kid, I just wanted to give you a quick update. I don't have a report written yet, but I thought you might want to hear what I have."

"I do, but I'm in the middle of something right this moment."

"No problem. I'll email you a report in the morning."

He was frustrated at himself for calling.

He was about to say goodbye when Sabre said, "Can you come by the office? I'm still here working, but I'm almost done with the case I'm working on."

"You're still at the office? Alone?"

"Yes. I'm alone. My doors are all locked. All is good."

"I'll be right there."

JP hated when Sabre worked late at night in her office. A few years back, she'd had a stalker and it had given her a good scare. For a long time after the man had been apprehended, she hadn't worked late there. But she hated the restriction on her, and he knew she had started extending her hours beyond those of the two men with whom she shared the building. Suddenly, JP was glad he had called her.

***

Sabre was talking on her cell when she unlocked the door and JP entered the building. She moved her head in a sideways motion, indicating that he should follow her. They walked back to her office, and JP waited until she finished her conversation.

"What a mess," Sabre said when she hung up. "I got a call from the father of one of my minor clients saying the child's mother is seeing an old boyfriend who uses drugs and he's been around when his daughter is there. The mother then called and was screaming that the father is abusing the child and filling her head with lies. The child says neither of those things is true, but I don't know if she's just trying to protect them or if the mother or father is making up things. The child had a bruise on her leg the size of a nickel, which she says she got from a fall when she was playing with her friend. For now she's been placed with the paternal aunt who says neither parent should have this child, but the aunt can't keep the little girl any longer because she's been diagnosed with cancer. The grandparents are like the Hatfields and the McCoys. Neither set will let the other parent see the kid if they have her." Sabre took a deep breath. "I'm sorry for babbling. What great news do you have for me?"

"I wish it was better, kid, but I feel like I've been hugging a rose bush so far."

"I'm guessing that's not so good."

"Too many thorns." He winked and nodded. "Jodi Ellis, the clerk at Albertsons, remembers Sister Maria being in the store because she's been going there a long time and she knows her by sight. She also remembers the incident, and by that I mean she remembers seeing the man. She also thought the nun was acting a little strange, but she didn't know why. She can't describe the man or the kid, except that he was a light-skinned black kid. I showed her several photos of kids and she couldn't pick out any one of them, with the exception of one photo which she eliminated."

"So all that witness will do is confirm that the sister was there and saw a man and a boy fitting Tray's description, which will help the jury believe the nun."

"Yup."

"What else do you have?"

"I discovered that there was a man in front of Albertsons trying to obtain signatures on a petition that day. I managed to track him down, but he just barely remembers being at Albertsons. He did not remember seeing Irving, couldn't recognize his photo, and did not remember seeing any white man with any kid, white or black. He sniffs a lot, which might mean he has a cold, but I think it's more likely that it's from previous drug use."

"He's out."

"I met with Irving's sister, Suzanne, who lives with and cares for their ailing mother. Suzanne knows Irving had a problem but never had any real evidence of it. She told me about an incident in Orange County, which I will follow up on, but it's a long shot. Their mother has Alzheimer's and thinks her son is still alive, but when I asked her where he worked, she mentioned *Dale* and went on to say that it wasn't a good place for him. As it turns out, he worked at Dale Elementary School for a very short time last year."

Sabre shivered. "How do these creeps end up in schools?"

"They go where the cotton is tall," JP said. "He was let go because he 'didn't meet probationary standards.' I'll try to see what that means, but it's hard to get into those kinds of records."

"Even if you were able to find out that he was let go for some sexual misconduct, it'll take a court order to get the name of the child. And we would need some pretty hard evidence to get the order."

"I'm still trying to find Anthony, the kid at the skatepark who was hanging out with Drew while he waited for Tray to come from therapy. I went with Drew to the skatepark on Saturday and looked for him, but he wasn't there. I had Drew look around to see if he recognized anyone else who was there that day, but no luck."

"By the way," Sabre said, "they still haven't identified the second body that the police found when they discovered Irving. Some woman came forward and tried to claim him as her husband. But when she claimed her husband was President Ronald Reagan, they pretty much discounted anything she had to offer." Sabre paused. "What else do you have?"

"The good news is that I found Tray's father,

Horatio Whisenant. He's probably not our killer, although I haven't had a chance to check his alibi. However, he's willing to perjure himself and give the kid an alibi if we think that will help. And he wants to congratulate the guy who 'ganked the goof,' as he put it."

"And he used the term *goof*?"

"It rolled right off his tongue."

After JP received some direction as to where Sabre wanted him to spend his time on this case, he said, "Are you finished with your work here?"

"Just about."

"How about if I wait around until you're done? It's getting late and Bob wouldn't like it if I left you here alone."

Sabre smiled. "You're right." She packed up her things and they walked toward the door.

"Have you had dinner?" JP asked.

"No."

"Are you hungry?"

"I'm starved."

Chapter 22

JP was in Sabre's office delivering a report he had recently finished. She wondered why he didn't just email it, but she never minded seeing him in person.

"I'm meeting with Dr. Bell, Tray's therapist," Sabre said. "He has worked with other clients I've had in the past, and although I've spoken with him many times, I've only seen him once before. That's when he testified at the dispositional hearing for Tray's placement. He made an excellent witness, was very believable, and he didn't buckle under pressure. He's a super nice guy, very friendly, and my minors all seem to like him." Sabre heard the front door to her building open. "That must be him now."

"Then I'll get out of your hair."

As JP was leaving, Elaine was escorting Dr. Bell to Sabre's office. The doctor was wearing a t-shirt, and a bit of blue ink was exposed below the sleeve. JP nodded to the doctor and said, "Nice tattoo."

"Thank you," Bell said and kept walking.

"Good evening, Ms. Brown," he said, as he walked into her office. He was an attractive man in his sixties who stood about five foot eight. Sabre remembered from the last time they met that he was always fighting to keep his weight off. He seemed to be doing better with it because he was in pretty good shape.

"Good evening. Please call me Sabre."

Elaine started to close the door, and Sabre said to her, "Chris Firmstone will be here shortly. If you have to leave, just leave my door open so I hear him come in."

"I'm in no hurry. I can wait until 'young surfer boy' gets here."

Sabre chuckled. Elaine liked to call the attorneys

by nicknames, most of which Bob had named, but she had come up with a few on her own. There were two "surfer-boys"—Wagner and Firmstone. She distinguished them by calling Firmstone *young surfer boy* and Wagner *old surfer boy*. There were others too, like *Ichabod Crane,* who was a tall, lanky, Harvard graduate. Her favorite was *Cruella De Vil*, a tall, bossy woman with short, gray hair.

"Please have a seat," Sabre said. "How was your trip?"

"It was amazing. Always is."

"You've been before?"

"Yes, many times. I go to Tanzania to work with children with albinism about every three months. They have such a plight. The witch doctors claim that albino body parts are magical, so their belief consequently puts all albinos at risk. People hunt them down and chop off their fingers, ears, or other appendages and sell them. Sometimes, the families even sell their own albino children so they can afford to feed the rest of their family. It's a very poor country. The majority of children with albinism now live in special schools because it's too dangerous to live at home. There's a philanthropist from Canada who has formed a non-profit organization called Under the Same Sun. He does so much for the kids. I volunteer with that program whenever I can."

Sabre stared with fascination at his comments.

"I'm sorry," Dr. Bell said, "I'm on my soap box again, aren't I?"

"I'm just amazed and appalled at what you are saying. It's hard to believe that this sort of thing goes on in the world today. Why Tanzania? Does the government allow it to continue?"

"They have laws against the maiming and killing, but so far those laws haven't really deterred anyone.

Thanks to the many efforts of organizations like Under the Same Sun, they're starting to enforce the laws more. But for some reason, Tanzania has an inordinate amount of children with albinism, more than most countries, and no one knows for certain why that is."

Sabre shook her head. She didn't know what to say. Just then the door opened and Chris Firmstone entered. Sabre introduced the two men, and Chris took a seat next to the therapist.

"Have I missed anything?" Chris asked.

"Not a thing. The doctor was just telling me about his fascinating trip." She turned to face Dr. Bell. "We have a number of questions about Tray. The prosecutor wants to try this child as an adult, which we think is ridiculous. We'd like to hear your take on that. We'll be able to put the fitness hearing off for a few months, but we need to know what kind of battle it's going to be. Have you ever testified in a 707 hearing?"

"Yes, several times."

"You know what we have to show in order to keep the case in juvenile court?"

"I'm quite familiar with the statute."

"Very well. I've shared what I know with Mr. Firmstone about your background and the length of time you've been working with Tray, so we don't need to get into all that."

"Good."

"Chris, would you like to start the questioning?" Sabre asked.

Without answering Sabre, Chris began. "Tray is fourteen years old. Would you consider him to be mature for his age?"

"Quite the contrary,"Dr. Bell said. "Tray is far younger and less sophisticated than most fourteen-year-olds. He's very much a kid. He still likes kid play, and the kind of friends he's drawn to are immature as well."

"How do you think he would do in an adult criminal environment?"

"He wouldn't survive. It would be like putting a kitten in a lion's den."

"But Tray has had to fend for himself a good part of his life. Hasn't that prepared him for adult interaction in a prison setting?"

"Tray's not the typical result of a child of addicted parents. Although he has seen far more than any child should see over the years, he has also had long bouts of good parenting. When his mother is clean, she's a responsible, loving parent. Unlike most children who are raised in a drug-addicted environment, he hasn't transferred his survival needs to his everyday life. He only shows maturity when it comes to taking care of his little sister. As soon as he doesn't have that responsibility, he reverts to childlike behavior. For that reason, I wasn't anxious to have his sister placed with him in the foster home, but he quickly trusted the foster parents to do their job, so he doesn't have to."

"Doesn't that in itself show maturity? Wouldn't he just adapt, like he does with his sister?"

"I don't believe that he would. He hasn't shown any real maturity in any other aspect of his life, nor does he plan ahead to take care of her. He only reacts in the moment to her needs."

Sabre spoke up. "Dr. Bell, if we go beyond the fitness hearing, do you think Tray could have planned this elaborate crime that they are suggesting? Could he have set Irving up to meet him, then lured him to the crime scene, killed and buried him, and then gone about his daily life?"

"No. I do not believe Tray would do that. He reacts to his sister's needs. If she's hungry, he gets her food. If she's sad, he comforts her. If she were in danger, he would try to protect her. But he doesn't anticipate her needs, or his own for that matter. Where he would protect Shanisha, he may not do the same for himself because he has a different set of fears. If Irving came to him, he could react in two ways. He could slip into a state of fear and do nothing or say nothing. Or, at this point in his therapy, he would likely be stronger than that and at least run."

"Or perhaps fight back?" Sabre asked.

"Yes, he could do that if he felt threatened. But most likely, I would expect him to flee and tell someone."

Another hour of questioning brought more of the same. The therapist was very adamant that Tray should be tried in juvenile court, and both Sabre and Chris were confident that he could explain his stance well in court under direct or cross.

"While you're here, I would like to clarify a few things about your last session with Tray."

"What would you like to know?"

"The best the medical examiner can determine as a time of death is a twenty-four hour time period that ranges from about one o'clock in the afternoon on Saturday, the eleventh of May, until noon or one the next day. Part of that time frame is based on the fact that a witness saw Irving at around eleven or twelve on Saturday morning. So if that is correct, Irving was still alive at that time. Supposedly, Tray was with him at that time. But according to Tray and his foster mother, Tray had an appointment with you at the same time he was allegedly seen with Irving. We need you to verify that Tray was with you."

Dr. Bell wrinkled his brow for the first time. He removed his phone from his pocket and looked at his calendar. "Tray is mistaken. I did have an appointment with him, but I had to cancel it."

"Are you sure? I know the foster mother didn't bring him, but she had it in her calendar and Tray is adamant about being there."

He shook his head and sighed. "I saw Tray for the last time before my trip on Wednesday. I told him that I couldn't make the Saturday appointment because I was leaving for Africa on Friday. I even tried to get a colleague, Dr. Debra Clark, to fill in for me, but she wasn't available. Tray was supposed to relay the cancellation to his foster parents. I'm afraid I had so much to do that I didn't follow up."

Chapter 23

Sabre, Bob, and JP finished their lunch at Pho's and walked out to the parking lot.

"I've got to run," Sabre said. "I have a trial this afternoon. Later, guys."

JP watched as Sabre walked to her car.

"Why don't you just ask her out?" Bob said.

"What are you talking about?" JP said.

"You're ogling like a pimply-faced teenage boy in the girls' locker room."

"I'm not ogling."

Sabre pulled out of her parking space and drove past where JP and Bob were standing. She rolled down her window and said, "See you tonight, JP."

Bob slapped him on the shoulder. "You dog."

"Yeah, she invited me to her house to watch a video."

"So she had to take the first step. What's the matter with you? Well, it's about time anyway. Now, don't screw it up."

"Let it go, Bob. I'm going to her house to watch the security video on the Copley case. It's not a date." JP turned to walk away, then stopped and said, "By the way, my cow died last night, so I don't need your bull." He walked toward his car.

Bob laughed and then yelled after him. "I can't believe you already screwed up the date before you got a chance to have one, McCloud."

JP shook his head. *I never should've told him about DuBois and the "McCloud" story. He gets a hold of something and he doesn't let go.*

***

Sabre had the flash drive in the computer and ready to go when JP arrived. He was feeling a little uncomfortable because he kept thinking about what Bob had said. He did care for Sabre, but that didn't mean he could do anything about it. *What would she want with this old cowboy?*

"Would you like something to drink? Water, tea, coffee, beer?"

"A beer. Thanks."

"Coors Light okay?"

"Is there any other kind?" He wondered if it was a coincidence or if she knew what kind of beer he drank. *Of course she didn't.*

JP sat down on the sofa in front of Sabre's laptop. Sabre returned with a beer and handed it to JP.

"Just push *Enter* and the video will start," Sabre said.

"Have you watched it yet?"

"No, I haven't had a chance." Sabre picked up a keychain flash drive shaped like an airplane and handed it to JP. "I made you a copy in case you want to watch it again later."

JP looked at the object. "An airplane?"

Sabre pointed to the side of it. "See, it says *Boeing* on the side. A friend of mine works for Boeing and he got them for me. It was some promotional thing." She wrinkled up her face. "Sorry, it's the only flash drive I could find in the house except for a Sylvester and a Tweety Bird. I thought you'd prefer the plane. Next time I'll try to get you a boot or a cowboy hat, or perhaps a pistol shape."

"That's all right, the plane is fine. I just never saw one before. And I'm glad you didn't go with the Tweety Bird. If Bob saw it, he'd never let me hear the end of it."

Sabre took a seat mid-sofa next to JP.

"How about we fast forward it until we see Sister Maria and then we can work backward from there?" JP suggested.

"Good idea," Sabre said as she reached for the mouse, accidentally brushing JP's leg as she did. "Sorry."

He moved his leg. "No problem." He tried to control his breathing that suddenly seemed heavy to him. He removed his hat and set it on the end table, just to have something to do.

Sabre fast-forwarded the video. "Watch for Sister Maria."

"I am." JP watched attentively. "Stop. There she is. She just stepped into the line to check out. Back it up just a bit."

Sabre backed up the video.

"There's a man in a baseball cap and sunglasses in front of the nun, but I can't tell if it's Irving or not."

"I don't see anyone with him," Sabre said as the video moved forward. "Oh no, there is a kid with him." The kid's back was to the camera, but his dark, curly hair stood out and he was about the right height for Tray.

The man in the baseball cap reached for the boy's arm. He caressed his bicep but stopped at his elbow, where he gripped a little tighter. Then he moved the boy closer to him. She hit *Pause* and *Rewind* and replayed the video from the time the nun came into sight.

"It could be them, but I can't be certain. Keep it rolling so we can see if there is a clearer shot of either of their faces."

JP and Sabre both moved to the edge of their seats as they watched the security video. The man in the baseball cap turned toward the camera, but his face was shadowed from the hat. Sabre stopped the video and zoomed in on his face and upper body.

"It sure looks like Irving," JP said. "And see that shirt he's wearing. Look." He reached for the mouse. "May I?"

"Sure," Sabre said.

JP zoomed in on the logo on the shirt. "There's the faded *In-N-Out* logo on his shirt, just like the crime scene photos."

"If that's not Irving, someone went to a lot of trouble."

"To do what, Sabre? Frame Tray? That doesn't seem very likely."

"I know he didn't do it."

"Or maybe he did."

"Roll the video," Sabre barked, a little harsher than she intended.

JP looked directly at her and said softly, "I know you're madder'n a mule chewin' on bumblebees, but I think you'd better start considering the possibility that he did do it."

His comment made her chuckle. She took a deep breath and said, "I apologize. You're probably right. Besides, I don't need to take it out on you. I'm just frustrated."

"When you have me investigate, you always tell me you want the truth, no matter what it is."

"Maybe this time I don't." She sighed. "Besides, even if that is Irving, it doesn't mean it's Tray."

"You're right."

JP started the video again. The man was paying for the items and the young boy turned towards the nun, showing a good three-quarters of his face. When he did, Sabre gasped. "Oh, no!"

JP pushed *Pause* and Tray's sweet face illuminated the screen. Sabre's eyes looked wet and she swallowed. JP wanted to take her in his arms and comfort her, but instead he reached across and put his hand on her shoulder. "We're going to figure this out."

Chapter 24

"Tray, we need to talk about the evidence the DA has against you," Sabre said as she sat in the interview room once again at juvenile hall with Tray. "There are some things that we need to clarify."

"Like what?"

Sabre removed some photos she had printed from the still shots of the security video. She showed Tray a photo of the young man in the store.

"Do you know who this is?"

Tray looked at her with a wrinkled brow. "That's me."

"You're sure?"

"Yeah, those are my clothes. Where did you get the picture?"

"This photo is from the security camera at Albertsons. It was taken the day that Irving died."

"No, it's not," Tray argued. "I wasn't there. Why don't you believe me?"

"So, this isn't you?"

"I guess not." His voice grew stronger and louder. "It can't be 'cuz I wasn't there."

Tray was so adamant about it not being him that Sabre started to wonder if there was another kid running around this town who looked just like him. But that made no sense either. *Another kid with Tray's clothes? There had to be another explanation.*

"We're going to figure this out." Sabre found herself repeating what JP had recently said to her. She hoped she was more convincing than he had been.

Sabre showed him another photo. This one was of the man in the store. "Do you recognize him?"

He glanced at the picture, quickly turning his head

away from it. “Was that Irving?”

“I don’t know. Do you think it was?”

“I think so.”

The next photo was of the nun. “What about her?”

“I don’t know who that is.”

“Does she look familiar at all?”

“No. I’ve never seen her before.”

The same thing happened when Sabre showed him a photo of the clerk. He denied any recognition of her.

Sabre watched as Tray became more frustrated and eventually started to cry. “You don’t believe me, do you?” he said.

“Tray, I’m sorry you have to go through this, but I need to find out what happened. If you killed Irving, I’m sure it was in self-defense.”

“But I didn’t. You have to believe me,” he pleaded.

“I believe you don’t remember anything about what happened. I think maybe you blacked out and you’ve repressed what happened. That’s why you can’t remember being at Albertsons.”

“But I was at Dr. Bell’s office and then the skatepark. I remember being there. Ask Dr. Bell and Drew. It must be someone who looks just like me.”

“Maybe it is,” Sabre said. She didn’t want to remind him that Dr. Bell already said Tray wasn’t at the therapy session. He was too distraught already. *Perhaps Dr. Bell has an explanation. I’ll go see him right after I have lunch with Bob.*

***

Bob and Sabre sat in Pho’s eating their #124s, a dish of rice noodles with pork.

“You’re quiet today,” Bob said. “Is something wrong with my little SOB?”

"I'm struggling with Tray's case. I don't think any jury would convict him if we could show self-defense. But I don't think we can provide evidence on the required elements."

"And the elements of self-defense are what?" Sabre started to respond, but Bob said, "No, don't tell me. I think I remember these from law school. There are three of them, right?"

"Right."

"You would have to prove that Tray was in imminent danger of suffering bodily injury."

"That's correct, but it could also be *of being touched unlawfully,* which is more likely in this case. And the second element?"

"He would have to reasonably believe that the immediate use of force was necessary to defend himself against that danger. And third, that he used no more force than was reasonably necessary."

"How can you remember that stuff from law school? I barely remember *taking* my tests, much less what was on them."

Bob pointed to his head with his index finger. "It's all up here. Sometimes it's just a little harder to find it." He wrinkled his brow. "So how can you show that it was self-defense if Tray claims he wasn't even there?"

"That's the problem, of course. If Tray would tell me what happened, I'd bet we could make a case for self-defense."

"And if you presented evidence on each element, that would shift the burden to the prosecutor to prove that it wasn't self-defense," Bob added.

Sabre shook her head. "You're amazing. Have you ever done a case claiming self-defense?"

"I've never handled any criminal case, except for one DUI, but we settled that."

"Then how do you remember those things?"

"Beats me. My mind is filled with useless information." He smiled. "You have been so adamant that Tray was innocent. Do you now think he may have killed him?"

"I don't believe he murdered him, but he may have been protecting himself—although, I can't for the life of me figure out how he could have ever been alone with him. There's something wrong and I'm beginning to think that Tray is telling the truth as he remembers it."

Chapter 25

Sabre asked Siri for directions to Dr. Bell's office and then drove directly there. There was no receptionist, and the door to the office was closed. She waited in the small waiting area until he had finished with his patient, which was only about ten minutes. The doctor's office door opened and a tall, thin woman came out and exited through the main door. The doctor could see Sabre once the door was open and he came right out.

"Hello, Ms. Brown," Dr. Bell said with a smile.

"Hi, Doc. Do you have a minute? I need to talk to you about Tray."

"Is he okay?"

"Yes, well...sort of."

"Come into my office." He led her inside.

"I'm sorry for just stopping in, but I didn't know what else to do."

"It's fine," Dr. Bell said. "I don't have another session for an hour and a half. Have a seat and tell me what's going on."

Sabre informed the doctor about the security video and asked if Tray could have somehow blocked everything out.

"That's very possible."

Sabre suddenly had a bit of hope again. Not only did the doctor say it was possible, but *very* possible.

"However," the doctor continued, "that defense is not without problems. I would be more than willing to testify that I believe that is what happened because, like you, I can't believe that Tray could have killed Irving with malice aforethought. But if I remember from other self-defense testimony, there are a number of elements you must prove. Correct?"

"Yes, and it's almost impossible without his testimony, and if he testifies, he's going to say he never saw Irving and he didn't kill him."

Dr. Bell rubbed his chin, almost as if he were stroking a beard that was not there. "What can I do to help?"

"Don't people often block out traumatic events?"

"Yes, it happens."

"Let's assume that Irving got Tray alone and attacked him. Let's also assume that Tray reacted and hit him with something that killed him. Couldn't he have blocked it out?"

"Sure. He could have psychogenic amnesia."

"And then he wouldn't know that it happened, right?" Sabre asked.

"True. When a person has psychogenic amnesia they often can't remember events leading up to the traumatic event, which would explain why he can't recall the trip to Albertsons."

"And couldn't you testify to that?"

"I could, but…."

"No." Sabre stood up, shaking her head. "I don't want to hear a *but*."

"I know." The doctor tapped his pen on his desk. "I wish I could do more for him. I hate that he's going through this. I could testify that he could very well have psychogenic amnesia and I could sound pretty convincing. However, Tray can account for his time, so instead of having a loss of memory, they will bring in an expert to dispute anything I say."

"So, how do we make him remember?"

"Sometimes psychotherapy helps, but not always. I certainly wouldn't recommend therapy for him at this point with a new therapist. If you can get a court order for me to continue, I will gladly go to the Hall to work with him. It's not an ideal setting, but I'm willing to do anything I can to help." He dropped his head down for just a second.

"Are you okay?"

"I'm fine. I just feel like I've failed Tray somehow."

Chapter 26

Three months later…

Sabre and Bob sat outside Department Four waiting for their next hearing.

"If we don't get this case done before 9:30, can you cover it for me? I have the 707 hearing for Tray Copley."

"Sure, we're on the same side. You're just submitting on the recommendations, right?"

"That's it."

"So just how does the 707 work? I should know these things in case I ever decide to take delinquency cases or if I have to cover something for you."

"When a child is at least fourteen years old and has committed certain crimes, and murder is one of those, the prosecutor can bring a motion to have the case heard in adult court. The defense has to show why the child is fit to be tried as a juvenile. Deputy District Attorney Marge Benson brought the motion, and now Chris and I have to prove that Tray is fit to stand trial in juvenile court. We're prepared to put up a good fight. Our biggest concern is Judge Palatini. Although we couldn't be certain, we knew we at least had a chance with Judge Trapnell. With this judge, anything could happen."

"How do you show Tray's fit?"

"There are about five different criteria, and since he would do less time if he's tried in juvenile court, we must show that he could be rehabilitated by the end of his jurisdiction."

"Tray is a really good kid overall. He sounds like just the kind who should stay in juvenile. Besides, he's a little guy. He's going to have a really hard time if he goes to a facility with hardened criminals."

"I know. He's struggling to hold his own even at the Hall." Sabre sighed. "How's his mother doing?"

"She's back in rehab. She would've been here for the hearing, but she's in her first thirty days of sobriety and they don't like them leaving the rehab facility for any reason. She would've come anyway if it would make any difference."

"We'll inform the court, and hopefully the judge will be more impressed that she's back in rehab. The foster parents are here and that looks good."

Sabre checked the time and stood up. "It's 9:25. I'm going to Department Three and see if they're ready. If I don't come back, start without me."

***

When Sabre walked into the delinquency courtroom, the bailiff said, "Right on time, Ms. Brown. I'll get your client."

A few minutes later, the bailiff seated Tray Copley at Sabre's right at the defense table. Attorney Chris Firmstone was to her left as they waited for Judge Thomas Palatini to take the bench. Neither Sabre nor Chris knew what to expect of this judge since he was new to juvenile court. When Judge Trapnell put in for a leave of absence, they brought Palatini in from trial court downtown.

Chris whispered to Sabre, "I hear he's a no-nonsense judge who doesn't like theatrics. He pays a lot of attention to the defendant's behavior, and he doesn't put up with bad attitudes."

"Then he should like Tray."

"I hope so."

A round-faced, short, bald man in his sixties took

the bench. His robe covered the few extra pounds he was carrying.

"This is my first fitness hearing, but I'm very familiar with the requirements," Judge Palatini said. "I have presided over many a young man downtown who had lost in their 707 hearing here in juvenile court. For most, the order seemed to be appropriate. Occasionally, I couldn't understand the basis for the order. That said, I expect to hear good arguments and solid evidence from both sides."

DDA Marge Benson had initiated the fitness hearing. She alleged that the minor was at least fourteen years old and was charged with murder, an offense covered by Section 707 (b) of the Welfare and Institutions Code.

"Although Tray Copley is only fourteen years old, he is charged with the heinous crime of murder," Benson began. "The evidence will show that Copley would not be amenable to the care, treatment, and training available through the juvenile facilities based on the following criteria:

"Number one is the degree of criminal sophistication exhibited by Copley. He planned a very sophisticated crime. He led his victim to him, and then killed and buried him. And before leaving him in a shallow grave, he desecrated his body.

"Second, Tray Copley would not have the time to be rehabilitated before the expiration of the juvenile jurisdiction if he were tried as a minor. We will present evidence through expert testimony to those criteria.

"Third, it is true that Copley has no previous delinquent history that we have been able to determine. However, the crime was premeditated and committed with no remorse.

"The fourth criterion is to show that previous attempts by the court to rehabilitate Copley have been unsuccessful. However, since there have been no previous crimes for which he was convicted, there have been no attempts to rehabilitate.

"Which leads us to the fifth criterion, the circumstances and gravity of the alleged offense. It doesn't get graver than murder. And in order for this crime to have been executed, it would have taken very careful planning."

"Thank you, Ms. Benson," Judge Palatini said before she could continue, "for that lesson on the requirements for a fitness hearing. However, I'm well aware what needs to be proven here today. Please call your first witness."

Chris caught Sabre's eye, and she saw his lip turn up just a little. The defense bar wasn't fond of Ms. Benson, so even the slightest slam by the judge was entertaining.

"Of course, Your Honor," Ms. Benson said. "I would like to call Marcia Woolard."

A woman about fifty-five years old with short, blonde hair and oval glasses took the stand and the clerk swore her in.

"What is your profession, Ms. Woolard?" Benson asked.

"I'm a San Diego County probation officer and I work with juveniles. Tray Copley is one of the minors on my caseload."

"Where did you receive your training?"

"We'll stipulate as to Ms. Woolard's training, Your Honor," Chris said.

"Ms. Benson?" the judge said. When she hesitated as if she were not going to agree, he continued, "There's no jury here, Ms. Benson. And I'm aware of Ms. Woolard's credentials."

"So stipulated," Ms. Benson said, and turned to her witness. "And you investigated this case?"

"Yes."

"And did you write a report after you completed your investigation?"

"Geez, this could take all month," Sabre whispered to Chris.

Chris spoke up. "We'll stipulate that she wrote the report. We do not object to it being submitted as the probationary report for the alleged crime, as long as it's not submitted for the truth of the matter asserted."

"Thank you," Judge Palatini said with a sigh.

"I'd like to play poker with this guy," Sabre said to Chris. "He doesn't mind showing his cards."

"The report is admitted into evidence as Exhibit #1. Please continue, Ms. Benson."

Ms. Benson's questions to Woolard established that Woolard had been an adult probation officer for five years before moving to juvenile for the past twenty-two years. She had investigated over a thousand cases and written as many reports. Homicide had become her specialty, and the number of homicide cases she had had over the years was somewhere between forty and fifty.

"How much planning would it take to commit this murder?"

"Objection," Sabre said. "Speculation. There is no way to know if the crime was planned or if it happened on the spur of the moment."

"Overruled," Judge Palatini said.

"Nice try, but I've heard he doesn't sustain many objections," Chris whispered.

"Ms. Woolard," Benson said, "please answer the question."

"In my opinion, Tray would've had to lure Irving to the spot where he was killed. He would've had to bring the weapon with him, and he would've had to come equipped with a shovel to bury him—all of which required careful planning."

When Woolard mentioned Irving's name, Tray winced. Sabre looked up at the judge and saw that he was watching Tray's reaction.

Ms. Benson questioned Woolard for nearly an hour, attempting to establish that a crime had been committed, and that it would have taken a great deal of planning. The questioning was an attempt to meet the first criteria that proves unfitness for juvenile court.

On cross-examination, Chris asked, "Tray has no criminal record, correct?"

"He has no convictions that I'm aware of," Woolard said.

"And you've done a thorough investigation, correct?"

"Yes, of course."

"And he has no arrests, correct?"

"Correct."

"Are you aware of any other crimes that Tray has either planned or committed?"

"No."

"In fact, he has never so much as received a referral for misconduct in school, correct?"

"That's correct. However, he has missed a lot of classes."

"And do you know the reasons for those absences?" Chris asked.

"I can't be certain."

"You are aware of Tray's mother's drug addiction, right?"

"Yes, I am."

"Is it unusual for children of drug-addicted parents to miss a lot of school?"

"It happens."

"The majority of Tray's absences have been during first period, correct?"

"That's correct."

"Were you aware that Tray often had to take his younger sister, Shanisha, to preschool?"

"I heard that." Ms. Woolard squirmed in her seat.

"And even in spite of his frequent absences, Tray has continued to maintain good grades?"

"There's no question that he's smart and sophisticated. That's my point."

Chris's face turned red. "What, besides this alleged crime, has Tray done that demonstrates his sophistication?"

"He acts more like a parent to his younger sister than his mother does. By his own admission, he takes care of the household when she isn't capable. As you said, he takes her to preschool."

"That is normal for children with addictive parents, correct?"

"I've seen it before, but I'm not an expert."

"Do you have any other examples of Tray's sophistication?"

Silence ensued as if she were trying to think of some.

"Do you understand the question, Ms. Woolard?"

"Yes, I do."

"And do you have any other examples?"

"This murder took a great deal of sophistication."

"You stated that Tray 'would have had to lure' the victim to the spot where he was killed. Is that correct?"

"Yes, that's correct."

"You do not have any evidence to suggest he was lured there, do you?"

"He had to…."

Chris interrupted her. "Please answer *yes* or *no*."

Ms. Woolard shifted in her seat and looked at Benson. Then she said, "No."

"Do you know how much time passed between

Irving's death and when he was buried?"

"No."

"So whoever did this may have gone to Home Depot and bought a shovel after he was dead and then dug a hole and buried him?"

"I suppose."

"So, other than a few missed classes, his love and care for his younger sister, the only other evidence of sophistication is the crime itself, correct?"

"I guess so."

"So if he didn't commit the crime, you really have no evidence of his maturity or sophistication?"

"Objection," Ms. Benson bellowed.

"I withdraw the question."

Ms. Benson's next witness was Detective Jack Plummer, one of the investigators on Tray's case. The detective continued with another hour of testimony explaining what kind of planning it would have taken to commit this crime, implying that Tray Copley was indeed sophisticated.

On cross-examination, Chris asked, "You never actually questioned Tray Copley about this crime, did you?"

"I tried, but he wouldn't talk to me."

"So he said nothing to you at all?"

"He said…."

"Please just answer the question *yes* or *no*."

"Yes, he did say something to me."

"Didn't he say that Ms. Brown was his attorney and that you should probably talk to her?"

"Yes, that's what he said."

"And from that you decided he was too sophisticated for juvenile court?"

"Partly. Most kids don't ask for an attorney right away unless they've already had experience with the law."

"But you're aware that Tray does not have a criminal record, correct?"

"Yes."

"And that he has an attorney because of his parents' actions, not his, correct?"

"Yes, but…."

"No further questions," Chris said.

"I have no further questions, Your Honor, but I reserve the right to recall this witness at a later time."

"We will adjourn for today," Judge Palatini said. "I'll see you all back here tomorrow morning."

After they left the courtroom, Sabre turned to her colleague and said, "You've done these before, Chris. How do you think it's going so far?"

"I'm not sure. Palatini is different. It's fun watching him put Benson down, but I think he would do the same to me if he got the chance."

"She does give him plenty of ammunition." Sabre noted the strain on Chris's face. "You're worried, aren't you?"

"I think we've made some good points so far, but I still wish we had Judge Charlie Bozo."

Chapter 27

Chris's first witness was June Longe, Tray's foster mother.

"Please state your name and spell your last name for the record," the clerk instructed.

"June Longe. L-O-N-G-E."

"Please raise your right hand." June did so. "Do you solemnly state, under penalty of perjury, that the testimony you may give in the case now pending before this court shall be the truth, the whole truth, and nothing but the truth?"

"I do," June said.

"How do you know Tray Copley?"

"He's our foster child. He came to live with us about six months ago. He's been a wonderful child. His sister, Shanisha, came a couple of months ago as well."

"Can you tell us a little about Tray's behavior at home? What kinds of things does he like to do?"

"He likes video games, such as *Mario* and *Angry Birds*, jigsaw puzzles, and he reads age-appropriate books."

"Does he ever play video games with violence?"

"No, not that we would allow them, but he doesn't like them anyway."

"How do you know that?"

"Because he has friends who play them, but he does not."

"You said he likes jigsaw puzzles?"

"Yes, he always has one set up on a table in his room that he works on. He likes family board games as well. His mother used to play Monopoly with him when he was living at home."

June Longe made an excellent witness. On cross-examination by Benson, she held her own. When Benson asked, "Ms. Longe, you have nothing but good things to say about this young man. Could it be that you are overly attached to him?"

"I don't know what that means. How could I be too attached to a child under my care? If you mean, do I love him? Yes, I do. I love him very much because he is a sweet, kind child who can't even kill a bug. If he finds a bug in the house, he picks it up and takes it outside."

Sabre and Chris both grinned at her response. "Way to go, June," Sabre muttered to Chris.

Benson continued to cross-examine the foster mother, but no matter what she asked, it made the child look either innocent or very lovable, neither of which helped the prosecutor's case.

Chris's next witness was Dr. Charles Settle, the psychologist who tested Tray and was there to offer his opinion regarding Tray's level of sophistication and whether or not he could be rehabilitated in a short period of time, if he in fact committed this crime.

"Do you have any more witnesses, Mr. Firmstone?" the judge asked.

"Just one, Your Honor, but he just returned from a trip to Africa. We're meeting with him later today. I'd like to continue this until tomorrow morning, so Dr. John W. Bell, Tray's therapist, can testify."

"Very well. You are all ordered back tomorrow morning at 8:30." The judge looked at Benson. "Do you have any rebuttal witnesses?"

"Just one, Your Honor: Dr. James Foley."

"Good. We should be able to wrap this up tomorrow morning."

Sabre turned to Tray. "I'll see you tomorrow morning. You doing okay?"

"Yeah, I'm okay," Tray said, but he had a distant look in his eyes. Sabre watched as the bailiff escorted him out the back door.

Once Sabre and Chris were out of the courtroom, Sabre asked, "So how do you think it's going?"

"It's hard to say. I think we've more than made our case, and if Trapnell were on the bench, I'd sleep better tonight, but I just don't know this guy. I never bet on a sure thing. Did you touch base with Tray's therapist?"

"Yes, Dr. Bell will be at my office at 5:00 to go over his testimony," Sabre said. "Can you make it?"

"I'll be there. I can't believe he went to Africa again. He's quite an interesting guy."

"Yeah, he went to help the albinos again. He told me he had a twin brother with albinism."

"Had, as in the past tense?"

"Yes, he passed away when they were teenagers. He didn't explain what happened and so I didn't push it."

"Have you talked to the doc about the case since he came back from Africa?"

"Not really, but I met with him just before he left. He was having sessions with Tray once a week before then, but Tray was still claiming he had no contact with Irving after he went into foster care. Dr. Bell has always only had good things to say about Tray. He firmly believes this child should not be tried in adult court. He's really vested in him and has assured us that he will do whatever he can to see that Tray gets a fair deal. That's about all I know."

"See you this afternoon."

Sabre walked down the hallway to Department One to see if Bob was still there. She opened the door slightly and peeked into the courtroom. She took a seat outside and waited until the hearing was completed. It was nearing lunch so the courthouse had far fewer people in it than earlier. Only about ten people remained waiting for their cases to be heard.

Sabre studied the people who waited. It brought a mixture of sad and angry feelings to the surface as she watched. One woman ranted at her attorney as he tried to speak to her. She strutted around waving her arms, her voice escalating as she spoke. He tried to calm her, and when she wouldn't lower her voice, he walked away. She followed him, yelling at him to listen to her.

A man sat on a bench holding his head in his hands. Every few seconds, Sabre heard him sob. She wondered if he was crying for his child or for himself.

Bob walked out. "Hi, Sobs. Are you ready for lunch?"

"I sure am." She saw Bob glance at the man on the bench. "Do you know what his story is?"

"Collicott represents him. She told me that his ex had custody of their three kids and she was living with some lowlife who beat one of the kids to death. He's been sitting there like that all morning."

Sabre sighed. “That poor man.”

They reached the front door and Bob opened it for Sabre. "Pho's for lunch?"

"Sure."

"How's Tray’s hearing going?"

"I've never done one of these, so I can't know for sure, but it seems like we're winning on every point so far. Chris is concerned because he doesn't know the judge. I think it would be a slam dunk with Judge Trapnell, but I still think we're doing well. Tray is one of those defendants whom I believe the statute is designed to protect. But we'll see."

***

Dr. Bell made an excellent witness. He explained to the judge how unsophisticated Tray was and how amenable he was to rehabilitation, as shown by his good work in therapy. He listed the many ways Tray had grown and the behaviors the boy was able to change through the work that he had already done. All was evidence that he could be rehabilitated in a short period of time. Chris was very careful to stay away from any questions that might open the door to Tray's last therapy session. They weren't sure how they would proceed at trial, but they didn't want what appeared to be a lie by Tray in the record, at least not yet. Sabre knew it would eventually come out because of the security videos, but she was hopeful that the videos wouldn't become an issue until the trial.

After Chris called Dr. Bell, Benson brought in an expert to rebut Dr. Bell's testimony about Tray's rehabilitation and his maturity level. Her expert testified that it wasn't likely that he could be rehabilitated within the short time allotted by juvenile court facilities. In spite of Chris's cross-examination pointing out that the prosecutor's expert had never even met Tray Copley, Sabre didn't feel comfortable about the testimony. Unfortunately, Judge Palatini seemed pretty impressed with the expert doctor's credentials.

"Do you have any more rebuttal witnesses, Ms. Benson?"

"No, Your Honor."

"Closing remarks?" the judge said.

Chris summed up the evidence they had presented. "Your Honor, Tray Copley is not a sophisticated criminal. In fact, he is neither sophisticated nor a criminal as shown by his lack of delinquent history. There have been no failed attempts to rehabilitate him because he has not committed any crimes. Dr. Bell, who has worked with Tray for more than nine months, testified to his ability to learn from his therapeutic experience.

"Tray is a young boy who has had one of the most horrific things happen to him, and yet, he continues to do well in school and gets along well in his foster home. His foster parents have been here throughout these proceedings and welcome him back into their home. Without listing each criterion, we believe we have met the burden of proof for each one, with the exception of the alleged crime, which we deny was committed by our client."

However, Benson argued that in spite of all that, the crime alleged in the petition was too heinous—that Tray would've had to plan it all out, which required a sophisticated, criminal mind. She continued to state the same thing in several different ways. Judge Palatini shifted several times in his chair. On two occasions it appeared that he was going to interrupt her but didn't. At some point, he just seemed uninterested and turned his attention to watching Tray. Unfortunately, every time Benson mentioned Irving's name, Tray's eyes would narrow and what appeared to be hatred that Tray felt for the man came across on his face. A couple of times, Sabre tried to get Tray to relax, but he was nervous and scared. Sabre was concerned that Judge Palatini might misread him.

"Consequently, Your Honor," Benson continued, "we ask that the court make a finding that Tray Copley is not fit to be tried as a juvenile and send this case to the Superior Court downtown."

"Thank you, Counselors," Judge Palatini said. "I will notify you when I have my ruling." He stood up and walked out of the courtroom.

Chapter 28

"I hope you have some good news for me," Sabre said to JP when he walked into her office. She never failed to think how handsome he was whenever she saw him.

"Sorry, kid," JP said. "I feel like I've been pushing a wheelbarrow with rope handles up a hill. Everyone I talk to makes the case worse instead of better. I checked again on the identity of the other dead guy to see if we could point the finger in a different direction. But they still don't know who he is, and the MO is entirely different from this one."

"Yeah, I didn't think that was going to get us anywhere. What else do you have?"

"I can't find any more of Irving's molest victims. The only lead we had was the boy who lived near him in Orange County, and he was a bust."

"You couldn't find him?"

"Oh, I finally found him. At least I'm pretty sure I have the right kid. His name is Roderick Jones. The owner and landlord of the apartments hasn't changed in fifteen years. He told me that Roderick and his mother lived together in the apartment. The kid apparently never knew who his father was, and shortly after his mother passed away about a year ago, the kid joined the army. I was able to follow up on his military record and discovered that he's been in Afghanistan for the last eleven months. So he's pretty much off the list."

"What about Tray's father?" Sabre asked. "I know you said he had an alibi, but maybe he was lying."

"I spoke to his 'old lady,' as he referred to her. I'm not sure if it's his wife or girlfriend. She corroborated his story and so did their neighbors."

"What about Tray's mother, Jeannine Copley? Does her alibi hold up?"

"No one has seen her since Tray and Shanisha's review hearing when we set a trial date. She left the rehab center on Friday and never returned. No one knows where she is. I've been to the center several times and questioned everyone who would give me the time of day, but Jeannine hasn't been back there and I haven't learned anything new."

"Does Tray have anyone else close to him who might have sought revenge?"

"His foster parents care a lot about him, but they were both at the hospital with June's father who had had a heart attack, not that they would go kill anyone."

JP started to say something else, but before he could, Sabre said, "If Tray did this, I don't know how he could've done it alone. We already know that Tray was at Albertsons with a guy who was most likely Irving. Let's assume for a minute that Irving somehow got Tray to meet him and that Irving then took Tray to the location in Coyote Ridge where they found the body. If Irving did something and Tray fought back, Tray could have accidentally killed him, but how would he bury him?"

"That bothers me too. Where would he even get a shovel?" He paused. "Unless he brought it with him."

"Which means Tray would've had to plan the murder, and that just does not work for me. Besides, he had to be in someone else's car. How could he have a shovel?" She shook her head. "No, if Tray did kill him, it was an accident or self-defense. I don't believe this was a pre-meditated murder—not by Tray anyway."

"The only other person that Tray is close to is his friend Drew Fletcher. Maybe Drew was with them.

Drew could've helped Tray bury the body."

"You talked to Drew. Do you think he was telling the truth?"

"He appeared to be, but I've been wrong before. He may have been a little hesitant with some of his answers, but I thought it was because he was afraid he would say something that might hurt Tray's defense. I don't think he totally trusted me."

"Did you get the feeling that Drew and Tray are close enough friends that Drew might have defended him?"

"If you mean, do I think Drew killed Irving? I have no reason to think that, but if Tray killed Irving and had an accomplice, Drew would be the first place I would look."

"Maybe you should have another go at Drew. See if you can get anything new out of him. If that's what really happened, we can still change our strategy to self-defense when we go to trial. I think Tray might stand a better chance with that anyway. Eventually we're going to have to do something to explain those security videos."

When the phone rang, Sabre said, "Excuse me." She answered her desk phone and said, "I'll be right there."

"I take it you need to go," JP said, standing up.

"That was Judge Palatini's clerk. He wants us to come for the ruling. Want to come?"

JP wanted to say he would go anywhere with her, but he didn't. "Sorry, kid, I'd better hit the pavement and see what else I can dig up for this case. I'll start with Fletcher." He opened her office door. "Let me know the ruling." And he left.

Sabre watched as he went out the door. Then she gathered her things and went to court.

***

Chris stood at the defense table when Sabre arrived. No one else was in the courtroom except the bailiff, who was just walking out the back door. Sabre laid her file on the table.

"I'm nervous," Sabre said. "Are you?"

"More anxious than nervous," Chris said. "I don't really like this judge. By all rights we should win this hearing, but I don't know what to expect from him. If we lose and are sent downtown, then we'll get a jury trial. I do think Tray would have a better shot at an acquittal with a jury. It would be a lot easier to convince a jury that Tray was the victim, no matter how the DA spins the case, than it would be to convince Palatini. But if he loses at trial downtown, he could get life in prison. This kid doesn't deserve that, no matter what he's done."

"Is there any word on when Judge Trapnell will be back? Maybe we can hold out for him."

"The word isn't good. He's pretty sick. Chances are he won't be coming back."

"Does that mean we get Palatini for trial if he keeps the case here?"

"I'm afraid so, unless we can come up with a reason to challenge him."

DDA Marge Benson walked in and took her seat at the table without making eye contact with either Chris or Sabre. Sabre started to say something but stopped.

The court clerk entered through the rear, then the bailiff, and finally the judge.

"Are you ready for the defendant?" the bailiff asked.

"Yes, please," Judge Palatini said.

A few minutes later the bailiff entered with Tray Copley. Sabre had spoken to him in one of the holding cells just before she had entered the courtroom. She had explained again to Tray that being tried in juvenile court meant that the most he could get for a sentence was a little over ten years, which would make him twenty-five upon his release. If he were tried as an adult, he could get life. She hated scaring this young man any more than he already was, but he needed to understand what was happening. He was still denying that he was ever at Albertsons, in spite of the security videos. And he still claimed to have had a therapy session with Dr. Bell, even though the doctor was in Africa. It concerned Sabre that Tray wasn't opening up to her. She had told him over and over again how she needed to know the truth so she could give him the best defense, but a confession of any kind had never come.

The bailiff seated Tray on the end next to Sabre. She touched his shoulder and encouraged him to relax. His face was very tight and his breathing was heavy.

The clerk called the court to order.

"Murder is a heinous crime," Judge Palatini said. "When it's premeditated, it's even worse."

Sabre didn't like the way the judge started his ruling. She didn't look at Tray because she didn't want him to see her concern.

"I find that Tray Copley has no previous delinquent history, and therefore, there have been no previous attempts to rehabilitate him."

Sabre hoped he would keep going and there wasn't a *but* following these remarks.

"However," the judge continued.

Sabre saw the look of concern on Chris's face and her heart beat faster. *He was ruling against them.*

"I have been hearing murder cases for over twenty years and the one thing that I have learned is that dead is dead. It doesn't change. When someone is killed, someone else grieves. Whatever Irving did while he was alive cannot enter into my decision. I expect that no matter how evil this man may have been, his mother still grieves for him, and for that, I am sad. I'm even sadder over the effect Irving's behavior had on Tray Copley. His life is tainted forever by the victim's crimes. But again, I cannot let that influence my decision."

Sabre wondered where he was going with his statement. He seemed to lean one way and then another until he said, "I find that Tray Copley is unfit to stand trial in juvenile court; that he was fourteen years old at the time of the alleged offense; that the offense is listed in Section 707(b); and that Tray Copley would not be amenable to the care, treatment, and training program available through the juvenile court because of the degree of criminal sophistication exhibited by him. I find that the circumstances and gravity of the alleged offense are such that he could not be rehabilitated before the expiration of jurisdiction."

"He covered his bases," Chris whispered to Sabre.

Sabre reached over and squeezed Tray's arm.

"Thank you, Your Honor," Attorney Firmstone said. Sabre couldn't get herself to mutter the words.

"Thank you, Your Honor," DDA Benson said. "We have filed an accusatory pleading against Tray Copley in violation of Penal Code Section 187(a). It's on hold, but my office will ask to release it."

"The 602 petition is dismissed upon release of the pleading in criminal court," the judge ruled. "The minor will remain in the juvenile hall detention facility."

"We asked that no bail be set for this minor," Benson argued. "He is a dependent of the court, has no real ties to the community, and will be likely to flee the jurisdiction."

"Your Honor," Sabre said, without waiting for Chris. "I have known Tray for nearly a year and I know him to be a responsible young man. His foster parents care a great deal for him. They have been to every hearing. They're willing to take him into their home and take full responsibility for him."

"I'm sorry, Counselor, but I'm not willing to do that at this time. No bail is set. You can argue it again at the arraignment." The judge looked directly at Chris and then at Sabre. "I'm willing to remain on this case and follow it downtown unless you object."

Sabre raised her eyebrows, and then whispered to Chris, "I don't know how he was able to find him unfit. We better take our chances with someone else."

"I agree," he whispered back.

Sabre explained to Tray what was going on and he was in agreement.

Sabre stood up. "My client would like a new judicial officer."

"Very well." The judge stood up and left the courtroom.

Tray looked confused. "Now what?"

"We'll go to trial downtown and we'll get a jury. This isn't necessarily a bad thing. A jury is more likely to acquit you than a judge. You need to stay strong."

Chapter 29

Three-and-a-half months later...

Attorneys Chris Firmstone and Sabre Brown sat in Chris's office preparing for Tray's trial.

"I wish we had more evidence on our side for trial tomorrow," Sabre said. "I don't see how we can win with the 'other dude did it' defense. We don't have any substantial suspects to point the finger at."

"I agree, but we have nothing else. We'll have to create 'reasonable doubt' by pointing the finger at enough people with a motive and no solid alibi."

"But the crime had to be self-defense. Are you sure we shouldn't just go with that?"

"We can't just make a self-defense argument without some kind of evidence. And the only witness we would have to self-defense would be Tray, and he continues to deny that he ever saw Irving."

"We could put Dr. Bell on the stand, and he could testify that Tray may have blocked out whatever happened. He told us that's a possibility and he's willing to testify to that."

"But how are we going to prove the elements of self-defense? We have zero evidence that Tray was defending himself, or that he did it with reasonable force. Our best bet is to point the finger at someone else; otherwise, we're done before we get started."

"I know you're right. I just know Tray, and I know he wouldn't have planned a murder."

***

June and George Longe, Tray's foster parents, sat in

the front row directly behind the defense table in the Superior Court on Broadway. Tray's mother sat next to them. At the other end of the row was Tray's father. At the table were Sabre and co-counsel, Chris Firmstone. Since bail had been denied and Tray had remained in juvenile hall, the bailiff brought him in and seated him next to Sabre. She acknowledged Tray's presence and then turned to Chris.

"What do you know about Judge Shirleen Miller?" Sabre asked Chris.

"I know a few attorneys who've appeared in front of her," Chris said. "The word is that she has no tolerance for attorneys who show up late. She knows the Rules of Evidence inside and out, and apparently she teaches Evidence at USD Law School at night."

"That's a good thing. I hate when the judge doesn't make a good evidentiary call. Does she tend to lean to one side or the other?"

"She has a reputation for not being too conservative or too liberal, but she hates civil rights violations. Also, she loves to talk about her little dogs, Missy and BJ."

"What kinds of dogs?"

"I think they're both poodles. Some kind of little furry things."

Judge Shirleen Miller walked into the courtroom. She was a large woman with short, white hair; thin, slightly crooked lips; and a friendly smile that she flashed at the people at the counsel table. It put Sabre at ease. She hoped it did the same for Tray.

The judge called the case and heard the motions that both the prosecution and the defense had requested before bringing in the jury.

Five men and seven women filed in and took their seats in the twelve assigned seats. Another two jurors, one man and one woman, sat in the two end seats.

These were the alternates in case someone had to be replaced. Sabre and Chris both tried to load the jury with men, hoping they would be quicker to understand why someone would kill a molester. However, it was difficult to get them on the jury because those same men were too open about their views, and when questioned, they stated such to the judge, which disqualified them.

Marge Benson made her opening statement claiming that the evidence would show that Tray killed Irving. She claimed she would show that his alibi was not sound, that experts would testify that it was his handwriting on the body, and that he had motive to kill Irving.

Preparation for the opening statement was much different for a jury trial than it was for a judge trial. In juvenile court, there was no point spending much time on emotional issues since there was no jury. The judge just wanted the evidence and the law. Since the defense had lost the 707 motion, Sabre had spent a great deal of time on her opening statement to the jury. Sabre and Chris agreed that it would be best if she gave the opening statement since she knew Tray better than Chris did. So she began.

"Tray Copley is the real victim here. He is innocent. The evidence will show that he is a quiet, well-behaved, child with no prior record. He attends school regularly, gets good grades, and helps care for his younger sister.

"Tray's father left him when he was approximately eight years old, and Tray hadn't seen him until his recent visits while Tray was in custody. His mother struggles with a drug addiction and has not always put Tray's best interests first. His mother met and fell for Glen Irving, and after a two-month relationship, she moved him into her home with her two minor children.

Shortly thereafter, Irving molested Tray and continued to do so for several months. When Tray's younger sister told a neighbor what was happening, CPS became involved and removed the children. Tray never saw Irving after that, nor did he have any contact with him of any kind.

"The prosecution has a witness, Sister Maria Luisa Hilasco, who will testify that she saw Irving and my client, Tray, in an Albertsons supermarket on the weekend of Irving's demise. For some of you, it may be difficult to believe that someone of her religious stature could be incorrect. We're not saying that she's lying. I'm sure Sister Maria is telling the truth as she believes it to be. However, that is simply not possible because Tray Copley was elsewhere. And we will provide evidence as to the inaccuracies of eyewitness testimony. We ask that you consider her testimony in that light. You will also see a security video of a young boy at Albertsons who looks a great deal like Tray, which will explain why Sister Maria was so sure she saw him.

"We are certain that Tray was not Irving's only victim. Plenty of other angry parents and young men had a motive to kill him. Irving's own sister will testify to behaviors she witnessed.

"You will hear testimony that the word *GOOF* was written on Irving's forehead. You will also hear that goof is a street or prison term for a pedophile, suggesting that he was killed because of his pedophilia. However, we don't know that for certain because we don't know exactly when the marker was applied or how much time elapsed between his death and when the words were written on him. One may not have anything to do with the other.

"You'll also hear testimony that material was found in my client's possession with the word *GOOF* written on it. We will show that too many variables exist to prove that the handwriting on the body was that of my client's.

"Tray Copley is the victim here, and if you find him guilty of this crime, he will be victimized once again. He is a young, innocent boy who fell prey to a horrible man. The medical examiner is unable to pinpoint an exact time of death, but he has narrowed it down to a twenty-four-hour period. All of Tray's time is accounted for in that time period. Therefore, Tray could not have killed Irving. Please do not victimize this child again."

Marge Benson stood to make her rebuttal statement.

"Please do not blame the victim here. Glen Irving is dead. He cannot speak for himself, so the people of the state of California have to do that for him. We know that Glen Irving allegedly did some despicable things in his life, but that doesn't give this young man the right to take Glen's life. Tray's not claiming that it was an accident or self-defense. His defense is that it wasn't him at all. However, the evidence will contradict that. We will show that he wasn't where he claimed to be, that a witness saw him with the victim shortly before his death, and the evidence on the body was in fact that of Tray Copley. Listen closely to the evidence that is provided to you and you will know he is guilty."

Chapter 30

"A medium coffee and a cranberry bagel," Sabre told the clerk at Einstein Bros. Bagels on Friars Road.

Bob ordered a coffee and plain bagel with cream cheese. He took out his wallet, but Sabre stopped him.

"I've got this," she said. "It's the least I can do for your covering my dependency cases this week while I do the Copley trial." She paid, they took their food, and sat down.

She took a stack of files out of her bag. "Once we had this trial date set, I didn't schedule anything else unless I was forced to, so it's mostly review hearings that were set six months ago. These are the files for today and tomorrow. The rest are in the car. I'll give them to you before you leave here since we're going different directions. My record sheets for the hearings are in the front of each file with all my notes on what I want you to do."

"Of course they are," Bob said.

Sabre ignored his remark. "The sheets are all color-coded, so it's easy to see what kind of hearing it is, and they are marked at the top if you forget the code."

"Doesn't everyone color-code their files?" Bob said jokingly.

She frowned at him. "Here is a list of the hearings with notes. I've seen all the minors, and the notes are in there on the home visits as well."

"I'd expect nothing less."

"Stop making fun of me. You'll be glad when you get into court and you don't have to go searching through the files."

"I'll just wing it," Bob said.

She knew he could do that, but she also knew he would do what she wanted him to do. And if the case went south, he would either deal with it or get a continuance. Her cases were in good hands.

"Thanks for stopping here this morning," Sabre said.

"Anything for you, Sobs." He took the wrapper off the bagel and opened it. "Are you nervous about your trial?"

"I'm not nervous about doing it, but I'm scared to death of the outcome. What if Tray is found guilty?"

"You still think he's innocent?"

"I do. It would be a lot easier if I thought he did it because then if I lose, it's his fault for not having the right facts to support his case. But now if I lose, I'll feel like it's my fault for not giving him the best defense." Sabre took her bagel out and set it on top of the paper sleeve.

"Yeah, I know what you mean. That's why I like representing the parents instead of the kids. Most of the time the parents just screw themselves, no matter how much I try to save them. The mental patients are hardest for me because they really have little control over what they do." He picked up his coffee cup. "You and Chris will do just fine. I know you're prepared, and JP has thoroughly investigated. Speaking of JP, have you two been out again? I know you said you had a dinner date months ago, but I haven't heard you mention anything in a long time."

"We had dinner, not a dinner date. We were working late and we were both hungry. That's all it was. And no, we haven't had any more 'working dinners' since then. We've both been so busy with this case that I can't think of anything else. I'll be so glad when it's over."

Bob finished eating his bagel.

"Are you going to eat? You haven't touched your food."

Sabre put it back inside the paper sleeve. "I think I'll take it with me. We had better get going."

They both stood up and walked out.

"Hey, I hear Judge Charlie Bozo is back at work," Sabre said.

"Yes, he's doing really well. I understand that the cancer is in remission."

"That's great. He seems like a really good guy. I'm just sorry he didn't get back a little sooner. If he had, we may not even have had to be downtown on this trial."

They reached their cars and Bob gave Sabre a little hug. "You're going to do just fine."

"Thanks." Sabre got in her car and drove away. She didn't feel fine. All she felt was concern and fear that she hadn't done enough, that she hadn't found the real killer, and that she had failed Tray.

Chapter 31

"Please call your first witness," the judge said to the DDA.

Benson called Detective Greg Nelson to the stand. He testified that the body was found in a shallow grave in a remote area. He went into great detail about the word *GOOF* on his forehead, the positions of the word, the type of marker, and the lettering.

"Do you know when the word was written on the body?"

"Not for certain. We have a witness that saw Irving on Saturday, May 4, around 11:00 a.m. Our best guess is sometime between then and when the body was found."

"The medical examiner determined that the body was there about a week before it was found. Could the word have been written on the body after the body was buried?" Benson asked.

“That was a dumb question,” Chris whispered to Sabre.

Detective Nelson shifted a little uncomfortably in his seat. "If someone dug it up and wrote on it and then re-buried it, then it's possible but not likely," he responded.

Nelson continued to testify as to the time and circumstances under which they found the body. He testified that the grave was dug about a foot-and-a-half deep and that the dirt was spread out in a slight mound over the body.

On cross-examination, Sabre asked, "What direction was the word on his forehead written?"

"If you were standing in front of the body, it was written from left to right."

"So the person who wrote it would have had to be in front of him."

"Most likely. If the body was on the ground and the writer was behind his head, it would have been upside down. We surmised that it was written from the front."

"You stated that the grave was dug about a foot-and-a-half deep, correct?"

"That's correct."

"Could you tell if an instrument was used to dig the grave?"

"It was not done by hand, if that's what you mean. Forensics determined that a medium-sized shovel was likely used."

"How large a man was Irving?"

Nelson looked down at his notes before he answered. "He was five foot nine and weighed 193 pounds."

"My client is five foot two and weighs about 105 pounds." Sabre expected an objection since she was testifying, but when none came, she continued. "As you can see, he is not muscular. Do you think it would be difficult for him to move a body the size of Irving?"

"It would be difficult for him to lift the body, but he could have possibly dragged him."

"There was no evidence that a body had been dragged to the spot where he was buried, was there, Detective?"

"No, but some time had passed and he could have had help."

"Do you have any evidence that two people were involved in this crime?"

"No, I do not."

Sabre looked at Chris and he nodded. "No further questions," Sabre said, and sat down.

Benson called Detective James Smothers, the other detective who was at the scene, but she didn't get anything new from him. Defense declined to cross, but left it open for later questioning in case something arose.

Next up was the medical examiner, who established the time of death to be within a twenty-four-hour span between noon on Saturday and noon on Sunday.

On cross, Chris asked, "You're basing the noon on Saturday on the alleged sighting of Irving at Albertsons, correct?"

"Yes, the time we determined had many factors which I explained earlier, but that is one of them."

"Thank you. So if there was no witness, you might have a different time frame, correct?"

"Based on his coloring, the bloating of the body, and the condition of his hair, teeth, and nails, we were able to pinpoint a time of death of around three on Saturday afternoon. From there we go several hours on either side, but since he was seen sometime between eleven and noon, we estimated within the next twenty-four hours. It's not an exact science. The longer the victim has been dead, the harder it is to pinpoint an exact time."

"So if the witness made a mistake and didn't actually see Irving around eleven or eleven-thirty, he could have been dead around midnight on Friday night."

"That's possible, although we believe it was closer to mid-afternoon on Saturday."

The prosecutor then called Jerry Bartlett, the man who discovered the body. All Bartlett did was describe the crime scene and explain how his son found the body, making it a little more dramatic for the jury. It appeared Benson hoped his testimony would show the trauma it caused his son when they discovered the dead man, but it backfired. JP had done his homework.

"How old is your son?" Sabre asked.

"He's eleven," Bartlett answered.

"Did you know Glen Irving?"

"No."

"Did you ever hear of him before you found his body?"

"No," he said, shrugging his shoulders and cringing.

"What school does your son attend?"

"Objection," Benson said. "Relevance."

"If the court will allow me a couple more questions, I'll show the relevance."

"Proceed," the judge said.

"He attends La Mesa Middle School."

"Where did he attend last year?"

"Dale Elementary in La Mesa."

"Where Glen Irving worked as a custodian?"

Jerry Bartlett wrinkled his brow and paused for a second, and then said, "I didn't know that."

"No further questions," Sabre said, and sat down. They needed to create reasonable doubt and who better to point a finger at than the person who found the body. JP's investigation showed that Bartlett was at an ophthalmology conference that weekend, but she could at least show that there were other possible suspects. It was weak, but they didn't have much.

The judge looked at the clock and then at the prosecutor. "Do you have redirect for this witness?"

"Not at this time, Your Honor."

"It's already 4:30," the judge said. "How long do you need for your next witness?"

"About an hour on direct, Your Honor."

"We'll adjourn for today." Judge Miller faced the jury. "Ladies and gentlemen of the jury, I stated earlier that you are not to discuss this case during breaks with fellow jurors or anyone else. That still holds. When you go home tonight, you may be tempted to tell your family or friends what happened today. Do not do that. Also, do not do any research on your own, either about the case or the law pertaining to it. If that is understood, we'll see you all back here tomorrow morning at 8:30 sharp. I start my trials on time."

Chapter 32

"The State calls Sister Maria Luisa Hilasco," Benson said.

She took the stand and the clerk swore her in.

"What is your occupation?"

"I'm a Sister Servant of the Blessed Sacrament, a religious order in which we are devoting our lives to the Holy Eucharist and to educating our youth. Presently, I'm a teacher at St. Kieran Catholic School."

"You are a nun, correct?" Benson asked the witness who was wearing her habit.

Sister Maria glanced down at her clothes and said, "That's correct."

Sabre did all she could to keep from chuckling. The court clerk snorted.

Benson ignored it. "How long have you been a nun?"

"She's driving that point home," Chris whispered to Sabre.

"Twenty-three years," Sister Hilasco said.

She went on to testify that she had seen Irving at the Albertsons supermarket with Tray somewhere between 11:00 and 11:30 on Saturday, May 4. She recognized Irving because he had been hanging around the school the previous week. She explained that when she saw his picture in the newspaper, she told the police about seeing Irving on that Saturday.

“Do you see the young man who was with Irving at Albertsons on Saturday, the fourth of May?” Ms. Benson asked the witness.

“Yes,” Sister Hilasco said.

“Will you point to him, please?”

The nun pointed at Tray Copley sitting at the

defense table.

"No further questions," Benson said, and sat down.

"Ms. Brown or Mr. Firmstone, who is cross-examining this witness?" Judge Miller asked.

Sabre stood up and responded, "I am, Your Honor."

"The man you saw in Albertsons whom you identified as Glen Irving, how was he dressed?" Sabre asked.

"He had a gray t-shirt, a light brown jacket, a baseball cap, and I think he was wearing jeans."

"Was he wearing glasses?"

"He had sunglasses on."

"Long or short hair?"

"Kind of long, just below his ears."

"Was his cap on backward or forward?"

"Forward with the bill down."

"So his hair was around his face, he had sunglasses, and a cap on, correct?"

"Yes, that's correct."

"I believe you stated earlier that he kind of kept his head down, is that right?"

"That's right."

"So you never got a good look at his forehead, correct?"

She paused for a second. "No. I never saw his forehead."

"So you wouldn't know if anything was written on his forehead at that time, correct?"

"No, I wouldn't."

"No further questions."

"It's nearly twelve o'clock. We'll break for lunch. Jurors, remember you are still under the same instructions. I'll see you all back here at 1:30."

"No surprises in the nun's testimony," Chris said.

***

Sabre was back in court before anyone else. She spent a few minutes going over her notes before the other parties arrived.

"The State calls Dr. John W. Bell to the stand," Benson said, giving Chris and Sabre a smug glance.

"Damn it," Chris whispered to Sabre. "They must know that Bell didn't have that last therapy session with Tray."

"I guess we'll find out," Sabre said. "Bell called me last night and I missed the call. When I tried to call back this morning, it went to voicemail. I'll bet that's why he was calling."

After Dr. Bell was sworn in and his credentials were established, Benson asked him about the timeline of the therapy sessions. Dr. Bell explained that the sessions had started about nine months ago and had continued until Tray was incarcerated.

"When was your last therapy session with Tray Copley?"

"About a week ago."

"So you have continued to work with him while he has been incarcerated?"

"Yes. He still needs therapy, probably more so than ever. He's a good kid."

"Objection. Nonresponsive," Benson said.

"Sustained as to everything beyond 'yes,'" Judge Miller said.

"Move to strike the last sentence."

"It will be stricken." The judge proceeded to admonish the jury to ignore the last sentence.

"Prior to Tray's incarceration, when was the last therapy session you had with him?"

"I don't recall just when it was."

"Would it help your recollection if you reviewed

your calendar?"

"Yes." Dr. Bell pulled out his phone and looked at his calendar. "It was on a Wednesday."

"And the date?"

"May 1."

"Of last year?"

"Yes."

"And that was your last appointment with him before his arrest?"

"Yes, that's the last time I saw him."

"He's trying not to tell about the canceled appointment," Sabre whispered to Chris.

"I see that, but Marge knows; you can tell by her questioning," Chris said.

Marge took a deep breath. "Yes, Doctor, it's the last time you saw him for therapy, but were there any canceled appointments after that?"

Sabre stood up. "Objection. Asked and answered."

The judge hesitated for just a second. "Overruled. You may answer the question."

"We were scheduled for another appointment on Saturday, but I had to cancel it."

"You canceled the appointment?" Benson asked.

"Correct."

"Did you notify Tray's foster parents of the cancellation?"

"I don't believe I did."

"You're not sure?"

"I intended to, but time got away from me. I had to get ready for my trip to Africa."

"Did you tell Tray that it was canceled?"

"I believe I did."

"When?"

"At the last therapy session."

"The Wednesday before you left?"

"Correct."

"No further questions," Benson said.

Sabre leaned over to Chris. "You can see he wants to help Tray. I'm asking a few questions."

Sabre stood up and took a couple of steps toward the witness.

"Dr. Bell, do you have a receptionist?"

"Yes, I do. She only works three hours a day, so I usually schedule my own appointments."

"Do you share the office with anyone?"

"No."

"Are there other offices in your building?"

"Yes. There's an accountant, a couple of lawyers, and a consultant of some sort."

"Is there a waiting area outside your office?"

"There's a little bench by the window between my office and the accountant's."

"Objection. Relevance," Benson said.

"Overruled," the judge said without waiting for a response.

"Is it possible that Tray went to your office and waited outside for you to show up?"

"That's very possible. In fact, on two occasions I was a few minutes late and Tray did exactly that. He's a good kid. I'm sure if he forgot about the cancellation, he would've waited a long time."

Chapter 33

Sabre and Bob sat at Einstein Bros. Bagel Shop at 7:00 a.m. on Thursday, the fourth day of the trial.

"How have my cases been going?" Sabre asked.

"Nothing I couldn't handle. The Mayhall case went south when the father came forward and accused the mother of making porn films with her boyfriend while the kids were visiting in the home. The judge ordered supervised visits and continued the case for two weeks so you and DSS could investigate. Personally, I think the father is making stuff up, but if not, I'd like to represent the mother."

"You're such a dog," Sabre said. "Anything else?"

"No, just a bunch of review hearings set. The dates are all on your court hearing sheets in the files. You don't need to worry about that. Tell me about the trial."

"The State has rested. We moved for a directed verdict, hoping the judge would rule that Tray was 'not guilty,' but it was denied. We start our defense case today. Most of their witnesses didn't hurt too much, except for the therapist. We had considered putting Tray on the stand to testify, but because of something the therapist said, we can't do that."

"Did the therapist tell you something in confidence?"

"No, but if we put Tray on the stand he'll look like a liar. They have totally contradictory statements about the last therapy session, and I'm afraid the jury will believe the doctor over Tray. Frankly, I'm having trouble reconciling it myself."

"But now you can put on your defense," Bob said. "That should help."

"I hope so. We're calling Dr. Bell again. We're pretty sure he can't do any more damage. He seems to really want to help Tray, and he throws in positive comments every chance he gets. June Longe, the foster mother, will testify as to his character and to how he was never alone except when she was at the hospital, which is likely when Irving was killed. Mrs. Fletcher, Drew's mother, will testify that she took Tray to therapy that day. And then we have Drew, who is his alibi for most of the rest of the day." Sabre sighed.

"You have concerns about Drew's testimony?"

"He's a teenager for starters. JP has talked to him three times, and Chris and I went over his testimony just last night, but you never know about kids. Besides...."

"Besides what?"

"If Tray actually committed this crime, he likely had an accomplice and the most likely person would be Drew."

"Are you having second thoughts about Tray's innocence?"

"No. I'm just befuddled by the whole thing. It doesn't make sense. We must be missing something."

***

The defense called several expert witnesses. One disputed the time of death of the victim. Another questioned the ability of someone Tray's size to commit this crime alone. And a third was a handwriting expert, Barbara Foltz, who testified that the handwriting of the word *GOOF* found in Tray's locker was his. However, the word written on the body was similar in many respects, but not necessarily Tray's. She also stated that it would be difficult for anyone to be absolutely sure about the writing on the body because of the texture and the contour of the surface upon which it was written. That testimony got them through to lunch. When they returned, Sabre called Drew Fletcher to the stand. The clerk swore him in.

Sabre stood up and stepped to her left so she was closer to the witness before she started her questioning. "How do you know Tray Copley?"

"He...he's my neighbor and my best friend," Drew Fletcher said. His mouth twitched as he spoke.

"Are you nervous, Drew?"

"A little."

"Try to relax. This won't take too long. How long have you known him?"

"About nine months. Since he went to live with the Longes."

"Do you live close to him?"

"We live only a few houses from the Longes." Drew seemed to breathe more evenly.

"On the fourth of May last year, did you see your friend Tray Copley?"

"Yes, we had plans for that afternoon, but he came over early."

"To your house?"

"Yes."

"What time did he come there?"

He shrugged. "I'm not exactly sure, but it was around 9:00 in the morning. Mrs. Longe's father had a heart attack and she had to go to the hospital, so Tray came to stay with me."

"What plans did you have for the afternoon?"

"We were going to the skatepark."

"Did you go?"

"Yes."

"Were you with Tray the whole day?"

"Yes," Drew said, but the word didn't sound final, like he had something else to say but stopped.

Sabre wasn't ready for him to add anything, so she continued. "How did you get to the skatepark?"

"My mom took us."

"Do you know what time you went to the park?"

"We left the house about 10:45 because Tray had a therapy appointment at 11:00."

"Did you go to the appointment with Tray?"

"No. We dropped him off at the therapist's office, which is only about a block away from the skatepark, and then Mom dropped me off at the park."

"Did your mother go in with Tray?"

Drew accidentally bumped the microphone and it made a loud noise. He looked at Sabre and then the judge with a scared look on his face.

"Sorry."

"It's okay," Sabre said. After a short pause, she added, "Do you remember the question?"

He shook his head.

"Speak up, please," the judge said.

"No, I don't remember the question."

"Did your mother go into the therapist's office with Tray?" Sabre asked again.

"No."

"Did she stay at the park?"

"No, she went to work." He quickly added. "We go there all the time."

"Do you ever go to the park without permission?"

Drew hesitated.

"Just tell the truth," Sabre said.

"We went once after school when we weren't supposed to."

"Who are 'we'?"

"Me and Tray."

"Did you get into trouble for that?"

"No, my mom didn't know."

"Did Tray get into trouble?"

"No because I told them he was helping me with my homework."

"Did you ever do it again?"

"No because Tray didn't want to lie to his foster mother."

"Thank you for your honesty," Sabre said. "That Saturday on the fourth of May, how did you get home from the skatepark?"

"Mom picked us up."

"What time was that?"

"Around five o'clock."

"Do you know how Tray got to the skatepark after his appointment?"

"He walked. It's only, like, a block away."

"When Tray arrived, what did you two do?"

"We just skated, did tricks, carved the bowl, ollied the steps—things like that. We competed with a couple of other kids there." He shrugged. "That's it."

"Did Tray leave the park before your mom came to pick you up?"

"No."

Sabre stepped toward the defense table and checked her notepad. "Where did you go after the park?"

"We went to my house and had dinner."

"Did Tray stay the night?"

"No. Mrs. Longe picked him up after dinner."

"No further questions, Your Honor." Sabre sat down.

"Ms. Benson," the judge said.

Marge stood up and gave the witness a strained smile. "Tray is your best friend, right?"

"Yes."

"And you don't want to get him into trouble, do you?"

"No."

"You would do just about anything to help him, right?"

"If he needed me."

"You stated earlier that you lied for him about being at the skatepark when you weren't supposed to be. Are you lying now?"

"No."

"Did you go with Tray to Albertsons on May 4?"

"No."

"Were you with Tray when he lured Mr. Irving to Coyote Ridge?"

"No."

"Objection," Sabre said. "Assumes facts not in evidence."

"I'll rephrase," Benson said. "Did you go with Tray to Coyote Ridge that day?"

"No."

"He went alone?"

"Yes, I guess. No, he was with me."

"You both went then?"

"Objection, badgering," Sabre said.

"Sustained."

"I withdraw the question," continued Benson. She took a step forward from the table and lowered her tone. "Drew, you don't know where Tray was when he was not with you that day, do you?"

"I know we dropped him off at the therapist's office."

"But you don't know if he actually stayed there, do you?"

"No."

"Tray's therapist's office is a block and a half from the skatepark, correct?"

"Yes."

"And in fact, he was gone several hours before he returned to the skatepark, right?"

"I don't think it was that long."

"But you don't know for sure because you lost track of time, right?"

"It wasn't that long."

"Do you have a cell phone?"

"Yes."

"Did you check the time while Tray was gone?"

He didn't answer.

"Drew, did you check the time while Tray was gone?"

"Just once."

"And what time was that?"

"It was a few minutes until twelve."

"And then it was quite a while before Tray actually showed up, right?"

"It was a while, but I don't know how long. Anthony, this other kid, showed up and we started carving the bowl."

Her young assistant whispered something to Ms. Benson. She nodded.

"How many times did you 'carve the bowl,' as you call it, before Tray showed up?"

"A few, I guess."

"You mean two? Or was it more like twenty? Or a hundred?"

"It wasn't a hundred."

"But more than two?"

"Yeah, I guess. I don't know how many."

"So, somewhere between two and one hundred?"

"Objection, asked and answered," Chris said.

"Overruled," the judge said. She looked directly at Drew. "You may answer the question."

"I didn't count them."

"Was it closer to two or closer to a hundred?" Benson asked.

He sighed. "It wasn't anywhere near a hundred."

"So, maybe fifty?"

"Maybe. No, less than that."

"Does twenty sound closer?"

"Yeah, I guess."

"Did you do any other tricks before Tray showed up?"

"A few."

"What kind?"

"We jumped a few steps."

"How long were you doing that?"

"I don't know. Not long because the manual pad opened and that's what we were waiting for. And then Tray got there."

Benson looked at a note her assistant had scribbled and then took a breath before her next question. "Has anyone told you what to say here today?"

"Just Ms. Brown." Drew nodded toward Sabre. She was careful not to make eye contact for fear the jury would think she was coaching him.

"What did she tell you to say?"

"She said that I should just tell the truth, no matter what I'm asked."

Sabre sighed. *Benson asked one question too many, but at least we made that point.*

"Redirect, Counselor?"

"One second, Your Honor," Sabre said. She whispered to Chris, "Do you think I should try to get Drew to narrow the timeline some?"

"He could make it worse and that'll just call more attention to it. Besides, we ended on a positive."

"I agree." Sabre looked up at Judge Miller. "No more questions, Your Honor."

***

JP was waiting for Sabre when she came out of the courtroom. "Hey, kid," he said in his usual tone.

"What are you doing here? That didn't sound right. I guess what I really mean is, do you have some news for me?"

"Remember Anthony, the guy at the skatepark?"

"Yes, what about him?"

"I've gone to the skatepark with Drew about three times, and another five or six by myself. I asked every dark-haired, dark-skinned kid I met if he was Anthony and then I listened for an accent. I finally found him last night."

Sabre smiled and her face lit up. "Do we need a subpoena?"

"I'm afraid if you call him to testify, you'll be diggin' up more possums than you can kill."

Sabre's face lost the brightness it just had. "What did he say?"

"He said that he didn't get to the park until almost noon. He and Drew were carving the bowl for a half hour to forty-five minutes, and then the steps opened up and they were jumping the steps for another forty or fifty minutes. They were on the manual pad when Tray arrived and they had been there quite a while before he showed up."

"Which means Tray was gone a couple of hours without Drew. Drew was trying not to tell how long, but Benson got to him today."

"He said the same thing as Anthony?"

"Not quite as bad, but I'm glad I didn't continue to question him or it may have gotten worse." Sabre sat down on the bench outside the courtroom. "I just don't get it. Tray swears he was at therapy for an hour and then went straight to the skatepark."

Chapter 34

Sabre and Bob were in her office looking through the files of the cases Bob had covered all week, but Sabre kept forgetting what she was doing and asking Bob to repeat things.

"What time did you finish the trial yesterday?" Bob asked.

"It was nearly six because the judge wanted to keep going until it was done, so we did."

"You're worried about the verdict, aren't you?"

"This is the worst. I've never been this anxious. I'm so afraid that we didn't do enough. I'll be glad when the verdict comes in and I can put this behind me." Sabre checked the time. "It's only three. It could still come in today. I hope so; otherwise, we'll have to wait the whole weekend." Bob started to say something, but Sabre continued to talk. "If he goes to prison for something he didn't do, I'll never be able to forgive myself."

"Sobs, you and Chris did the best you could. JP has been investigating this case for months and he's the best."

"I think we missed something because Tray swears he didn't kill Irving, but nothing matches up. He says he was at therapy. Dr. Bell says he wasn't. Tray says he went straight to the skatepark. Yet the witnesses say it was at least an hour or two before he got there. He says he hadn't seen Irving, but Sister Maria saw Tray at Albertsons with Irving and he's on the security video. I don't get it."

"Sabre," Bob said.

It sounded odd to hear him call her 'Sabre' since he never called her by her real name.

"Yes, Robert."

"Maybe Tray is lying to you. Maybe he killed him. And if he did, you don't have to beat yourself up. If he murdered someone, he deserves to go to prison."

She cocked her head to one side. "You don't believe that."

"You're right. I don't believe that if he killed that low-life scumbag, he should rot in prison. Irving got what he deserved as far as I'm concerned. But you can't change the facts. You just don't have them in your favor."

Sabre looked down at her cell phone when it rang. "It's the court," she said as she answered it. "Attorney Sabre Brown." She listened. "I'll be right there."

"The verdict's in?" Bob asked.

"The verdict's in."

***

When the jurors entered the courtroom, none of them looked at Tray.

"That's a bad sign," Chris said quietly to Sabre.

Sabre frowned at him because he had spoken a little too loudly and she feared Tray had heard him. She touched Tray's trembling hand.

"Take a deep breath," she told Tray.

"I'm scared."

"I know, but if something goes wrong, we'll keep trying. For now, just try to be brave."

The jurors took the same seats they had been in for the last week.

The judge said, "Madam Forewoman, do you have a unanimous verdict?"

"We do, Your Honor," a short, stout woman in her fifties said.

"Please hand it to the bailiff."

The bailiff walked over to her, took the piece of paper that she handed him, and walked it to the judge. Although the process took only a matter of seconds, to Sabre it seemed to take a really long time. She kept asking herself if they had done enough. She believed Tray was innocent, but the evidence kept stacking up against him. She wondered if they should've taken a chance and put Tray on the stand to testify. They would have if it weren't for Dr. Bell's testimony. It wasn't the doctor's fault. He did everything he could to keep from saying that he had canceled the appointment. Tray still maintained that they had a therapy session in spite of what the doctor said. And then there was Drew's testimony. That had really hurt because it opened up the timeline and basically destroyed Tray's alibi.

If Judge Shirleen Miller was surprised by the verdict, she didn't show it. She maintained her poker face as she read the jury's decision. Then she folded the paper and handed the verdict to the bailiff, who carried it back to the jury forewoman.

"What is your verdict?" the judge asked the forewoman.

"In the charge of First-degree Murder, we find the defendant *not guilty*."

Sabre sighed.

"In the charge of Second-degree Murder, we find the defendant *guilty*."

Sabre felt heaviness in her chest. She told herself to breathe. As prepared as she thought she was, this hit her hard. She immediately turned to Tray. Tears were already rolling down his cheeks. Sabre could barely hear the words he muttered.

"We lost," he said. "That's not what was supposed to happen."

Part II

The Oscar Hazelton Case

Chapter 35

Present day...

The news anchor announced the name "Ruben Parks," grabbing Sabre's attention. She recognized the name from a recent report she had obtained from JP. Reaching for her remote, she turned up the volume. "Ruben Parks was discovered in a shallow grave a few hundred feet from another body found approximately three years ago. Although the discovery took place on the twelfth of May on Coyote Ridge in El Cajon, it has taken more than three years to determine Ruben's identity. Ruben's widow, Rachel Parks, and her alleged boyfriend, Larry Norbit, who is still on parole, were arrested today in Parks' home on Mt. Helix. Well-known criminal attorney, Jerry Leahy, is representing the widow. Leahy told Channel 10 News that 'my client is innocent and she's grieving the death of her husband. We're confident that the truth will come out and my client will be exonerated.'"

"Of course you are, Leahy," Sabre said with a smile at the television.

Sabre was still watching the news when Bob called her. "Did you see they arrested someone for killing that guy who was buried near Irving?"

Sabre muted the sound on her television. "Yes, I was just watching it. I guess some good came out of this case. They may never have found the body if that kid hadn't peed on Irving."

"There are just so many things I could spin off of what you just said," Bob said.

"But please don't."

"Did you see that?"

"What?"

"Wait. It's something about another body."

Sabre turned her volume back up.

"...found less than two miles, as the crow flies, from the bodies of Irving and Parks," the news reporter said.

"They found two more bodies. That makes four in that area. It looks like El Cajon has a new burial ground," Sabre said.

"It's a lot cheaper than the cemeteries," Bob said. "I think I'll put that in my trust. *Just dump my body in the hills in El Cajon. Give the wild animals a feast. They have to eat too.*"

"Listen." Sabre turned up the volume.

"Our sources say that based on evidence found on the two new bodies, there may be a connection to Glen Irving's death, whose body was found more than three years ago on Coyote Ridge."

"What? Do they think Tray killed those guys too? Isn't he still locked up?"

"He's in Northern Youth-to-Adult Conservation Camp. It's a special program for violent offenders who have proven to be low risk. It's a higher security level than most of the camps. I was able to have him transferred there after he was beaten up twice at Division of Juvenile Justice in San Bernardino. I tried to get him moved sooner, but there wasn't anywhere available any better than where he was. Shortly after he turned seventeen, that's the minimum age requirement for the camp, I managed to get him sent to Northern Youth—but only because he almost died the second time he was beaten."

Sabre paused for a second to listen to what they were saying on the news. "Unless the bodies have been there more than three years," Sabre said, "law enforcement can't blame these on Tray."

"I don't think the reporter said how long ago the men were killed. The coroner likely doesn't know that yet."

"This could be good news," Sabre said.

"How's that?"

"Maybe the real killer will be caught."

"You still don't think Tray did it?"

"No. I don't. I'm sure he didn't murder Irving. Maybe he killed him in self-defense, but we'll probably never know that. He still hasn't changed his story."

"The news reporter said Parks' body was *connected* to Irving's, but he didn't say what the connection was," Bob said. "It could be someone Irving associated with at some point. Or maybe it's a copycat killer. A lot of information came out about the murder during the trial."

"True, but if there is an actual connection, we may get enough for a new trial for Tray."

"Any word on your last appeal?"

"I heard yesterday. It was denied. We've filed every appeal and writ available. We've exhausted all our avenues for release. The only thing left is if we can find new evidence, and even then it would have to be substantial."

"This *connection* could be anything, Sobs. I'm worried about you getting your hopes up."

"I always do. I'd better call JP and see what he can find out."

***

Private Detective JP Torn stood in the doorway at Sabre's office, waiting for her to notice he was there. She was focused on the file in front of her. When she finally looked up, she smiled at him.

"Hey, kid," said JP. "I hear you're looking for a good private eye."

"Yeah, you know any?"

He sauntered over to her desk, removed his black Stetson, and kissed her gently on the neck. "Good enough for you?"

"I'm not sure yet." She turned her head toward him so their lips met. "Yeah, you'll do."

JP had been working with Sabre for several years, but they hadn't started dating until recently. They were drawn to each other right from their first meeting, but both denied the connection until they couldn't any longer. He was the yin to her yang. Sabre was an "A-type" personality; JP was a quiet, no-nonsense cowboy, boots and all. Previously, he was a San Diego deputy sheriff, but now he freelanced as a private detective. Their age difference of eighteen years seemed to bother him more than her.

He moved around the desk and took a seat across from her.

"So, what's the connection between Irving and the two new dead guys?" Sabre asked. Before he could answer she added, "Have they been identified yet?"

"I think the police know who they are, but I couldn't squeeze that information out of anyone. They're still notifying family, or trying to." He paused.

"And the connection to Irving?"

"At least one of them had GOOF written in black marker on his forehead."

Sabre sighed. "Maybe they'll find the real killer."

JP shook his head. "They think they already have Irving's killer. They're looking for a copycat. Tray's case has been all over the news and the Internet and they're talking about the word *GOOF*. Anyone could have seen that and copied it."

"Is there anything else that is similar?"

"Not that we know of yet. We're not even sure if the other men who were murdered are pedophiles because they haven't yet been identified. As soon as I find out, I'll let you know. Then we can see if there's anything else that may connect all three of them."

Chapter 36

Sabre entered Mary Ellen Wilson Group Home. When Sabre first started practicing at juvenile court, she was curious about the name of this group home. After doing a little research, she discovered the group home was named after one of the first children in New York to receive protection from the court system. In Sabre's opinion, this was one of the better group homes in San Diego County. As a rule, she tried to keep her minor clients out of group homes because placing the children with family or in foster homes seemed like more natural, normal settings. Most of her clients did not fare well in the group homes. But for some there was no alternative. If no family came forward and if the foster homes refused to take a child because of the child's behavioral issues, a group home was the next step or often the only option. Sexually abused children were harder than usual to place because parents feared what might happen to their own children. Wilson was opened to house children who were victims of sexual abuse.

Sabre was greeted at the door by the group home facilitator, Jesse Alder, a tall man with an athletic body, a chiseled face, and a thunderous voice. Most of the children came to respect him after being in the group home for a short time. She found him to be caring and gentle with the boys, but he didn't put up with any nonsense. When he spoke, they jumped. She wondered how much that had to do with his deep, commanding voice.

"Hello, Ms. Brown. Nice to see you again."

"You too, Jesse. How's my boy doing?"

"Oscar's a handful, but he's coming around. He's

been looking forward to your visit."

Sabre shook her head. "It's pretty sad when your attorney is the only constant in your life."

"I know, but it's more than that. He seems to like you, and he doesn't like many people. He hasn't warmed up to any of the social workers. Admittedly, they keep changing. You, on the other hand, have been with him from the start, almost a year."

"There are times when he has opened up to me about things that happened to him when he was very young, but most of the time I get nothing."

"From what I understand that's more than he's done in therapy. I'm glad you're on this case. He needs you."

Sabre sighed. "Thanks. Anything I should know before I see him?"

"He was in a fight yesterday with a new kid, a fourteen-year-old. The new kid was a lot bigger than Oscar, but that never stops him. From all accounts, this time Oscar didn't start the fight, but he's on disciplinary action just the same since we have a zero tolerance rule about fighting."

A young man about twenty-five with a full, dark beard who stood approximately six-foot-four and weighed about 300 pounds walked up with Oscar. It made Oscar look even shorter than his five feet. He was an angry, twelve-year-old boy with an angelic face; a sandy, Beatles-style haircut; freckles; and cornflower blue eyes. He was the kind of kid you would like to hug when you first meet him. But then he'd open his mouth and spew out his rage. Then, he'd seem more like a grizzly bear than a teddy bear.

"Have you met Callum?" Jesse asked Sabre.

Sabre turned to the big man. "I saw you last time I was here, but we didn't actually meet." She extended her hand. "Nice to meet you, Callum."

"You too," he said. He looked at Oscar. "Now, you mind your manners and no swearing. You hear?"

Oscar mumbled something that Sabre didn't understand.

"Hi, Oscar," said Sabre.

"Hi."

"Let me know if you need anything," Jesse said, and he and Callum walked away.

Sabre sat down on a chair near the table in the twelve- by twenty-foot room they used for interviews. It contained a small table with four chairs and a love seat. One wall was lined with windows, two of which were open. The other walls were bare and had no pictures. The room contained no plants or any other decor. It was supposedly a work in progress, but it hadn't changed in the four years that Sabre had been going there. The money was always needed elsewhere.

Oscar didn't sit. Instead, he walked around the room, picking up speed with each pass.

"Would you like to sit down and talk with me?"

"No. I'm good."

"How are things going here?"

"Terrible."

"How's that?"

"I got in a fight yesterday and now I'm on restriction."

"Do you want to tell me what happened?"

"No."

"Okay, you don't have to tell me about the fight. What is your restriction?"

"The new kid is a fu..." he paused, "stupid ass…." Oscar fidgeted and struggled for the words as he rounded the table. He slowed down and looked at Sabre, and yelled, "He's a stupid jerk!"

Sabre had to give him credit for trying not to use

the cuss words. The last time she was here, he'd sounded like a drunken sailor.

"What did he do to you?"

"He kept calling me 'Pipsqueak,' and then he put his hand on my head and tried to hold me down. But I kicked him real hard in the leg so he let go. When he lost his balance and fell down, I jumped on him. I was getting him pretty good when Hagrid broke us up."

"Hagrid? Who's that?"

"The giant from the *Harry Potter* books. That's what everyone calls Callum. He's big like him, but he's real nice."

"But you shouldn't call him names."

"Callum doesn't mind. He likes it. We watch the *Harry Potter* movies all the time, and Hagrid is his favorite."

"If you're sure." Sabre paused. "And then you got put on restriction?"

"Yes."

"Both of you?"

"Yes, but he got more than me. It's a point system and you lose points for each offense. I only got in trouble for fighting. Junior got it for fighting, calling names, and insatgating, instantgating, or something."

"Instigating?"

"Yeah, he instigating-ed the fight. And that's worse." Oscar moved quickly around the room. As he circled, he bounced one foot against the wall and kept going almost as if he were walking along the wall.

"Oscar, could you come here and sit for just a few minutes? It won't take long."

He scowled but sat down across from Sabre. Instead of looking at her, though, he faced the window. This is how their sessions usually went. Oscar would start out like she was a stranger but before she left, he was talking to her like she was his friend. The only subject she could never get him to open up about was the molestation. One of his mother's drunken boyfriends had abused him on several occasions. That and his mother's alcohol abuse is why he and his brother were removed from the mother's home.

"So, what was your punishment?"

"I lost game room privileges for three days." He wiggled around in his chair.

"Other than your recent fight, how have things been going here?"

He bobbed his head. "It sucks, but it doesn't suck any more than other places I've been."

Sabre's heart ached for this young man. He had never really had a childhood. His mother and father were both mean, angry alcoholics. The domestic violence in that household was non-stop for the first six years of Oscar's life. He would get so scared when they started fighting that he would hide under his bed with his ears covered to drown out the noise. She knew that because he had told her about it some time ago.

Oscar looked out the window and his eyes narrowed with contempt. Then the color suddenly drained from his face. Sabre turned to see what had brought on the anger or fear she was seeing in his face. Two cops were outside talking to Jesse.

"Do you think I'll be arrested?"

"Why would you be arrested?"

"For fighting yesterday."

"I'm sure they're not here to arrest you for fighting. Jesse already dealt with all that." Then Sabre considered that the other child's parents may have called the police, but she didn't think it very likely.

"I hate cops," Oscar said. He stood up and came closer to Sabre.

"Why?"

"Because they took my dad from me."

"But your dad is not in jail."

"Not now, but when I was little my mom and dad got into a fight. I started to go hide under the bed, but my mom was holding my baby brother and I was afraid he would get hurt."

"So what did you do?" Sabre asked.

"I grabbed him from my mom and I hid him under the bed. One of the neighbors called the cops, and when they showed up, my dad was furious."

"What did he do?"

"I forgot to shut the door, so I could see them from where we were hiding. My mom and dad were punching each other. There was blood everywhere. They were both swinging and screaming, and the cops were trying to get them apart. I saw my mom fall to the ground. Blood was shooting from her mouth. One cop pounded on my dad with his billy club."

"Did you come out from your hiding place?"

"No. I wrapped the pillow I kept under there around my brother, and I hid until the cops found us. My mom went to the hospital and my dad went to jail. If those stupid cops hadn't shown up, my dad would never have left us."

"But your mom could've been hurt really bad."

"The cops made him madder and so he hurt her more. He was always worse when they came."

"How long did your dad stay in jail?"

"I don't know because when he came out he went to a rehab center, and he never came home to stay after that. He got married about a year later, and then he stopped seeing us kids completely. He just left us and made a new family." Oscar kept his eyes on the cops outside as he spoke, and then he moved closer to Sabre.

Sabre told him, "Sometimes parents do things that aren't right, but that doesn't mean he stopped loving you." Sabre searched for anything that might make this boy feel better.

"No." He shook his head. "He didn't love us anymore. I used to beg to go see him, but he didn't want to see me. Then one day he came by the house and I thought he was coming to get me, but he was there to pick up something he had left in the garage. My mom asked him for some money, and he told her he didn't have any—that he had his *own kids* now to take care of. I hate cops."

Oscar was standing right next to her now. Sabre wanted to reach out and wrap her arms around him and tell him that everything was going to be okay, but she knew that wouldn't really be the truth. She considered explaining that it was not the cops' fault, but he didn't want to hear that right now. She guessed that his fear and hatred for cops stemmed from more than the issues with his father. The man who molested him was a security officer. It made Sabre angry to think what his parents had done to their son: the fear and the abandonment that he felt for most of his life, and the neglect and the abuse by his mother's boyfriend. He never had a chance to be a normal child.

The two cops followed Jesse toward the building where Sabre and Oscar were talking. Oscar's eyes darted from the window to Sabre.

"Don't let them take me to jail," Oscar blurted.

Sabre stood up. "I'll see what's going on."

Jesse opened the door and walked in with the two deputy sheriffs.

"Ms. Brown, these officers are here to talk to Oscar," Jessie said.

Sabre walked around the table toward the door, but Oscar stayed behind. "What about?" She looked from one officer to the other.

The taller of the two cops spoke. "We just want to

ask him some questions, ma'am."

"I don't know what this is about, but I'm his attorney and no one will question him without me present."

"That's fine, ma'am."

"What is this regarding?"

"It's regarding a man named Sammy Everton."

Sabre knew how much Oscar hated to talk about the man who had molested him. "Why now? Has Everton hurt someone else?"

All of a sudden, both officers dashed forward, almost knocking Sabre down. She turned just in time to see Oscar fling himself head first through the open window. The taller cop ran toward the window. The other spun around to run out the door, but it took him a few seconds to get around Jesse, who had been standing there. Oscar ran across the road and behind a building. The tall cop dashed back from the window and out the door to join the other one. But Oscar was nowhere in sight.

Chapter 37

JP sat down in the chair across from Sabre's desk. "You have a job for me?" he asked.

"Yes." She sighed. "I have a twelve-year-old dependency client, Oscar Hazleton, who I expect will soon be in the delinquency system. I visited him a couple of hours ago at Mary Ellen Wilson Group Home where he's been living for about a year. A couple of cops came to the group home to question him about Sammy Everton, the man who molested him. Oscar is really afraid of cops, so he bolted. They're looking for him now."

"He got away from them?"

"He dived right out the window, rolled onto his feet, and took off running before they could get out the door."

When JP chuckled, Sabre gave him a stern look.

"I know it's not funny, but the visual in my head was."

Sabre smiled. "It actually was almost comical for a moment. All I could see was the bottom of the kid's feet as he flew through the window; the two cops trying to figure out which way to go; and the dance between Jesse and the one cop as Jesse tried to get out of his way. Jesse was unintentionally blocking the door. At least I think it was unintentional."

"Where is Oscar now?"

"They haven't found him yet."

"Or you just haven't been notified, if they have."

"I'm sure Jesse, the director at the group home, would've called me. I've already invoked Oscar's right to counsel, so they shouldn't be questioning him without me present."

"Do you want me to go look for him?"

"Not yet. They probably don't want your help right now. I hope they find him soon, though, because it's not safe for him out there by himself. Oscar knows those hills pretty well because the staff from the group home takes the boys on a lot of hikes around there. But that means the staff knows the area even better. Before I left, the department had enlisted the help of Jesse, Callum, and two other staff members, as well as a few other deputy sheriffs." She handed JP a file. "This is Oscar's dependency file. Jot down the information you need and copy his photo and that of his perpetrator, Sammy Everton. I want you to find out everything you can about Everton, including any new arrests. The cops wanted to question Oscar about Everton, so something has come up."

"Do you want me to try to interview Everton?"

"If you can find him, although I doubt he'll talk to you."

"I take it he's not in custody."

"No, he disappeared before he was ever charged with anything, so either this is about an old crime or Everton has resurfaced."

"Okay, boss, I'll get right on it." He stood.

Sabre didn't like JP to call her 'boss,' but she gave him a fake smile. "And be forewarned: you're not going to like what you read in that file, so keep your cool." Nothing made JP angrier than a child molester. He often suggested his own "red-neck justice," as he called it.

"If you have to warn me, I don't make any guarantees," JP said. "Can I use David's office to look through the file?"

"Yes, he's not here."

JP returned about twenty minutes later, his eyes narrowed with contempt. "You're right. I don't like it one bit." He handed the file back to Sabre. "I think I have everything I need to find that polecat."

"Good. Please call me in a couple of hours and let me know what you've found out. If they haven't found Oscar by then, I may want you to join the search."

JP walked around the desk, reached for her hand, and gently pulled her up. She leaned against his body and he kissed her passionately.

"Whew. I'm not complaining, but what was that for?"

"Just for bein' you, darlin'." He placed his hat back on his head and walked out.

Chapter 38

JP started his investigation from his home office by running Everton through the criminal database. His beagle, Louie, stood next to him with his head draped across JP's knee. JP reached down and patted his head between clicks on his computer. According to the social worker's report, Everton had lived most of his life in the San Diego area. About five years ago he moved to Las Vegas, where he lived for about two years before returning. JP checked to see if there was anything in the local database first. Everton had no convictions in California except for a "drunk in public," two years previously. Next, he checked in Nevada but found nothing.

JP spent the next hour attempting to find a more recent address than the one he had when Everton lived with Oscar's mother and the children. He had lived there for approximately eight months, but left when the children were removed due to the alleged molest on the case. It didn't appear that anyone at the Department of Social Services had tried very hard to find him. Nor would they.— Their job was to protect the children, not prosecute the perpetrator. JP wondered how much effort the police had made. He made a note to contact the mother's attorney to see if he could question her client regarding Everton's whereabouts, hangouts, and friends.

The next call was to JP's good friend, Ernie Madrigal, with whom he had been on the force for many years. Ernie was still working for the sheriff's department and was a good source of information for JP when possible.

"What's up?" Ernie asked.

"I'm trying to find a guy named Sammy, or Samuel, Everton. The last known address I have was about a year ago."

"What kind of case?"

"Dependency. Sexual abuse."

"Prior record?"

"Just a PC 647(f) about two years ago. Nothing else. According to the reports from DSS, he has lived in two other homes with women who had young boys. At least one of them suspected molest and kicked him out, but again, he was never charged with anything."

"Let me see what I can find," Ernie said.

"One more thing you ought to know. A couple of hours ago, two deputies from East County came to question our client, Oscar Hazleton, about Everton. I don't know what they were seeking because the kid bolted. They're searching for him right now."

"Why would the kid run?"

"Sabre says he's really afraid of cops because of some things that happened to him and to his family when he was younger. He also got in a fight yesterday with a boy at the group home, and he may've been afraid that he was in trouble for that. But he didn't run until Everton's name was mentioned, so it might be that he just didn't want to talk about him. Who knows what goes through these kids' minds?"

"I'll let you know as soon as I find out something."

Louie fetched a toy and brought it to JP to play with him. JP tugged at the toy for a few minutes. When he dropped the toy, Louie picked it up and laid it on his lap. JP stood up. "Sorry, Louie, but I have to go see a man at work."

JP got in his car and drove to Smart & Easy Self-Storage on Jamacha Road where Everton had worked security. He pulled into the small parking lot outside the gated facility and up to an office door. Once he stepped inside, JP saw windows along the back wall that provided a good view of the entire facility. JP glanced around and estimated it to consist of eight hundred exterior units. A man in his late sixties, as best JP could tell, spoke to him from behind the counter. "May I help you?"

"Is the owner here?"

"I'm the owner."

JP extended his hand. "I'm JP Torn."

He reciprocated. "George Ingle."

"I understand you have twenty-four-hour security. Is that right?"

"That's right. Are you looking to store something valuable? Because we haven't had a single break-in or theft since I bought the place, and that'll be ten years next month."

JP decided to tell him the truth. Sometimes, it just worked best. "No, I'm not looking for storage. I'm a private investigator on an abuse case in juvenile court. I can't give you any details on the case because that's all confidential, but I'd like to get a little information from you if you don't mind."

"I can't imagine how I can help," Ingle said, "but if it will help the kids, ask away."

"I'm looking for Sammy Everton. Does he still work here?"

"No, he doesn't. Left about ten months ago."

"Did he say where he was going or ask for a referral to another job?"

"Nope, he came to work one day. Everything seemed fine. He never said a word about quitting. He just never showed up again."

JP wondered if that was his usual pattern and this time he just moved on. "Did he miss much work?"

"Nope, never. Always here. Never late." He paused. "Some days he came in with a pretty good hangover, especially if he had the morning shift. I had to send him home once and write him up because he smelled like a distillery. I don't think he'd been drinking that morning. I think he was still looped from the night before. It never happened again. He was pretty determined to keep his job."

"Did he get along with his co-workers?"

"He seemed to. He wasn't the most social guy around. Didn't talk much. Kinda kept to himself, but no one complained about him or anything, if that's what you mean."

JP gave him a business card. "Thanks, George. Please call if you hear anything about him from the other workers or if you remember anything else you think I might want to know."

"Sure will." JP turned to leave when George said, "If you find him, you might want to let him know I still have a check here for him. It's only for three days' work, but unless he won the lottery or suddenly came into a trust fund, I expect he could use the money."

Before he started back toward San Diego, JP called Sabre. "Have they found Oscar yet?"

"No, they told me they were still combing the area. That's about all I could find out. They don't seem to want to tell me anything else."

"Do you want me to go there and see what I can find out? I'm still in East County so I'm not far away."

"Would you? I'm starting to get worried. I was sure they would've found him by now, and it'll be dark soon."

"Do you want me to help with the search?"

"I'd like you to just go and find out what they're doing and what this is all about. If you can, talk to Jesse and see what they told him."

"Okay."

"And JP, don't stay out there too long. I don't want you to go missing too."

"No worries. By the way, I just found out that Everton left his job without his last paycheck. No one does that unless they can't get back to it…or they're running away."

Chapter 39

Within fifteen minutes JP had reached the group home. There were two police officers outside the office. The male cop was on the phone. JP introduced himself to the female and said, "I'd like to help."

"How do you know about this?"

"I work for the minor's attorney and she was here when Oscar ran away. Don't get me wrong, I think it's great that they're out there looking for a lost boy, but I can't help but wonder if there's something else. Is the boy in trouble?"

"Fortunately, two officers happened to be here when he ran away or we wouldn't know he was missing."

"It appears that they were the reason he ran away," JP said. "He's very afraid of the police. It might be better if I were to find him."

The officer's eyes narrowed as she looked at JP. "We're not taking volunteers at this time because it's a police matter."

"Is he going to be arrested when he's found?"

"He's a person of interest at the moment."

JP removed his "retired deputy sheriff's card" from his wallet. "I was with the sheriff's department for twelve years, and now my job is to protect this child who is a dependent of the court. I'm requesting to be part of the active search. I know you already have laymen from the group home out there who are a lot less qualified than I am. And, unless he's under arrest, he's a minor who needs protection. Are you really going to turn away help to find him?"

"Let me check." She made a phone call. "You can go, but if you find him, you need to bring him in."

"Is he under arrest?"

"No, but he's wanted for questioning."

JP was relentless, and she remained evasive.

"As a suspect?"

"He's a person of interest," she repeated.

"Fair enough. Any suggestion on which way to go?"

"We have a helicopter in the air that was in place shortly after the search started, so we're pretty sure he didn't go south. The chopper would've spotted him because there's so much open ground in that direction. We also would've seen him if he went west unless he got into a vehicle somewhere before the highway; otherwise, he wouldn't have had time to get to the highway on foot. If he got a short distance from the group home to the north or to the east, there are a lot of trees that would make it difficult to see him from the air. So, I'm guessing he went north or east; take your pick."

"And there have been no reports of any sightings of him?"

"Not one. The kid knows the area. Apparently, he's been hiking those woods for quite a while, so I'm sure he knows the hiding places. The K-9 unit was delayed for some reason, but they're now on their way."

JP called Sabre with an update as he headed northeast in search of Jesse, watching for signs of Oscar along the way.

***

Sabre's cell phone rang.

"It's on the news," Sabre said without saying hello.

"What is?" JP asked.

"About Oscar being missing."

"I don't understand. Kids run away from group

homes every day. Why is this one newsworthy?"

"I found it strange too. Maybe some reporter picked up something on the radio and went with it, or someone called them from the group home. The cops are playing it down. They said they went to question Oscar and he got scared and ran. Now they just want to find him before it gets dark."

"Or there's more to this than they're telling. The cop was real evasive when I asked why they wanted to talk to Oscar. She just kept saying he was 'a person of interest.' We both know that usually means a lot more. And a helicopter and dogs are a lot of resources to put into a 'person of interest.'"

"I hope you find him. Keep me posted."

Sabre stayed at her office working and waiting to hear back from JP or Jesse. She turned on the television in David's office to watch the six o'clock news to see if any information had been released to the media. The headliner was a seven-car crash on I-15 near Lake Hodges. Traffic was at a complete standstill. There was at least one casualty, and three others were in critical condition. That was followed by news of a fire at a facility that housed Alzheimer patients. In the chaos, three patients had wandered off and a K-9 unit had been called to help find the patients. Sabre wondered if that's why it took so long to get the dogs on Oscar's search. She had no idea how many active dogs they had altogether.

The next bit of news was a follow-up to the story a couple of days ago about the two bodies that had been recently found in El Cajon. The news reporter said, "According to the San Diego County Sheriff, the bodies have been identified, but the names have not yet been released. Nor would they comment on any possible suspects or motives for the murders." When it went to the commercial break, Sabre shut off the television and returned to her office.

She pulled the file for Oscar and contacted the social worker on the case. When she reached voicemail, she left a message and then drafted an email to let her know that Oscar was missing. Then she called the father's attorney, Regina Collicott, and left a message. Richard Arroyo, the mother's attorney, picked up when Sabre called him.

"I see you're still working too," Sabre said.

"Yes, I have a big trial tomorrow. What's your excuse?"

"I have a missing kid. I called because you represent the mother."

"My client didn't run off with him, did she?"

"No, nothing like that. It's the Hazleton case. Oscar ran away from the group home."

"How long has he been gone?" Richard asked.

"About three hours, but the cops are searching for him." Sabre related the story about Oscar jumping out of the window. Richard also found the image of the kid diving out of the window head first pretty funny. "I'm not sure if he has done something and that's why he ran, or if it's his general fear of cops."

"His mother has that same fear, so I'm sure she has instilled it in him as well. Actually, I think hers is more a hatred than a fear."

"For so many of these kids, the only contact they have with law enforcement is negative. It's no wonder."

"And it starts so early." He sighed. "I'll inform my client—or at least try to. She's on the streets most of the time, and she doesn't have a phone. Let me know if there is anything else I can do."

Chapter 40

JP walked up a slight incline, avoiding the boulders and bushes. When he reached the top, he saw a deputy coming toward him. As the man got closer, JP realized he recognized him. He and Vincent DuBois were on the force together many years ago.

"Well, I'll be. What are you doing here, McCloud?"

JP smiled. "No one has called me that since I left the force. How the heck are you, DuBois?" Someone had given JP that nickname early on in his law enforcement career. There was a series on television in the seventies starring Dennis Weaver as Sam McCloud, who was transplanted to New York City from Taos, New Mexico, and he had arrived there with full western dress. The first time JP was seen with his cowboy hat and boots, the name was pinned on him and it stuck.

"I'm six months away from retirement. Life is good. I hear you're in the PI business. Is that what brings you out here?"

"Yes, I'm working for the attorney who represents the runaway. Has anyone seen him?"

"Not yet." He looked up at the sky. "We don't have much daylight left. I'm heading in. They'll keep the K-9 unit out here for a while, if it ever gets here, but most of us on foot are packing it in."

"I understand the program director of the group home, Jesse Alder, is out here looking. Have you seen him?"

"I saw him earlier with another big guy with long hair and a full beard. I didn't get his name."

"That's Callum. Do you know where they are?"

"They headed into those woods over there. Callum said he had an idea where Oscar might've gone, but as far as I know, he hasn't returned. I'm taking these tired feet home." DuBois slapped JP on the shoulder. "It's nice to see you again, McCloud."

"You too."

It took about ten minutes for JP to reach the edge of the woods. The trees were sparse for about thirty feet and then they began to fill in. He knew there was little point in getting into the thicket of trees. He wouldn't likely be able to see Jesse even if he were in there. JP was considering turning back. He knew the dog had arrived because he could hear him in the distance. That was their best shot at finding Oscar anyway.

JP glanced around once more and spotted Jesse, Callum, and Oscar coming through the trees. *Well, I'll be.* He waited for them to approach.

"Hello, Jesse. Callum," JP said. He knew them from other visits to the group home when he had investigated cases in the past for Sabre and other juvenile court attorneys. "Is he okay?"

"He was just scared. We had a long talk. I think he's going to be fine."

"Hello, Oscar. I'm JP. I work for your attorney, Sabre Brown. We were all pretty worried about you."

Oscar shrugged his shoulders. "I'm okay."

As they walked toward the group home, JP turned to Jesse. "Can I talk to you a minute?"

"Sure. Callum, go on ahead. We'll be right behind you." When Callum and Oscar were about twenty feet ahead, Jesse asked, "What do you need?"

"You talked to the cops who came to the group home before Oscar bolted, right?"

"Yes."

"Did they tell you what this is all about?"

"They just said they had to ask Oscar some questions about Sammy Everton, the man who molested him. They said that's all they could tell me. I told them he was really afraid of cops and that I should go in and pave the way, but they wanted to do it their way. That didn't go so well."

"Did Oscar have any idea what they wanted?"

"No. He thought at first he was in trouble for the fight he had yesterday. And then he heard them mention Everton's name and he freaked. He's in therapy, but I'm not sure he has really dealt with that horrible incident."

A dog started barking. They could see it now in the distance heading their way. "We better catch up before the dog gets here," Jesse said.

They reached Callum and Oscar just before they started down the hill. By then they were less than thirty yards from the dog. JP said, "Why don't you slow down a little bit? I'll go ahead to let them know what's going on."

He reached the K-9 officer and explained that Oscar was coming in with the group home staff. "The kid is real gun shy. You might want to back the dog off and wait until Oscar gets to the facility so he doesn't get spooked again."

"And who are you?" the K-9 officer asked.

"I apologize. I'm JP Torn. I work for Oscar's attorney. Who's the detective in charge?"

"Greg Nelson is handling this case."

"Nelson? He's homicide." JP winced. "That polecat, Everton, didn't kill a kid, did he?"

"I can't discuss the case with you."

"Is Nelson here?"

"Yes, he just got here. Apparently you know him."

"We worked together when I was on the force. We'll take the kid to him."

"I'll check with him." He radioed Nelson. "I'm here with a guy named JP Torn. He says you know him."

"I do," Nelson said.

"He says the kid is really afraid of cops, and he wants to get him back to the group home so he doesn't run again. Can he meet you there?"

"That's a good plan. Take the dog to the car, and I'll get the rest of the force away from here."

"Are you sure, sir?"

"Yes, I'm sure," Nelson said sternly.

The K-9 officer walked away and JP returned to Oscar, Jesse, and Callum.

"Everything okay?" Jesse asked.

"We're good now."

***

When they reached the group home, there were only two extra cars in front of the office. Detective Nelson greeted them as they walked in the door. Oscar pulled back, but Jesse put his hand on his shoulder. "It's all going to work out. Remember what I told you. It'll be a little scary at first, but it'll get easier."

"Hello, Greg," JP said.

"Hello, Torn. Is this Oscar?"

"Yes." He turned toward Oscar. "This is Detective Nelson. He's really not a bad guy."

"I'll need to question him," Nelson said.

"Can you tell me what this is about?" JP asked.

"Not at this time."

"Sabre needs to be with Oscar when you question him. He has that right. I can call her and she'll come right over here."

"Considering what has already gone down, I think it would be better if we take him in for questioning."

"Is he under arrest?"

"No. I just need to ask him some questions. Tell Sabre to meet me at the station."

Chapter 41

JP called Sabre and told her about Nelson.

"So someone was killed?"

"Apparently, or Nelson wouldn't be on the case. He wouldn't tell me anything, which makes me wonder what they want to question Oscar about."

"I'm on my way. Can you meet me there?"

"Of course. I'm leaving for the station now. I should arrive about fifteen minutes before you do. I'll wait in the car. Text or call me when you get there."

When JP arrived, he opened his tablet, and using his mobile hotspot, did another search on Everton to see if there was anything new or if he had missed something. He came up empty. His cell phone rang and he picked it up without looking at it, thinking it was Sabre.

"Are you here, kid?"

"No, Torn, I'm not," a deep voice said. JP pulled the phone back and looked at the caller ID. It was his friend, Deputy Sheriff Ernie Madrigal.

"Sorry. You got something for me?"

"I thought you might want to know that Everton is dead. One of those bodies they found the other day in El Cajon was the guy you're looking for. Is that a coincidence or do you know something I don't?"

"Neither, but it explains a lot. Greg Nelson just took one of Sabre's minors in for questioning. Since Everton's dead, I'm not sure if Nelson thinks Oscar can help with the investigation or if he's a suspect."

"You know everything I know, not that I could tell you anything more right now anyway."

JP hung up just as Sabre pulled into the parking

spot next to him. JP told her the news.

"He probably just wants to find out anything he can about Everton," Sabre said. "Perhaps he suspects someone close to Oscar."

"Like who? His mother? From what I read in the file, she doesn't stay sober long enough to pull off something like that."

"You're right, and I doubt that his father cares enough to do it. He hasn't seen the kid in years. He didn't even participate in the case when it came into the dependency court."

"You know what that means?"

"Yeah, it's Tray Copley all over again. Let's go find out." They went inside and spoke to the clerk.

"Please tell Detective Nelson I need to speak to my client, Oscar Hazleton, alone."

The clerk returned about five minutes later and led her to an interview room where Oscar and a female cop were waiting for her.

"I got this," Sabre said.

The cop nodded and left.

"Are you okay, Oscar?" Sabre asked.

Oscar stood near a chair. "I guess."

"Do you want to tell me what's going on here?"

"I don't know. They haven't told me anything."

"Did they ask you any questions?"

"No." Oscar held on to the back of his chair and swayed back and forth.

"Why don't you sit down for a few minutes? This won't take long." He sat down facing Sabre. "Did they tell you anything about Sam—about Everton?"

"No." Oscar wiggled uncomfortably.

"Did you know that Everton is dead?"

Sabre watched for a reaction, not sure what to expect from Oscar. She thought he might feel relief; she certainly didn't expect concern. He seemed to flinch a little, as he always did at the sound of Everton's name, but nothing more. He didn't respond.

"Oscar," Sabre said, "Everton has been murdered."

"Good. He's a creep."

"Do you know anything about his death?"

"How would I?"

"I'm asking these questions because I'm pretty certain you're going to get them from the detective. I want to know before we talk to him."

"I can't tell him anything because I don't know anything."

"Okay, then we'll talk to him, but if you get too uncomfortable let me know and I'll stop the questioning. And Oscar, I know how difficult it is for you to sit still for any length of time, but when the detective is talking to you, please do the best you can."

Oscar shrugged.

***

The questioning took place in Nelson's office. The detective sat behind his desk and Oscar sat in a chair between Sabre and JP. Nelson tried to make Oscar comfortable, but Sabre still wasn't sure where he was going with the questioning. She knew Greg well enough to know that he had a soft spot for kids.

"Oscar, you know who Sammy Everton is, right?" Detective Nelson asked.

He wrinkled his face. "Yes."

"Did he live in your home for a while?"

Oscar squirmed. "Yes."

"Greg, do you need to go into all this?" Sabre said.

Nelson took a deep breath. "I know he did some criminal things while he lived in your home. I'm not going to ask you any questions about that. Okay?"

"Okay."

"When was the last time you saw Everton?"

Oscar shuddered. "About a year ago."

"Where was that?"

"At our house when the social worker took us there."

"Did you ever see him anywhere after he moved out?"

He wiggled his shoulders in obvious discomfort. "No." His response had a tint of anger.

"Did you ever talk to him or hear from him?"

"No, I told you."

"I'm sorry, Oscar. I know this is hard, but I want you to think carefully. Other than your attorney, your therapist, and your social worker, have you ever told anyone else about what Everton did?"

"No." His response had the same angry tone.

"Okay, I think we're done here for now." He picked up his desk phone. "Can you send Jesse Alder in to take Oscar back to the group home?"

"I'll walk him out," Sabre said.

"Never mind. His attorney is bringing him out," Nelson said into the receiver and hung up the phone.

When Sabre and Oscar left, JP remained seated.

"What's going on, Greg?"

"With Everton?"

"Yes. He's dead, right?" He couldn't tell Nelson that he already knew that.

"Why do you ask?"

"Because you're a homicide detective and all your questions are about Everton. You don't have to be Sherlock Holmes to figure that one out."

"Right." Nelson gave JP a skeptical look. "Yes, he's dead. His body was found a couple of days ago in El Cajon."

"Not far from Coyote Ridge, right?"

"Yes."

"They found two bodies. Who's the other one?"

"I can't say."

"Are they connected?" JP asked.

"Only that they were both pedophiles."

"And you know that because?"

"We looked at their records."

"But Everton had no criminal record. His only charges were in dependency court."

"He was accused in two dependency cases."

"And the other guy? Did he have a record?"

"No, only dependency as well."

"And something prompted you to look into their dependency cases."

"JP," Greg said, "let it go. I can't disclose anything right now."

JP took a guess. "They had the word *GOOF* written on their foreheads, didn't they?"

Greg sighed. "You didn't hear that from me."

***

As JP and Sabre left the sheriff's station, JP shared the information he had received from Nelson about the bodies that were found a few days previously.

"So they must know who both the dead guys are. Did he tell you anything else?"

"No, and he asked us to keep it quiet. Of course, we already knew about Everton, which explains why they questioned Oscar. And since he was one of Everton's molest victims, they suspect Oscar—or someone close to him."

"I'm sure there are even more victims. These guys don't just molest once or twice. We know Oscar wasn't his first because they have that previous dependency case, and he has likely hurt someone else since then.

Hopefully, they're looking at the other dependency case. They can't possibly think Oscar killed him. He's been in a group home practically since his case started." She threw up her hands. "Of course they can. It's déjà vu all over again."

"Do you want me to keep working on it?" JP asked.

"I think you better. See what else you can find out about Everton's background. See if you can find any connection to Glen Irving. And as soon as we find out the name of the other victim, let's do the same for him."

Chapter 42

JP's investigation of Sammy Everton led him to Sammy's family home in Rancho Santa Fe. As JP drove into the area, he passed home after home built in Spanish or Mediterranean style, none of which was situated on less than two acres. The lack of sidewalks and streetlights gave a very country feel to the town with its quiet, clean streets. JP knew this town was once dubbed the richest town in America with an average residential income of a hundred thousand a year. That average included children and adults who didn't work. As far as he knew, the town still held a high income ranking along with a low crime rate, and it had an ideal location just thirty miles north of San Diego. In spite of all of Rancho Santa Fe's perfection, it also held the title as the site of the worst mass suicide ever to take place in the United States. In 1997, thirty-nine members of the Heaven's Gate cult killed themselves in order to catch a ride on a spaceship that was supposedly trailing the Hale-Bopp Comet.

JP passed the two-block downtown area and a plethora of eucalyptus trees before he reached the house where Everton was raised. He was surprised that Sammy's parents had agreed to talk to him, considering their recent loss and the circumstances surrounding the case.

JP pulled into the long driveway and parked on a slab adjacent to the four-car garage. As he walked across the driveway, he surmised that the garage probably cost more than his home. A stylish woman in her early sixties introduced herself as Mrs. Everton and greeted him pleasantly at the door. She escorted him into the living room, where they joined Mr. Everton.

"Thanks for seeing me," JP said. "I know these are difficult times. I'd like to offer you my condolences."

"Thank you. It is a difficult time," Mr. Everton said, standing to shake JP's hand. "Please have a seat." He pointed to a chair. "How can we help you?"

"As I told you on the phone, I'm the private investigator for the child who was convicted several years ago of murdering a man who was buried near your son. We're not convinced that our client murdered anyone. I'm trying to determine what the connection is, if any, between the two victims." He intentionally left out the part that Sabre represented the molest victim of their son. There was no reason to denigrate their dead son unless he had to. "I was hoping that something in Sammy's life might help us find the real killer of the first victim, and possibly Sammy as well."

"Was the child molested?" Mr. Everton asked.

"Yes, he was." JP was surprised by his bluntness. "I take it you were aware of Sammy's issues?" He suddenly wished he would've used another word.

"Yes."

"We also represent another young boy who was a victim of Sammy's."

Mr. Everton dropped his head and shook it. "I'm so sorry."

"Sammy had no criminal record that I could find for sexual misconduct. Did I miss something?"

"Probably not. We saved him the first two times he was accused. We hired good lawyers and believed him when he told us he was innocent—until he tried to molest his little sister. Even then, we spent thousands of dollars on therapy and drug programs, which he didn't take seriously."

"Were charges filed when he attempted to molest your daughter?"

Mrs. Everton just shook her head, not making any

comments.

"No," Mr. Everton said, "but Sammy was twenty-one and still living at home. He didn't have a job and he had dropped out of school. We finally told him he had to move out. We gave him a nice little stipend and set him up in an apartment. He only came home when he needed money. When we refused to provide him with more cash, he started stealing things from the house. We had the locks changed and he eventually gave up. We told him if he ever got drug free and started to live a decent life, we would gladly welcome him back. That was nearly twenty years ago. We haven't seen him in over fifteen years. This is a sad day for us, but we actually lost our son many years ago."

"Did you know where he was living or anyone who might know anything about the last year of his life?"

"No. As I said, we haven't seen or heard from him in over fifteen years." Mr. Everton frowned. "I'm sorry about your client. In hindsight we should have let Sammy get out of his own messes, and we probably should've turned him in when our daughter was molested. But we didn't want to put her through any more pain. You make choices and you do the best you can raising your kids. I know we made some mistakes. That's why we agreed to talk to you and to work with the police. We're sorry Sammy is dead, but at least he can't hurt anyone else."

***

JP discovered Sammy's job prior to working security at the storage place was at a small plumbing store in El Cajon. The owner fired him because supplies were missing and Sammy was the only one who could've taken them. He knew nothing about Sammy's friends or social life.

An apartment in Lakeside was Sammy's last known address and apparently where he was living when he was killed. When JP arrived at the apartment, a man in his thirties with no shirt was standing out front, smoking a cigarette.

"I'm JP Torn, a private investigator. I'm looking into the death of Sammy Everton. Did you know him?"

"Yeah, man. He was my roommate."

"Sorry about your loss. Was he a good friend of yours?"

"Not really. I met him through another guy. We lived together for a few months was all. I didn't even know he was dead, man, until the cops came around asking about him."

"I understand he wasn't reported missing. Why didn't you report it?"

"Because I thought he just left." He took a drag on his cigarette. "We had an argument that day about the rent. He gave me a couple of hundred dollars when he first came and then nothin' after that. I told him he had to get out. I thought he did."

"Didn't he have any belongings here?"

"Not much. He was on the streets before he came here. All he left was an old bag with a blanket and a shirt."

"Is it still here?"

"No, the cops asked for it too, but I threw it all out a couple of months ago."

JP removed a photo of Glen Irving and showed it to the roommate. "Ever see this guy before?"

He shook his head. "Nope, only when the cops showed me his picture."

JP was not surprised that the cops were asking about Irving. They knew as well as he did that somehow these cases were connected. Even if it was a copycat killer, it had to be someone with an inside track.

"Did Sammy ever have any friends over?"

"No. Not a one."

"Is there anything else you can tell me about him? Did he hang out anywhere special? Anything like that?"

"Not really." The roommate dropped the lit cigarette butt on the ground and stepped on it. "I was working some of that time. He was usually here when I got home. He went out sometimes at night and didn't always come back. Sometimes he'd be gone a couple of days, but I never knew where he went. He didn't say and I didn't ask."

***

Sabre and JP had a working dinner that evening. JP was almost finished with his food, but Sabre had been picking at hers. Her mind kept going to Tray and how he must be suffering in that camp.

JP handed her his reports on Everton. "They seemed like real nice people. All that money couldn't help them raise a son to be a law-abiding citizen."

"It happens in the best of families. I think most people do the best job they can and sometimes it works and sometimes it doesn't." Sabre tapped the folder JP had given her on the table. "What else is in here?"

"A lot of dead ends. I haven't found any connection between Everton and Irving, except that both molested your clients. You're the only common denominator we have."

"Maybe that's it," Sabre said.

"*You* are the connection?"

"Not me specifically. Maybe it was some program that both Everton and Irving attended or something."

"But neither of them were court-ordered into any

programs by the juvenile court because they weren't the parents of the kids who were molested. They were just ordered to stay away."

"What, then, do Tray and Oscar have in common?"

"I haven't found any relatives on either side who are connected in any way. If the mothers of these boys were in the same programs, it would've been at different times, but I can check to see if they even attended the same ones. It's a long shot, but worth checking out."

Sabre raised her hand and shook her finger at JP. "I know of one connection between Tray and Oscar. You know the group home that Oscar is in, Mary Ellen Wilson Group Home?"

"Yes, but Tray was never there, was he?"

"Yes, he was. It was for a very short time, only a couple of months, but it's a place to start."

"I'll get on it first thing in the morning."

Sabre pushed her half-empty plate back. JP had already finished his.

"You ready?" she asked.

Before she could stand up, her phone rang. She answered it and her face lost color as she listened to the caller. She said, "Thank you," and hung up.

"What's wrong?"

"They've arrested Oscar for the murder of Sammy Everton."

Chapter 43

Sabre placed her bar card and her driver's license down on the desk at San Diego Juvenile Hall Otay Mesa. "Attorney Sabre Brown to see Oscar Hazleton, please."

The clerk checked her IDs, glanced at something on the computer, and then handed the cards back to Sabre. "You know the way?"

"Yes, thank you."

Without saying anything else, the clerk hit the button that opened the door. Sabre walked down the long hallway. This facility was newer than the one at Meadowlark, where most of her clients had been housed, but other than that, it wasn't much different. There were lots of locked doors, bare walls, and windows with bars lining the corridors.

She couldn't believe she had another client arrested for murder. Tray Copley's image kept popping into her head. He was such a sweet young man and she still believed he was innocent. The system had failed him. *She* had failed him. Now she was confronted with another sexual abuse victim who may be in the same predicament. It was times like this that she wasn't sure she could continue on this career path.

She waited nearly ten minutes before they brought Oscar out. His shoulders slumped as he walked down the hall toward her. As he approached, he stuck out his jaw defiantly, and spit the words out of his mouth. "I didn't kill anyone. What the f…!"

Sabre interrupted him. "Stop. Watch your language. We'll talk in the interview room."

He gave her a scorching look and ground out the words between clenched teeth. "I didn't kill that ass...."

"Oscar, please. We'll talk in a minute."

The guard who had brought him opened the door to the interview room and led Oscar inside. Sabre followed. The guard turned to Sabre. "I'll be right out there if you need me."

"Thank you," Sabre said.

The guard shut the door.

"I didn't do anything." Oscar still spoke in a defiant voice.

"Okay, but why did you run when the police came?"

"Because they started talking about that goof. I hate him."

"Why did you call him a goof?" Sabre asked.

"Because he is."

"What do you mean by goof?"

"What do you want me to call him?" He wiggled uncomfortably in the small quarters.

"I'm just asking why you chose that word." She spoke calmly. "Do you know what it means?"

"Someone creepy. I don't know. I wanted to call him something else, but I keep getting in trouble for using those kinds of words."

"Where did you learn that word?"

"I don't know. I just know it."

"Have you ever heard anyone else use that term?"

"I dunno."

"Tell me exactly what you think it means?"

There was silence for a moment and then he spoke. "It's a creep who does stuff—like he did to me." He winced when he said the word *he*.

Sabre couldn't remember ever hearing Oscar say Everton's name, and he always shuddered when someone else said it. For that reason, Sabre avoided using his name whenever she could, but occasionally she had to for clarification and when she did, she used his last name only in an attempt to make it less personal. The sound of his name made her stomach turn as well.

"I'd like you to do something for me," Sabre said.

"What's that?"

"First of all, don't talk to anyone about this case without me present. No cops or attorneys or inmates. No one."

"Got it," he said, still sounding irritated.

"Please stop using the word *goof* to describe him. It can only get you in more trouble. I want you out of the habit in case we go to trial."

"Whatever."

"Do you know anything about how Everton was killed?"

"No." He snarled. "Why would I?"

"I know you're angry, but we need to figure out how to defend you, and right now I'm pretty much in the dark, so you need to calm down and talk to me. I'm on your side."

"I don't know anything about it." His tone was only a little calmer, but he was having a hard time sitting still as usual.

"When was the last time you saw him?"

"I don't know. A year ago. Whenever he was at my house before the social worker picked me up."

"And you haven't seen or heard from him since?"

"No." Again with a sharp tone. "When can I get out of here?"

"I don't know. It's going to be a while, I'm afraid. But I'm investigating and hopefully we can sort this all out." She hoped she sounded more convincing than she felt.

Chapter 44

Sabre arrived at court early enough to get a good parking spot. She had thirteen cases on her calendar this morning and only eight of them were reviews. In addition, she had Oscar's detention hearing on the Everton murder. She carried an armful of files through the metal detector and placed them on a shelf near the stairs. After sorting through the files and finding the cases for Department Six, she walked to the end of the hallway where Bob was standing.

"Good morning, Bob," Sabre said. "You're early this morning."

"Yeah, we had to meet with Judge Hekman this morning on a case that we're trying to settle."

"This early? Is she here?"

"Not yet, but the clerk said she was on her way."

"I have a horrendous calendar this morning, so you may be waiting for me for a while on our cases."

"I expect this settlement conference is going to take a while anyway," Bob said. "You know Hekman doesn't do anything too quickly."

Attorney Roberto Quiñones walked up to where Sabre and Bob were standing. Roberto was another juvenile court attorney who started in dependency a few years after Sabre did. Now he primarily handled delinquency cases.

"Hi, Roberto," Bob said, looking at his hair. "I think you're getting a little grayer around the edges."

"You should talk. You're way ahead of me."

"Good morning, Q," Sabre said. That's what she affectionately called Roberto. "How's your day going?"

"Always good, but I just got a new case that you might find interesting."

"What's that?"

Just then, a young, attractive social worker walked up and started talking to Bob. He entered the courtroom with her.

"He's such a dog," Roberto said with a snicker.

"He's harmless, all show and no go. What's your case?"

"It's a PC 187. I'm representing a child who was charged with killing his molester. The dead guy, Roy Harris, was found in El Cajon about three miles from Coyote Ridge. Apparently, they found another body as well, but it's been there so long it was nothing but bones. I guess they did a real thorough search after they found those two dead guys a couple of weeks ago. According to the files, you're the attorney of record on the Hazleton case, right?"

"Yes, I have the defendant in a dependency case and I'll be appointed on the delinquency at the detention hearing this morning."

"And didn't you have one a few years ago with the same M.O.?"

"Yes, I did. Firmstone and I both represented that minor, and we lost. The kid's serving time, but the more bodies that turn up with the strange similarities, the more I think our defendant was innocent."

"And they both had the word *GOOF* written on their forehead, right?"

"Right. Did your victim have it too?"

"He sure did, and the minor was also a dependent of the court."

"Just like Tray and Oscar," Sabre said. "We need to get together and compare all these cases and see what else they have in common."

"Can you meet this afternoon?"

"I have a trial."

Roberto removed his leather calendar from his

pocket. "I can meet tomorrow afternoon about three o'clock."

Sabre checked her phone calendar, and said, "At my office?"

"See you there." Roberto turned to leave.

"Before we meet," Sabre said, "can you check to see if your client was ever in Mary Ellen Wilson Group Home?"

Roberto turned back. "Will do."

"And also, if you have time, can you make a spreadsheet on everyone listed in your dependency and police reports and email it to me? We need to see how these kids are connected."

Bob returned without the social worker just as Roberto said, "I've requested Barlowe's dependency reports from DSS, but I haven't received them yet."

"Not Barlowe Carrasco?" Bob said.

Roberto looked at Bob. "Yes, do you know him?"

"He's my client. Has been for about a year. Has something happened to him?"

"I was recently appointed on his delinquency case. He was charged with homicide."

"Same M.O. as Tray and Oscar," Sabre said. "Where is Barlowe living?"

"He was placed with an uncle in La Mesa just a few days ago," Bob said. "Before that he was in Mary Ellen Wilson Group Home."

***

Sabre, Bob, JP, and Roberto sat around a small table in the reception area at Sabre's office. Her building was an old, two-story home that had been converted to offices. This room was once the living room of someone's home. The round conference table and six chairs were in front of a beautiful stone fireplace.

Against the wall was a sofa and a small armchair. JP had set up a whiteboard in front of the window for notes. The meeting time had been changed to five o'clock so Bob and JP could join them. Firmstone was invited but he was unable to attend, and it would have been another week before they could all get a block of time together.

JP agreed to take notes on the whiteboard because he was used to diagraming cases and he had the best handwriting. He put the names of the victims—Glen Irving, Sammy Everton, and Roy Harris—in a block under "Dead Guys." He drew three lines from the block to the right. The first he labeled Tray, the second Oscar, and the third Barlowe.

Sabre had her laptop in front of her at her desk. "One thing we know they all have in common is Mary Ellen Wilson Group Home," Sabre said. "JP obtained a list of all employees at Wilson for the past five years."

JP handed them each a copy of the list he had compiled. "Since the boys were there at different times, particularly Tray, I narrowed the list down to only the employees who were there when all three boys resided at the group home. That left us with Jesse Alder, Callum Bridges, Antonio Vargas, Cheryl Scobba, and Isaac Horne." He wrote the names on the whiteboard as he listed them. "If you've been to the group home you probably know Jesse, the manager, and Callum, who is now his assistant. Cheryl is their office manager. According to records, she's been there about ten years."

"She's the blonde woman who's about fifty-five with arthritis?" Bob asked.

"Yes."

"She's remarkable," Bob said. "She's never let her condition keep her from doing anything. And she's super friendly and helpful."

"Who are Antonio and Isaac?" Roberto asked.

"Antonio is the groundskeeper. He's been there since the group home opened about twenty-five years ago. He lives on-site in one of the cabins. He's sixty-six years old, short, thin, and friendly. The kids all know him and seem to like him." JP wrote their positions next to each of the employee names. "Isaac is in charge of the kitchen and dining area. He's forty-eight years old; is a big guy, tall and overweight; has a mustache, no beard; and wears his hair in a short ponytail. The kids say he's grumpy and yells a lot, mostly because they make a mess in the dining room."

Sabre looked from Bob to Roberto. "I've merged my list and the lists you two gave me with all the family and friends and other people mentioned in the reports into one to see who overlaps. I didn't get much there. The intake social worker, Sharon Wolfe, was on all three cases. Ed Cardenas was on Oscar's and Barlowe's cases, which isn't a surprise because he handles group home placements, but he wasn't working for the county when Tray's case came through. Other than the people at Wilson that JP has already mentioned, there are no others who overlap—except Detective Greg Nelson who came on the scene after the murders." Sabre paused. "Oh, and I'm on two of the cases, representing the minors. And Bob is on both Tray's and Barlowe's dependency cases."

"It sounds like someone at the group home is most likely involved in some way," Roberto said. "It's too big a coincidence that all three of these boys were dependents before the murders and all three became dependents because they were victims of sexual abuse."

JP stopped writing on the whiteboard. "The police are working on a theory that these boys are all involved in some kind of a 'gang' or 'secret organization' where they plot and kill their aggressors."

"Even if that's the case," Roberto said, "someone has to be organizing them. It's been over three years since the first victim and you said Tray is in camp, right?"

"Right," Sabre said.

"Let's assume for a minute that Tray was the ringleader. He couldn't be doing much from where he is."

"Unless Tray just led the way and the others are copycats," JP interjected. "Although, I'd be more inclined to believe someone else is either leading these boys or working on their own and blaming it on the boys."

"I'd have to go with the latter," Sabre said. "These are not gang members; at least Tray and Oscar are not. And Tray is a really well-behaved, loving, young man—or he was before he was imprisoned. I hate to think of what that has done to him. Oscar is a little more troubled, but I don't think he's a killer. What about Barlowe? What's he like?"

Bob spoke up. "He's a decent bloke. He's a people pleaser, afraid to upset anyone or do anything wrong that might get him scolded. He's not very big and looks younger than his thirteen years, but he's a scrapper. He doesn't talk much and keeps a lot inside."

Sabre turned to Roberto. "Has Barlowe told you anything that might indicate he was involved?"

"He denies ever seeing Roy Harris—that's the vic—after he was taken to the receiving home."

"That's the same thing the other boys are claiming," Sabre said. "Let's look at the dependency cases. How are they alike? For example, my kids were both molested by the mother's boyfriend who was living in the home at the time."

"Same with Barlowe," Bob said. "But in all fairness,

that's a pretty common scenario. They're all boys and about the same age, which is a little older than our standard molest victim. Barlowe's and Tray's attackers were never convicted for their offenses."

"Nor was Oscar's," Sabre said. "Do you think it's a vigilante?"

"Maybe," Bob said.

"But you would think if someone is killing sexual predators, they wouldn't want the blame to fall on the victims of the molests," Sabre said.

"You're giving them too much credit. If it's a sociopath, he or she won't care about the kids."

"You're right," Sabre said. "What else do we have? Location? The victims were all found in El Cajon and the dependency cases were all East County, El Cajon and La Mesa areas."

"How does all this help us?" Roberto asked.

"I don't know if it does," Sabre said, "but if we keep brainstorming, we may come up with something."

They continued to compare the dependency cases, the sexual predators, and the defendants, looking for similarities and differences. Nothing was giving them any great insight.

"Let's explore the timing of the murders for a minute," JP suggested. "The first was about three years ago, the second was a couple of weeks ago, right?"

"Actually," Roberto said, "our victim was found recently, but the time of death appears to be more like four months ago. He's been dead for a while."

"So, either there are more bodies, or our Goof Killer has really ramped up his killing spree," Bob said.

"Or maybe the rabbits had the gun," JP said.

Sabre and Bob both nodded. Roberto looked at Sabre and then at Bob and shrugged his shoulders. "I don't speak JP. What does that mean?"

"JP means that maybe it wasn't convenient, or easy enough, or timely for some reason to kill anyone in between the other murders," Sabre said.

"Which means he would have to be very calculating and more concerned about doing it right than just getting it done," Bob said. "That could be helpful. Then it would be more likely to be someone like Jesse, who runs the group home, than say, the groundskeeper."

"That's right, but I'll investigate them all."

Chapter 45

JP's background check on Jesse Alder came up clean with the exception of one incident. He had been in a bar fight when he was twenty-three and had hurt a guy pretty bad, but all the witnesses claimed the other guy provoked him. They were both arrested for being drunk in public, but no other charges were filed on Jesse. He was charged with a misdemeanor, given a diversion so he didn't do jail time, and the charges were erased from his record. That didn't, however, erase the police files.

Jesse's family background seemed normal enough. He came from a middle-class home. His parents were both retired school teachers who were living in northern California where Jesse was born and raised. He moved south to attend San Diego State, where he received a degree in Sociology.

"You've worked here since college, right?" JP asked, glancing around the office. Jesse sat at a desk made of plywood and pressboard. He surmised that no matter how old the desk became, it would never be considered an antique. The top of the desk was messy, piled with files, loose papers, and a huge stack of unopened mail, which Jesse was attempting to sort.

"Actually, I started here when I was still in college," Jesse said, as he emptied an envelope and placed it on a stack to his right. "My plan was to get a degree in education and teach school just like my parents. But once I interned here at Wilson, I knew right from the start that I had found my calling. I realized how lucky I was to be born into the family I had. Most of these boys don't stand a chance. And even though we lose a lot of them, I'm more impressed with how many succeed than the number who fail, considering their starts in life. Some of them have no one to love them. I get pretty attached sometimes, and I have had to learn to be careful or they'll take advantage. They discover pretty quickly that I mean business and that I can still care for them. The pay isn't great, but I have no interest in going anywhere else, at least not somewhere that I am not working with children."

"Did you come right in as director of the program?"

Jesse continued to open the mail. "I hope you don't mind, I really have to get this done, but I can talk and work at the same time."

"No problem."

"To answer your question: No, I didn't start as director. I started at the bottom and worked my way up. The truth is most people don't last very long in this kind of job, so I ended up as the director partly by default." He chuckled. "I just outlasted everyone else."

"I imagine you want to pummel some of these parents, or the people who hurt the children. I know I would."

"Not so much. I know they have their own problems too. I learned long ago that violence doesn't usually get the end result you want. I was kind of a hothead back in my drinking days, but I've been in a twelve-step program for over twenty years now."

"Any of your employees have an anger problem?"

"Callum gets a little hot under the collar now and then, but most of the kids think of him as a big, cuddly bear. He's never lost his temper around one of the kids, but I did see him put a parent in his place once when the father came here high and tried to take his kid with him."

"What did Callum do?"

"He took the guy's keys, called him a cab, and when the man refused to leave, Callum picked him up like a rag doll and threw him into the cab. He told the man he could leave in the cab and come back to get his car when he was clean or he could take his keys, leave, and the cops would be waiting at the end of the road for him, but either way he was going without his son. He left in a cab."

JP laughed.

"The one here who gets the most upset, especially with the sexual assaults, is Cheryl, our office manager. She's always talking about clever ways to punish the goofs, as she calls them." He made air quotes when he said *goofs*.

"She calls them goofs?"

"Yes."

"Was she calling them that before or is that since the media dubbed the boys Goof-Killers?"

"I'm not sure now that you ask. I think she always called them that, but I can't be certain."

JP made a mental note to talk to Cheryl about it.

"Oscar has been here for about a year, right?"

"Yes."

"How many boys live here?"

"There are eleven right now, counting Oscar. We were at our maximum capacity until Barlowe left last week. We were supposed to get a new resident tomorrow, but it was put on hold until the group home is fully investigated."

"Is licensing shutting you down?"

"No, at least not at this point." Jesse rifled through the remaining mail. "Nothing in here today that says they are. The police are investigating since three boys who have passed through here have been charged with murder. It doesn't bode well for our reputation. Licensing isn't doing anything until after the police investigation is completed."

"Have the cops been here?" JP asked.

"The day Barlowe and Oscar were arrested, this place was swarming with cops. Detectives have been out several times since then. Everyone has been interrogated—employees and residents—and criminal checks have been run again. They came with a search warrant and pretty much turned this place upside down. I don't know what they expected to find, or what they actually found for that matter, but they did leave with a few small bags of evidence and some computers. I got the impression they think these boys were all part of some big, teenage, vigilante, homicide ring."

"What do you think?"

"I can't imagine any of those boys doing what they've accused them of, but I'm no psychologist and I wouldn't begin to guess what goes on in their minds. For some of these boys, the anger goes real deep."

"Have you ever seen any signs of collaboration between these boys?"

"Tray was only here for a little while and he never knew the other two," Jesse responded without hesitation. "Oscar and Barlowe didn't really hang out together. Oscar doesn't get along that well with anyone, except for Callum and one of the older boys named Mario. Oscar's more of a loner."

"Has he lived here the longest?"

"No, this facility is considered long-term, so most of our residents stay a while."

"How long have the other boys been here?"

He pondered for a few seconds. "We have one boy who came here about six months before Oscar; three more who have been here about two years; two others who have been here for at least five years; and the other five arrived after Oscar."

"What's the story on the two who've been here the longest?"

"Jacob Lowe came when he was eleven and he just turned sixteen. Mario Robinson came a few months later. He was thirteen and he's about to graduate from the program. We can't keep him after he turns eighteen, which is next month. I, for one, hate to see Mario go. He's turned into quite a decent young man. It's almost like having another staff member the way he takes leadership roles in the group home, and not just with Jacob. I'm also concerned about what Jacob will do. We fully expect him to leave when Mario does."

"Why's that?"

"He wants to live with Mario and has threatened to run away if Mario doesn't take him with him. They're like brothers. Mario has looked after Jacob since he came into the group home. Jacob is pretty troubled. He has a lot of anger issues, and when he gets out of control, Mario can usually calm him down when no one else can."

"How could Mario take him?" JP asked. "The courts won't likely place Jacob with him, right?"

"No, they won't for sure. If they were actually brothers, then they might, but not this way. Besides, Mario plans to join the military. We've been working with recruitment and as soon as he's eighteen, he'll head to boot camp."

"I'm not asking for specifics, but all your boys have had some kind of inappropriate sexual experiences prior to being admitted here, correct?"

"Yes, this program only accepts sexually abused victims. Unfortunately, most of the time we are full, which tells you how rampant the problem is. We have three specially-trained psychologists who work with us at all times, and our staff goes through a thorough background check as well as a rigorous training program before working with the children. They're all trained to work with children who have been sexually abused."

Jesse opened the last envelope, placed it on a stack to his left, and then picked up the stack. He attempted to open a drawer on the side of his desk, but it stuck. He wiggled it and then gave it a little yank. He looked up at JP before placing the papers in the drawer. "Everyone knows their own piece of junk best," he said as he patted his desk. "Sorry, where were we?"

"Are the psychologists on staff here?"

"No, they all have private practices, but they're court-approved and come here to work with the boys. We've been very fortunate to have some extremely well-qualified therapists. Even then, they aren't always effective. From what I understand, Oscar refuses to ever talk about the molest, even in therapy."

"Who are the therapists?"

"Dr. Debra Clark, Dr. John Bell, and Dr. Prasad Bopardikar."

"Is each case assigned to one particular doctor?"

"Yes, but they each see the patient for an intake, and then the three of them decide who is the better fit. When one of them can't be there, one of the others covers for him or her. They are all very busy outside Wilson, so it works better that they can all work together. In addition, they have some group sessions and the therapists take turns leading those."

"I'd like to talk to the doctors. I'm familiar with Dr. Bell, but I'll get the contact information on the other two from Cheryl." JP paused. "Are Mario and Jacob here today?"

"Yes, would you like to talk to them?"

"That would be good. I'd like to start with Mario if I could."

"I'll get him. Would you like an interview room or if you'd rather, you can use the picnic table."

“Outside would be good. Thank you.”

JP walked outside and around the area surrounding the main entrance to the house. The sun was shining and the temperature was a comfortable seventy-three degrees, according to a thermometer that was nailed to one of the trees. Eucalyptus trees shaded most of the compound, keeping the area cool. Amongst the trees was a picnic table where JP sat down for a minute.

A few minutes later, he saw Jesse and a young, dark-haired man who was at least an inch taller than the director’s six-foot-tall frame. When they approached, Jesse made the introductions.

"Would you mind if we talked out here?"

"That's fine," Mario said.

"When you’re done, Mario, will you please get Jacob, so Mr. Torn can speak with him as well?"

"No problem, Mr. Alder."

JP asked Mario about his interest in the military and shared his own experience when Mario questioned him further about the time he had served. Mario seemed eager to start the next chapter of his life, and he had realistic expectations of military life, or as realistic as any eighteen-year-old could.

JP retrieved a photo of Tray from his folder and showed it to Mario. "This young man was once a resident here. Do you remember him?"

Mario studied the photo. "I do. He was here three or four years ago, but he didn't stay very long. We bunked together and we became pretty good friends." Mario pointed across the yard toward the woods where Oscar had been hiding. "Tray and I built a fort together back there. It wasn't on Wilson property and we weren't actually supposed to do it, but we built it anyway. The fort looked pretty good when we built it, but now it's in bad shape. No one is allowed to go in it anymore. We never were supposed to be in the woods back there, but over the years most of us have gone there at one time or another." He paused. "Tray was a good kid, but he was very sad most of the time. I heard him cry himself to sleep at night. He hated that he had to leave his home because of that creep, and he really missed his sister and his mom."

"Did he confide in you?"

"Some."

"Did he ever talk to you about Glen Irving?"

"You mean the guy he supposedly killed?"

"You know about that?"

"There's not too many secrets around here. But no, he never talked about him except to say that he hated him."

Chapter 46

Jacob refused to talk to JP at first, but Mario finally coaxed him into it on the firm condition that Mario stayed with him. Even then, it was of little use. He claimed he didn't remember Tray, he hated Oscar, and Barlowe was a dork. He said he didn't like it at Wilson and he was leaving when Mario joined the service.

"They can't make me stay here," Jacob said.

"It isn't that bad here," Mario said. "You need to be strong and finish school. You can do it."

"I'm going to join the military too. I want to be a Marine."

"There's nothing wrong with that," JP said. "I was a Marine myself, but you have a couple of years before you can join and you have to get your high school diploma first."

"I do?"

"I'm afraid so, but that's a good reason to finish school. What makes you want to be a Marine?"

"Because I'm tired of everyone telling me what to do," Jacob said.

JP did all he could to keep from laughing, but he knew Jacob was serious. He caught a glimpse of Mario, who was also trying to check his smile.

JP continued to question Jacob, but to no avail. The boy didn't provide any information that might help determine if there was a secret society or an organizer of such at the group home.

***

Callum Bridges, also known as Hagrid by the boys at Wilson, walked with JP around the property of the group home. JP picked up his pace because even his long stride was no match for that of Callum.

"They're all good boys, you know," Callum said. "Even Oscar. They're not killers."

"Do you remember Tray?" JP asked.

"Course I do. I remember 'em all. These are my kids. I don't expect I'll ever have any of my own. Most women seem to be a little afraid of me, so I can't see myself ever getting married. It's okay, 'cause the best part of marriage is being a father and I have my kids right here."

"Did Tray ever talk about Irving hurting him?"

"Not really, but I think he felt safe with me. I always told him I wouldn't ever let anything happen to him on my watch."

"Did you ever have to protect him?"

"I didn't kill Irving, if that's what you mean."

Callum may have moved slowly, but his mind was quicker than JP had thought. "Do you think there's some kind of secret club among the boys?"

"Nothing I've ever seen here."

"Is there one of the boys who Tray, Oscar, and Barlowe all looked up to?"

Callum stroked his beard and his eyes narrowed under his bushy eyebrows. "The only boy here that any of them seemed to respect is Mario, but he wouldn't do anything like that."

"Do the boys obey Mario when he tells them to do things?"

"Most of the time, but it isn't like that. He isn't controlling or a bully or anything. He never tells them to do anything bad. He's just kind to them and respectful of them. Most of the boys return the respect."

"Is Antonio Vargas here today? I'd like to talk to him."

"He's off today. He seldom takes any days off, but

he had to drive to Orange County to see his uncle in the hospital."

"I hope his uncle is okay." JP checked his notes. "How about the cook, Isaac?"

"He left already. He'll be back later. He works a split shift. Jesse tried to set up the hours with another cook, but Isaac wanted it this way. Apparently, working a split shift works for him."

"Thank you for your input. I'll stop and see Cheryl on my way out. I noticed she was in the office when I came by."

"She'll take care of you. She loves visitors."

***

The office assistant at Wilson, Cheryl Scobba, took a liking to JP right off and told him she'd help any way she could. She was blunt about her feelings toward child molesters and what she thought should be done with them. In fact, she was blunt about everything. Her idea of an appropriate trial and sentencing for the goofs didn't include a court of law. She grew up in Montana and was a card-carrying NRA member. JP got the impression that she wouldn't be afraid to use her gun on a goof if she needed to.

"Have you always called child molesters goofs, or did you start that after the media tagged the victims with it?"

"That was a household word as long as I can remember. My grandfather, as well as my father, used it. I think my grandfather picked it up when he was in prison in Canada in the 60s. But that's another story."

"Did you ever use it in front of the boys here in the group home?"

"Probably. I don't know for sure, but I tend to just speak my mind. I've been reprimanded for it, but I don't have much of a filter."

"Do you remember Tray Copley?"

"I do. He was one of the best to pass through here, but he was always sad. I couldn't believe it when he was convicted of that murder."

"What about the other two boys, Barlowe and Oscar?"

"Barlowe is a good kid for the most part and even Oscar has kind of grown on me. He often came to see me and just hang out. He preferred that over being with most of the other kids. That Oscar is a strange one." Then she quickly added, "Not like a killer or anything. He's just a typical, angry teenager. He just has more to be angry about."

"If you had to pick someone here that could've killed all three of these men, who would it be?"

Cheryl thought for a minute, and then chuckled. "Me."

"You?"

"Yes, I'm the most likely. I hate those goofs. Every day I see the damage they've done to these poor boys firsthand, and I just want to kill them all. But if I were going to do it, I would've shot them in the balls and let them bleed to death. And I sure as hell wouldn't have let Tray get convicted for it." She exhaled. "To answer your question, I don't see anyone here who has the temperament."

The phone rang and Cheryl answered it. She took a file out of the cabinet behind her, answered a couple of questions, and hung up. She looked up at JP. "Is there any way I can help you with your investigation? I don't want to see any more of our boys charged with murder."

"I'd like to see the files on Mario and Jacob if that's possible."

"Now, Mr. Torn, you know I can't do that." She

stood up, opened the door to a closet, and rifled through a file cabinet. She returned with two thick files and set them on her desk. "Would you please excuse me for a few minutes? I need a break." She left the room with Jacob's and Mario's files sitting on her desk.

JP waited for a few seconds to make sure she was gone and then perused each file, taking copious notes and a number of photos. When he was finished, he closed the files and left the room. Cheryl was standing outside her office door as he left.

"Good day, ma'am," JP said as he passed her.

Chapter 47

Sabre had dinner ready for JP when he arrived, something she seldom did. She was not known for her culinary skills, not so much that she didn't know how, but mostly because she didn't like cooking. She had a few soups that she didn't mind making and often cooked those when the weather called for them. Today was one of those days. Clouds had set in by late afternoon, and by six o'clock rain had started to fall. Rainy weather called for soup. She hoped JP liked lentils. There is so much a couple doesn't know about one another in a new relationship, and theirs was still very new. Sabre and JP had only had a few dates, so she wasn't even sure if what they had qualified as a *relationship*. She did know that she was enjoying getting to know him. Unfortunately, she didn't make much of an impression with the lentil soup. She did discover that other than salad, there wasn't much that he liked to eat that was green.

His exact words were, "Sorry, kid, but 'cept for salad, I don't eat green."

"This isn't green. It's kind of brownish."

"Looks green to me."

"Do you want to just try it?" Sabre suggested.

"I will if you insist. The truth is I'm so hungry I could eat the south end of a northbound skunk, or I could eat this lentil soup, but I'd rather not do either."

Sabre laughed. "All I ask is that you taste it."

"Fair enough." Sabre handed him a spoon. He filled it up with the soup and swallowed it without making a face.

"Not bad." He kissed her on the forehead. "Mind if I order us a pizza?"

"Pizza it is."

While they waited for the delivery, JP gave her a rundown on what he had discovered in his investigation.

"I think Jesse is an unlikely suspect," JP said. "He's too normal. There was nothing he said or did that triggered any suspicion. For certain, Jesse didn't kill Roy Harris because he has an alibi. That doesn't mean he couldn't be their leader, but I highly doubt it."

"You said there were two residents who were there before Tray?" Sabre asked.

"Yes, Jacob and Mario. I couldn't get much out of Jacob. I doubt if he is disciplined enough to be a leader or an organizer. Mario, on the other hand, is sharp, efficient, and a born leader. I talked to some of the other boys at the school, and they all seem to respect and follow him. He may have some kind of strange, cult-like hold on them for all I know, although I didn't get a 'creepy' vibe at all. But I'm starting to distrust my radar since none of these people strike me as killers. Yet, it almost has to be one of them."

"We're running out of suspects."

"I suspected Callum more before my conversation with him," JP continued. "He's very protective of the boys. It's possible that he could have killed those men, and he could've picked them up and dumped them in a hole he had dug all by himself. But I find it highly unlikely that he would let the boys take the fall."

"Maybe it's someone connected to the group home some other way," Sabre said.

"Like what?"

"I don't know. I'm just stretching here."

The doorbell rang and JP answered it, discreetly paying for the pizza. Sabre started to object but then stopped. He set the box on the table. Sabre retrieved a couple of paper plates from the kitchen and handed a plate to JP. They each took a piece of pizza, and neither spoke for a few minutes.

"So you don't think Mario is the killer either?" Sabre said, breaking the silence.

"No, but he may be the organizer. He knew all the boys, befriended Tray, likes Barlowe, and gets along with Oscar, and from what I can tell, that's no easy feat."

Sabre looked at her list. "Did you talk to Cheryl?"

"I did and I drew the best bull at the rodeo on that one."

"Okay, tell me."

"Cheryl hates molesters and has called them goofs all her life. She learned it from her pappy. I'm starting to think that's where the boys in the group home picked it up. She even suggested it could be her. But she was joking. At least I think she was joking."

"Seriously, do you think she's involved with the murders?"

"No, but it would explain why the kids out of the group home use the term *goof*. Here's the best part." JP looked away.

Sabre lowered her voice. "What did you do?"

"I got some badly needed information. Do you want to hear it?"

"Was it legally obtained?"

"*I* didn't commit any crimes."

"Okay then."

"I found out the names of the men who violated Jacob and Mario, and I've been researching their whereabouts."

"And?"

"Ned Powell, Mario's goof, for lack of a better term, was serving time in Corcoran State Prison on eighteen counts of sexual misconduct with three different children. He was arrested after the incident with Mario, who was ready and willing to testify against him. They found another family he had lived with prior to Mario's and charged him with several counts of PC 288 from that living arrangement as well. He bought himself a twelve-year sentence."

"You said *was.* Is he out already?"

"Oh, he's out. He's pushing up daisies in the marble orchard. I guess the prisoners saw through his fake jacket and sent him out in a pine box."

"I've noticed that when these kids obtain justice through the court system, it seems to help them adjust better—like Mario, who seems to be the most stable one of these minors."

"Unless he's the murderer or the ringleader in this case, which would really destroy your theory."

"That's true, but I've seen it before. It's difficult for these kids to testify, but sometimes it empowers them as well when they get a good verdict. That can work both ways, though. It can be devastating when the perp doesn't get convicted." Sabre flicked her hand in the air in a dismissive manner. "Enough of my soapbox. What about Jacob's goof? What's his name?"

"Carl Murray. I can't find him. He has no criminal record, his California driver's license expired about a year ago, and he's not at his last known address. He could be incarcerated in another state, or he may have just moved."

"Or he may be dead—like the rest of them," Sabre said.

"That's possible, too, maybe even likely. He has a brother who works at an upholstery fabric company in National City. I plan to pay him a visit tomorrow, but first I'm going back to the group home."

Chapter 48

JP walked to the shed where Antonio Vargas, the groundskeeper, was putting away some tools. He found Antonio to be as friendly as everyone had suggested, and the man seemed genuinely interested in the well-being of the boys.

"You've probably seen a lot of what goes on around here over the years," JP said.

"I often see the kids sneak around doing things they shouldn't do. I don't report them unless I think it's dangerous, either to themselves or to the others. Most of the time, it's harmless."

"Did you ever see Tray sneak out?"

"He and Mario used to do it all the time and go off there in the woods. They'd take pieces of wood with them from a shed I was building. I didn't notice right away and when I discovered it, they had gotten away with about five sheets of plywood and quite a few two-by-fours. I also noticed that some of my tools were missing from time to time, but they always returned them at the end of the day. I knew it was Tray and Mario, so I followed them once and discovered they were building a fort among the trees. They did a pretty decent job. I was proud of them."

"Did you ever go in the fort?"

"Just once right after they finished it to see if it was safe. I added a couple of braces, but I'm not sure they ever noticed."

"Did you report them?"

"No, I didn't have the heart. I just replaced the wood myself and no one was the wiser. I heard them talking about it sometimes, and they were so proud of themselves."

"What happened to the fort?"

"A few other kids discovered it and used it from time to time over the years, but then Callum found it and shut it down. The fort had a small opening, so I'm sure Callum couldn't get inside. It was getting pretty rickety. I think Oscar used it a few times, in spite of warnings from Callum. I'm pretty sure that's where Oscar would go to hide when he had to get away. I saw him go in that direction a lot. He's a runner, that one."

"Do you think you could show me where the fort is?"

"Sure, let's go."

They headed northeast on much the same path JP had taken when he'd helped search for Oscar just over a week ago. They walked past the eucalyptus trees on the group home grounds and then into an open area with bushes and large rocks.

As they left the eucalyptus trees, Antonio said, "That's where the Wilson property ends. The boys are not supposed to go beyond the tree line."

"But apparently they do," JP said.

"All the time."

They walked for about five hundred yards at an incline until they reached a small forest of pine trees. When the trees started to get dense, JP was glad he hadn't tried this alone. He couldn't tell one tree from another. If he was judging their direction correctly, they were walking almost due north.

"Just a little bit farther," Antonio said.

After walking by another twenty or thirty trees, the fort appeared. Within a cluster of four trees, sheets of plywood were nailed together in an almost square shape to create the walls that extended from the ground up. The plywood stood upright, making the walls four feet long and eight feet high on the forest ground. A single sheet of plywood lay on top and was covered with palm fronds, which appeared to be tied together with zip ties and attached to the trees with rope. One side of the structure was a little shorter than the other because the trees were not far enough apart, so the plywood stuck out a few inches on each side. It was definitely not plumb, but not bad considering the ages of the carpenters. An opening, which acted as a doorway, was cut out of the boards at the bottom of one side about three feet wide and two feet tall. In order to enter, one would have to get on his or her belly and crawl. A removable wooden crate partially filled with rocks was in front of the opening.

"That's their work of art," Antonio said. "Not bad, huh?"

"Pretty clever, actually. Their door leaves a little something to be desired, but I like the roof."

"I'm guessing they didn't have any hinges to make a real door, but the crate probably kept the big varmints and large people out." Antonio looked admiringly at the structure. "Are you going in?"

"I may as well. I'm here."

JP pulled the crate aside, turned on the flashlight on his phone, and lay down on the dirt, sticking his head in the opening. "Looks safe enough." He scooted along the ground, wriggling his way inside. He stood up and shined his flashlight around the room. A couple of old blankets that appeared to have been chewed on by rodents were in one corner. Written on one wall in large, faded letters was the word *GOOF*. JP took a photo of it with his phone, and then took several other photos of the fort.

Two wooden crates were piled one upon the other in one corner. JP shined the light inside and saw four *Playboy* magazines; a deck of playing cards; a dark burgundy, spiral notebook; and a black permanent marker. The magazines had no mailing stickers on them, and the issue dates were all within the same year, about four years ago. He used his shirt to pick up the marker and stuck it in his pocket. He did the same to pick up the notebook in order to avoid leaving his fingerprints. As he turned the notebook over, he saw the word *GOOF* written across the front in black marker. He tucked the notebook under his belt inside his pants and crawled out.

Chapter 49

Siri navigated JP directly to National City Upholstery, where he parked in the small parking lot amongst several semi and box trucks. The opening to the store, which was really more of a warehouse, was through the roll-up doors. Once inside, he asked two men, who were standing at the entrance, for the store manager, Ryan Murray. One of them pointed to a slightly balding man in his forties who wasn't more than twenty feet away. JP started toward him, but before he could get there the man sped across the floor to deal with a crisis. By the time JP reached him, the manager was barking orders at a young, male employee. He was still reprimanding the young man when the manager's phone rang. He answered it. JP waited and then followed him while Murray talked on the phone and walked the other direction. By the time Murray stopped moving, he was back near the store entrance. He hung up the phone.

"Excuse me, Ryan, I'm JP Torn. You said I could come by this morning."

"That's right. Sorry."

"Thanks for seeing me."

"No problem, but you'll have to walk with me. Two people called in sick this morning, so I need to be on the floor."

They walked past rows of tables piled high with rolls of fabric in all colors and patterns.

"When was the last time you saw your brother Carl?"

Ryan stopped. "It's been four or five years. He stopped coming around or calling. I called him a few times after I hadn't seen him in a couple of months, but the second time I called, his phone was no longer active."

"How often did you see him before that?"

"Every few months we'd try to get together, usually when he needed something, but sometimes it would be as long as six months between visits. That's why I didn't think that much of it at first."

"And now?"

"I can't help but wonder if something has happened to him. I think he would've at least called me by now. We weren't that close. Even when we were young we had very different interests and friends."

"Do you have other family here who may have heard from him?"

"No. Our parents were killed in a car accident before we were out of grade school. We were raised by an aunt, but she passed away about ten years ago. We have an uncle and some cousins back east somewhere, but I don't even know what state they're in. I'm sure Carl didn't know either."

Ryan started walking at a rapid pace. "Hey," he yelled to two workers holding a large roll of green upholstery fabric. "That doesn't go there. Don't you see the yellow tag? Put it in the back." He stopped and shook his head from side to side. "They never learn. Look, I really should get back to work."

"One more thing."

"What's that?"

"Do you know anything about a family that Carl was living with about five years ago? There was a young boy named Jacob in the family."

"No, but then I never knew where Carl lived. He told me once about some woman accusing him of something, but he never told me what it was. And then it seemed to all go away because he didn't go to jail or anything." Ryan looked curiously at JP. "Unless he's been in jail all this time."

"If he is, it's not in this state. I've checked the system."

"Then I don't know what to tell you." He started to walk again.

"Have you reported Carl missing?"

"No."

"I'm sure you realize that there is a possibility that he's dead."

"I imagine a pretty good chance of it."

"Thanks for your help."

JP wondered why Ryan didn't ask for an update if JP found any information on his brother's whereabouts. Then he remembered his own brother. He probably wouldn't have asked either.

Chapter 50

Bob, Roberto, Sabre, and JP met at Sabre's office in the same room as they had met previously. JP had added Mario and Jacob to the list of suspects on the whiteboard as well as the three therapists. The attorneys remained seated at the table.

JP and Sabre had agreed that they should share the information about the fort and the notebook with the group. JP told them he had found a deck of playing cards; a black marker; an old, burgundy, spiral notebook; and four *Playboy* magazines.

"Where are the *Playboy* magazines?" Bob asked.

"Right, Bob," Sabre said, "because that's what's important here."

"I left them there," JP said. "I couldn't bring everything without Antonio seeing what I had, and I thought the notebook was a little more important."

JP went on to explain that he had already taken the marker and the notebook to a lab to check for fingerprints. He had managed to get prints from Callum, Jesse, Cheryl, and Antonio without their knowledge. No one in the room asked how he'd done it. JP looked at Roberto. "If you're willing, I'd like to check for Barlowe's prints as well. And I'd like a sample of his handwriting. By the way, the only word written throughout the notebook is the word *GOOF*, all in capitals. The letters were a little less than an inch high and about three to a page."

Roberto didn't answer right away.

"I know this is risky, Q," Sabre said. "If we can't figure this out, at some point we may need to start pointing the finger at each other. But I've been down this road once and failed miserably. I think the best thing we can do for our clients is to group together."

"Bob, what do you think?" Roberto asked.

"I'd do it, but it's your call."

"Okay," Roberto said. "I'll get both the fingerprints and the handwriting sample for you. If they are damaging, hopefully we can keep the information under work product."

"Unless someone has a better idea, we're going forward with three workable theories," Sabre said. "And these are in no particular order at this time."

"One scenario is that someone is killing these men and pointing the finger at the boys. Another is that the boys are organized and are killing their offenders. The last is that Tray killed Irving and the subsequent murders were done by copycats, possibly the boys. There are also some variations of these that we can hash out. Let's start with the first. We'll look at the suspects and see what we can come up with."

"Who are the most likely suspects for scenario one?" Roberto asked.

"In my opinion it's Mario, Cheryl, and Dr. Debra Clark," JP said. "The best we can tell is that none of them have alibis for at least one of the murders—specifically Roy Harris, Barlowe's goof. Everton's time of death is not exact and Tray's case is so old no one can remember where they were at the time of Irving's death. All three of the suspects are well liked by the boys and have good access to them."

"Do you really think it could be Cheryl?" Sabre asked.

"Cheryl came right out and said she didn't do it," JP said. "I tend to believe her, but I haven't written her off yet. She's a little different—sort of a cowboy. She doesn't strike me as a planner, but more of a 'shoot-from-the-hip' woman. She helped me obtain information from the files, but that might have been to throw me off—or if she's a real psycho, a strange kind of challenge."

"What about Dr. Prasad and Dr. Bell?" Q asked.

"Dr. Prasad had limited contact with the boys," JP said. "He had met Tray but never really worked with him, and he had very limited time with Oscar or Barlowe. And Dr. Bell was in Africa when both Irving and Harris were killed."

"And the second scenario?" Bob asked. "Who's most likely organizing them?"

"That list is a little longer, but at this point my money is on Mario," JP said. "He's smart, efficient, a leader, and the boys all trust him. Though it could be Callum, Cheryl, Dr. Deb, Dr. Bell, Dr. Prasad, or Isaac, and maybe even Antonio or Jesse."

"That narrowed it down," Bob said.

JP ignored his sarcasm and continued. "I don't think it's Isaac Horne, the cook. The boys all claimed he was grumpy, and they're right about that. I believe Isaac tolerates the kids. He doesn't seem to pay much attention to what they're doing unless they're in his dining hall. There, he is king and he makes that clear to them. He isn't particularly friendly with the staff, either, but he's a good cook and he keeps order during meals, so he keeps his job."

Sabre spoke. "But in both the second and third scenarios where the boys are doing the killing, they would need help. The group home is at least six miles from Coyote Ridge. How would they get there? They couldn't do it alone, could they?"

"Tray and Mario managed to build a substantial fort off the group home grounds using tools they 'borrowed' from the groundskeeper." JP made air quotes when he said "borrowed." "They built it without the awareness of any of the adults at Wilson with the exception of Antonio. Why couldn't they just as well get away to commit the murders?"

"They would need transportation for one thing," Sabre said. "They couldn't exactly take a bus with a dead body."

"They could've killed them at the place they were buried," Bob said, playing devil's advocate. "We really don't know where any of them were killed for certain."

"Besides, the buses don't run there," Sabre said.

"What about a bike?" Roberto suggested. "Any of those boys could have ridden a bike six miles."

"I thought of that, so I checked," JP said. "There are no bikes on the premises at Wilson."

"JP, do you think the boys managed to sneak away, kill, and bury these bodies?" Bob asked.

"No," JP said. "I certainly don't believe they did it on their own. I think it's highly unlikely that they did it without someone organizing them. One of the things that bothers me about this whole thing is that even though Mario is the most likely, he doesn't seem conniving or manipulative, and he certainly doesn't fit the profile of a serial killer. There are so many things that just don't add up."

"So if it's none of the usual suspects, who is it?" Roberto said. "Or what is it we don't know about the employees and the residents at Wilson?"

"Mario is still on both 'most likely' lists," Bob said. "I think we should have another look at him."

"We can, but we need to do it fast," JP said. "He's joining the Marine Corps on his eighteenth birthday. That's only a couple of weeks away. And another thing: as you all know, every boy at the group home has some sexual abuse history. I found out the names of the perps for Jacob and Mario, the only two residents of Wilson who knew all three of the defendants: Tray, Oscar, and Barlowe. I just discovered that Mario's assaulter was convicted and Jacob's has been missing for about four years. Any bets that he's dead too?"

Chapter 51

Sabre was driving when JP called.
"Hi, kid, got a minute?"
"Sure. I'm just leaving the courthouse. My trial settled so it freed my afternoon to work on something else. What's up?"
"I got the results back on the fingerprint tests. The prints on the pen belong to Oscar, Barlowe, and Cheryl."
"More than likely, the pen came from Cheryl's office, which means it doesn't necessarily implicate her."
"I thought the same thing, but I'm not ruling her out. The notebook had three sets of prints, none of which belonged to Cheryl, Callum, Jesse, or Antonio. The prints belonged to Oscar, Barlowe, and one other unidentified person."
"I'm meeting with Barbara Foltz, the handwriting expert, in about fifteen minutes," Sabre said. "I was supposed to go later, but I called her when my trial settled and she was glad to have me come in early. Do you want to join us? You might learn something."
"I can't. I'm meeting with Nelson in about half an hour. Good luck with your *expert*."
"I know you don't put a lot of stock in her expertise, but the courts recognize her as such, and hopefully she can lead us in the right direction."
"You're right. Call me when you're done."

***

The handwriting expert's office looked like a garden. Dried, preserved eucalyptus trees of all heights in decorative pots were scattered in clusters around the room. A small, western saddle surrounded by foliage and dried flowers created a beautiful piece of artwork and was hung on one wall. A mist smelling of lavender emanated from two small pots strategically placed in the office. Amongst the trees were two soft chairs and a desk with a swivel chair behind it. The swivel chair held an attractive, auburn-haired woman in her mid-to-late sixties. When she turned to the side, Sabre saw she was wearing the brightest, most colorful pair of leggings she had ever seen. From her feet to her knees was a bright red pair of cowboy boots covered with bling. Barbara Foltz was an interesting woman.

"Beautiful office," Sabre said, glancing around in an attempt to take it all in.

"Thank you," Barbara said. "We grow the trees on our ranch, dry them, and process them. My husband is the creative one. He did all the artwork you see in here. We still wholesale the plants, but we used to sell them at home shows, festivals, and fairs. Back then I did the handwriting analysis on the side. Now it's my full-time gig."

"I'm afraid if my office were this gorgeous I'd never get anything done."

"You'd be surprised how much a comfortable atmosphere can help you concentrate." She picked up the notebook JP had found in the fort. "But you didn't come here to talk about that. I spent a lot of time studying the writing in this notebook and the handwriting samples you brought me."

"And did you find a match?"

"It took me a while because there were so many pages, but I found two matches. The notebook had two distinctly different handwritings on the inside. One is neat and orderly; the other's hurried and messy. Toward the end of the notebook, the writing started to look more alike, but it was still by two different people. I couldn't testify to this part, but it looks like they were practicing."

"And do you know who wrote in it?"

"Yes, the writing matches that of the first two samples that JP brought me."

"And none of the others?"

"No."

"I pulled the file from the last case you brought me a couple of years ago, that of Tray Copley. I assumed they were connected, since you had me analyzing the same odd word. Is it related?" Before Sabre could answer, she said, "You can tell me to mind my own business if you want. Sometimes I'm just a nosey witch."

"They seem to be related, although we haven't been able to find the exact connection. Did you compare those old samples with the notebook?"

"I did, and they were not a match."

"I was pretty certain of that."

"Do they have another body with this word written on it? There I go sticking my nose in again."

"It's okay. They found *bodies*, plural. There are two of them. If the case goes to trial, I'll be bringing you the photos of the victim's forehead for you to analyze as well, but I hope it doesn't get that far."

"For what it's worth, I don't believe Tray wrote on that body. There was something wrong with it, but I don't know exactly what because we didn't have a good enough sample. It's far more difficult to determine from a photo than from an actual written object."

***

Sabre left the office and called Roberto Quiñones on her way to her car. She informed him of the fingerprint results first.

"That's not good news," Roberto said.

"It gets worse. I'm just leaving the office of the handwriting analyst. She says Oscar and Barlowe wrote the words in the notebook."

"Yet they claim to know nothing about the murders."

"If they're sharing a notebook and a fort, they must know something about one another's actions," Sabre said. "Maybe we need to put a little pressure on our clients and see what they'll tell us."

"I'm game if you are," Roberto said. "Maybe if we confront them with this new evidence, one of them will come around."

"That's the plan, then."

Chapter 52

Oscar seemed genuinely pleased to see Sabre, a behavior he hadn't exhibited often lately. She chalked it up to loneliness.

"Is that a black eye?" Sabre asked, looking closer at his face.

"I ran into a door."

"Did you get into a fight?"

"It wasn't that big a deal."

"What happened?"

"Some big, ugly kid called me 'Midget,' so I punched him." He demonstrated by slamming his right fist into his left palm. "I woulda beat him up if some dudes hadn't stopped it. They only stopped us because they didn't want marks against the unit."

"I should've heard about it. Didn't it get reported?"

"No. It didn't last long, but I got a couple of good punches in." This time he double-pumped his fist in his palm.

Sabre felt bad for this angry, small, twelve-year-old having to fight his way through juvenile hall and through life itself. She wondered if this was the way his life would always be.

"Oscar," Sabre began, after she'd been with him for about five minutes, "I need you to be straight with me. I'm struggling to find a good defense for you because I can't seem to get the information I need."

"Okay, but I've been telling you the truth."

"I'm thinking there may be a few things you left out. Anything you can tell me about your life since you went to live in the group home might be of help. Do you understand?"

"I think so."

"What boys at Wilson did you spend time with?"

"Most of those guys there are a pain in the butt." He moved his shoulders up and down, just to be moving.

"Why? What kinds of things did they do that make them a pain in the butt?"

"They called me names and teased me."

"How did you react when they did that?"

"I used to hit them, but I got in trouble for fighting too much."

"What about Mario? Did he tease you or call you names?"

"No. He wasn't so bad. But I didn't really hang with him. He was always busy doing stuff." Oscar started rocking back and forth. He had such a hard time sitting still; Sabre wondered how he would be able to survive in long-term confinement.

"What about Jacob?"

"He's the worst. He thinks he's so tough 'cause he's been there the longest."

"And Barlowe?"

He wrinkled his nose. "He's a chicken. You could call his *mother* names and he wouldn't fight."

No one spoke for a moment, and then Sabre said, "I know about the fort in the woods." Oscar looked up in surprise. Sabre continued, not wanting to give him too much time to think about it. "Do you know who built it?"

"I heard it was Mario and some other kid who was there years ago. I asked Mario once, but he never admitted it."

"Did you go there often?"

He shrugged. "Whenever I felt like it."

"Did the staff know you were gone?"

"I think Callum did sometimes, but he never told on me. He was kinda good that way."

"Did he ever go there with you?"

A smile flashed on his face and then it was replaced by his usual sour look. "No, Hagrid's too big to get into the fort."

"Did you ever go there with Barlowe?"

He wrinkled his nose and spat his words. "No. I wouldn't go there with that dork. I didn't go there with anybody."

"What did you do when you were there?"

He shrugged his shoulders. "I dunno. I just hung out. Sometimes I'd sit on top of the fort and throw nuts at the squirrels."

"Did the *Playboy* magazines belong to you?"

Again he looked surprised. Sabre was always amused at how little teenagers thought adults knew. "No, they were there when I went to the fort."

"And the playing cards?"

"They were there too."

"And what about the notebook?"

"What notebook?"

"Inside the fort, we found a burgundy-colored, spiral notebook with your handwriting inside."

He raised his voice. "I don't know nothing about no notebook."

Sabre showed Oscar a photo of the notebook. "Is this yours?"

"No."

"Have you ever seen it before?"

"No."

"I want you to think carefully. Have you ever seen anyone else with this notebook?"

He shook his head from side to side.

"Not Barlowe?"

"No," he said, sounding even more irritated.

***

Juvenile court had emptied out except for a few stragglers. It was already twelve-fifteen and almost everyone had gone to lunch. Bob and Sabre were walking out when they spotted Roberto.

"We're going to Pho's. Want to join us?" Bob asked.

"I wish I could, but I have to go over to the Hall and talk to Barlowe."

Roberto went through the door that led to the tunnel and then to juvenile hall. Sabre and Bob stepped outside into the misty air.

"Is it going to rain?" Sabre said.

"Naw. I think this is all we're going to get, but I have an umbrella in the car if we need it."

"Then you can drive." They walked to Bob's car and got inside. "Q told me earlier that you talked to Barlowe. Did you learn anything new?"

"Just that your client, Oscar, is always looking for a fight and he's a 'stupid idiot.' His words, not mine."

"Well, that's because Barlowe is a 'dork' and a 'chicken.'" Sabre laughed. "They obviously don't like each other much. Oscar denied ever going to the fort with Barlowe and any knowledge of the notebook."

"So did Barlowe. I can't see those two working together. I think it comes back to Mario. He seems to be the one who can work with both of them. Have you met Mario?"

"Yes, I've seen him a few times when I visited Oscar at the group home. The way Mario carried himself and the way the other residents reacted to him gave me the impression that he was staff. I didn't realize then that he was a resident. He just seems like a good kid. I don't remember him from when Tray was there, but I think I only went there once before Tray was moved."

***

Bob and Sabre ate their meals quickly at Pho's and went back to the car. They both had busy schedules for the afternoon. They had no sooner stepped into the car when Sabre's phone rang. "It's Q," she said to Bob as she looked at the Caller ID, and then answered the phone.

"I just saw Barlowe," Roberto said.

"Just a second, I'm here with Bob. Let me put you on the speaker." She hit the speaker button and held her phone between them. "Go ahead."

"I tried to pressure Barlowe a little, telling him we had fingerprints and his handwriting and he needed to tell the truth. But he didn't admit to anything either. He doesn't know anything about the murder. He has never been to the fort with Oscar, and he doesn't know anything about the notebook."

"That seems to be the party line," Sabre said. "Thanks, we'll just keep looking." She hung up.

"Do you find it odd that none of them has admitted to any part of this disaster?" Bob asked.

"That bothers me a lot. They deny being places we know they've been. They deny writing the word *GOOF* anywhere, yet their handwriting tells us otherwise. And they all do it with such conviction."

"You mean like it's true? Or like they've all sworn to stick to the same story?"

"I haven't totally discounted that it's true, but it's more than sticking to the same story. It's almost like they're brainwashed or something."

"You mean like aliens have invaded their brains? I think you might have something here."

"You tease, but there is something not quite 'normal' about it."

"Sobs, they're teenagers. They think and act like

aliens have invaded their brains. That is normal teenage behavior."

"You make fun, but I know who might be able to help me."

Chapter 53

"Thanks for coming by my office," Sabre said to Dr. Bell. "I would've gladly come to you."

"It's my pleasure. I had to pass right by here, so it worked out fine."

"It's really nice to see you again." Sabre escorted him to a seat. "Come sit, and tell me about your latest trip to Africa."

"I just got back about a week ago. I'm so lucky to be able to go so often. It gives me a great deal of pleasure to be able to help those youngsters. Over the years, I've gotten to know so many of them and watched them grow up into fine adults."

"How long have you been making these trips?"

"About ten years now. At first I was only able to go once a year, but now I manage to get there about every four months."

"Well, welcome back, and thank you for all you do for those kids and for the others here. I know how much Tray liked you. He felt so comfortable talking to you." Sabre was genuinely impressed with the work the doctor was doing with the albinos.

"Thanks."

"Have you heard about the latest *Goof-Killing*, as the media has labeled it?"

"I did. Apparently, the last one happened a few days after I left, so I didn't know anything about it until I returned. I saw it on the news, and of course the police contacted me since I've worked with Wilson Group Home. I really hate that these boys are entangled in this mess. They don't deserve to have to deal with this on top of everything else. I only wish there were something I could do to help."

"Maybe there is, but you can start by clarifying a few things for me."

"Of course, whatever you need."

"I know you've worked with Oscar, but have you worked with Barlowe as well?" Sabre asked.

"I've worked with every kid who's been through Wilson. As you know, there are three therapists who handle the caseload there. We each meet with every child and spend some quality time with them until we decide who the best fit is. It started out as a temporary system, but it worked so well we've continued with it. It helps when one of us has to fill in because we're not strangers to any of the boys."

"I know you are the primary therapist on Oscar's case. How about Barlowe?"

"No, we thought I might be at first, but he turned out to relate better to Debbie."

"Of course you know Jacob and Mario, right?"

"The old-timers. For sure. Jacob has been there the longest. In fact, Jesse, Callum, and I were talking just yesterday about how these boys have been in our lives for so long. They are our family—all of them." He paused as if to reflect on times past. He shook his head. "Mario has done so well. He's not mine, but I've certainly gotten to know him. I'm pleased with all the progress he's made. Even though he's Deb's patient, he'll stop by and see me sometimes just to chat after I've had a session with one of the other boys. He usually wants to talk about his life's decisions. Lately, it's been mostly about his military career choice. He knows that I served, so I can relate. I think the military will be good for him. He has talked to me a few times about his concern for Jacob when he leaves for the service. As for anything else about Jacob, you'd have to talk to Debbie about him. He's been on her caseload almost from the beginning."

"What can you tell me about Debbie?"

"What do you mean?"

"We have a theory that someone besides these boys, or in conjunction with them, has committed these crimes. Do you think she could be involved?"

He shook his head. "I don't think so. She's never given me any indication of any kind of bizarre behavior. She's not a fanatic about anything that I know of. She's one of the most organized people I've ever met, and if you need a job done, she's the one. She knows my clients well because she is usually the one who covers for me when I'm traveling. I don't know her outside of work, but in her profession she is extremely efficient and a caring and compassionate person. In my opinion, she's a very unlikely suspect."

Sabre shrugged. "You had mentioned her twice in connection with these boys, so I just thought I would ask. JP is doing a little investigating. I'm sure if there's anything unusual it will turn up."

"That's your PI, right?"

"Yes, you met him on Tray's case."

"Nice fellow."

"What I really wanted to ask you about was the denial of all these boys. There are things that we know have happened that they simply deny. I thought with Tray that he had blocked it out, but why would they all exhibit the same behavior?"

"You know, Sabre, these boys have all had very traumatic experiences and that does happen. It's a coping mechanism. I don't know if Tray blocked out being at the store with Irving, or if he denied it out of shame."

"It's hard for me to believe he was there with him and I saw the footage," Sabre said.

"I know. Me too. Can you imagine how hard it was for Tray?"

"But why was he there in the first place?"

"I doubt if we'll ever know that. Let me help you make sense of what we do know. You said the boys are all in denial. What other things are they denying?"

"We have a notebook with both Oscar's and Barlow's handwriting in it, but they both claim they never wrote in it. And, of course, they all deny any part in the murder itself or of having any contact with their molesters."

"You're right about one thing. It's highly unlikely that they have all blocked out whatever they've done in connection with the murders." He looked at Sabre and gave her a knowing smile. "Maybe it's because they're telling the truth—at least as they remember it."

"Oh, Doc, you don't know how much I want to believe that they're telling the actual truth. Most of the time I do believe it, but proving it is another matter."

"What else can I do to help?"

"I was thinking that maybe these boys had some help losing their memories."

"You mean like threats of some sort?"

"That's a possibility too, but I was thinking more like maybe they were hypnotized or something. I know I'm all over the place with possible scenarios, but I'm at my wit's end trying to figure this out. Could hypnotism be possible?"

"I'm sure you know that you can't be hypnotized to do something you wouldn't ordinarily do."

"I know, but these are teenagers who have been molested. Do you think maybe down deep they wanted to kill their offenders?"

"There are a lot of problems with that theory. First, someone would have to be incredibly good at mind control, like they are in spy movies, and I don't know anyone who's that good. Second, that person would have to have access to the boys for long periods of time. And third, and most importantly, I know all these boys and most of their fears and hates and I don't think any one of them is a killer. Whoever is doing this wouldn't be able to make them commit that kind of crime." Dr. Bell steepled his fingers and pointed them at Sabre. "I think they're denying everything because they didn't do anything. Maybe that's hopeful thinking on my part, but I'd like to think it's based on my years of training and my time with these boys."

"What if I were to have Oscar hypnotized. Do you think if he has blocked something out, he would tell us?"

"I'm no hypnotist, but we all had to study it as part of our degrees to understand the effects of hypnotism. To use it as a means of recovering information isn't usually very effective or reliable. And it's risky. As Oscar's therapist, I wouldn't advise it because you take the risk of someone planting the information that you're trying to summon forth. Then the memories get all mixed up, and you still don't know what's true and what's not."

"What if you did it?"

"As I said, I studied it in school. We actually had hands-on training, but I wasn't very good at it. I'm really not qualified, but more importantly, I think hypnosis could set Oscar back in his treatment."

Chapter 54

As JP waited in Detective Nelson's office, he hashed out his investigation in his mind. He couldn't remember a case quite as frustrating as this one. There were too many suspects and none of them was solid. Each piece of the puzzle made it more confusing.

Nelson walked in. "Sorry, I had to deal with an idiot rookie. Where were we?"

"Have you identified the body you found when you discovered Roy Harris?" JP asked.

"No," Nelson said, as he took his seat behind his desk.

"Do you have an estimated time of death for the second body?"

"Somewhere in the neighborhood of four or five years." Nelson removed a file from a wire basket on his desk.

"Was there any writing on him like the others?"

"Where are you going with this, Torn? Do you think this guy is a victim of the goof-killers?"

"Just humor me for a second. Was there any writing?"

"There wasn't enough of him left to see anything. The bugs and the animals did a number on him. He couldn't have been buried very deep."

"Could they test DNA?"

"They don't have anything to compare it to."

"What if they did?"

"Do you know something I don't?" Greg Nelson said.

"I've got a hunch."

"What is it?"

"It may be nothing."

"I'll make that decision. Tell me what it is."

"It may be about as useless as a screen door on a submarine."

"So tell me already, Torn."

"I think the body might belong to a guy name Carl Murray. He's been missing about four years. He has a brother who works for an upholstery fabric place in National City."

Nelson made a note on his notepad of the name. "Did he report him missing?"

"No, because Carl disappeared a lot, just never for this long. By the time he realized he wasn't showing up, time had just slipped away."

"Real close family, huh?"

"They didn't get along too well, but I think he'd be willing to give you a DNA sample just to find out if his brother is dead."

"Do you think the brother killed him?"

"No."

Nelson cocked his head to the side, and said, "But you know who did."

"Not exactly, but if Carl is the dead guy, I'll tell you everything I know."

"Torn, it doesn't work that way."

"This time it kinda does," JP said.

"You can be a real jerk sometimes, you know?"

"Only when the wind's blowin' in Dodge."

***

Surveillance was JP's least favorite part of the job, but Sabre had asked him to do it, so he did. JP was parked on a one-way street across from an office building. The parking for the office was a small lot adjacent to the building. Whoever left that lot had to pull out onto that street, so JP would be able to follow him or her. He waited until he saw a woman about five-foot-ten with shoulder-length brown hair. She was wearing a white blouse, a blue tailored suit, and blue pumps, and she was exiting the front door. He looked at the photo he had of Dr. Debra Clark. It was her.

JP tailed the 2009 burgundy Toyota Sienna minivan as it headed east on I-8 and exited on Greenfield Drive. He followed the car onto La Cresta Drive and to Mountain View Road, where she turned into the driveway that led to Wilson Group Home. JP passed the driveway and made a U-turn. He came back to a spot where he was hidden by trees but could see if the van left. Sixty-five minutes later, the van left Wilson's parking lot and turned right onto Mountain View Road. JP followed her into Alpine, where she stopped at the Alpine Tavern and Grill. He followed her inside. She sat at the bar next to a man in a baseball cap, had a glass of water, spoke briefly with the man, and then left with a to-go order. From there she drove the two miles to her house. JP watched her residence for about an hour but saw no activity in or around the house, so he left.

He drove back to the bar on the outside chance that the man in the baseball cap was still there. The bar was more crowded than it had been earlier, but the man remained seated at the bar. JP approached him, sat down, ordered a beer, and struck up a conversation.

"You lived here long?" JP asked.

"About ten years. I used to live in Lakeside, but it got too crowded there. I had to find some country, and this is as close as I could get and still be able to make a living."

"I was in here about an hour ago and I saw this beautiful woman sitting next to you at the bar. Do you mind my asking if that was your wife?"

"Oh no, that was Dr. Deb, but she's married, pal. Her husband travels a lot and her sons have moved away, so she stops here and gets food most evenings on her way home from work. She's a beauty, that one." He looked up and down at JP. "I'm afraid she's out of our league, pal. She's a classy lady. I don't mean snooty or anything. She's real nice and friendly, but classy."

"You had me at married," JP said. "I don't play in another rooster's hen house."

JP took another sip of his beer and decided to leave. Spending any more time watching Dr. Deb seemed like a waste of time and resources unless they had some idea if, or how, she may be implicated in the case.

***

Back at his home, JP spent the next few hours gathering information on the therapists that worked with Wilson Group Home. His research uncovered very little of consequence. Deb Clark had no criminal record, not so much as a traffic ticket. She was married to Bill Clark and had two sons named Adam and Alex, both of whom had completed college and moved away. Alex was teaching in Colorado, and Adam was successfully pursuing an acting career in Los Angeles. According to *Entertainment Tonight*, Adam Clark was the newest Hollywood rage. Dr. Deb's husband was also a psychologist and worked with a ministry. Dr. Deb was a member of the American Psychological Association and the Society for the Scientific Study of Sexuality. She was a board member of Soroptimist International, San Diego, and belonged to several organizations dealing with the fight against child abuse. There was nothing there that fit a serial killer profile.

Dr. Prasad Bopardikar was also an unlikely candidate. He was younger, divorced, had no children, and was not as active in the community. Just about the same time as Tray had become a resident of Wilson, Dr. Prasad started working with some of the boys. Consequently, he had only been there for about three years. He had spent very little time in therapy with Tray, Oscar, or Barlowe. Although JP didn't delete him from his list of suspects, he decided to make him a low priority.

Dr. Bell was already low on the suspect list, but it was JP's position that "everyone was a suspect" so he did a little more background check on him. He couldn't find any marriages or children of Dr. Bell, which he already knew. He verified each entry on the doctor's dossier. Everything was as he stated. Next, he looked into his trips to Tanzania. There was a lot of information and photos of the doctor on his quest to help the albino children. He had received several awards and recognition from various humanitarian groups for his efforts.

JP failed to uncover anything suspicious or helpful to his investigation on any of the therapists. He would talk to Sabre about taking another tack.

Chapter 55

JP's flight to Sacramento was uneventful. He rented a car and drove to Northern Youth-to-Adult Conservation Camp, where he expected a decent reception from Tray. Since the boy's family was so far away, he assumed there had been few visitors. As far as he knew, no one had been to see him since he left DJJ in San Bernardino, a facility that had since closed. JP didn't know what he hoped to gain from talking to Tray, but Sabre thought it was worth the trip. If nothing else, Tray deserved to know that they were working on his case.

With the directions from the website, the camp was not too difficult to find. It was only a few miles off Highway 88 east of Sacramento and about twenty miles west of the Sierra Nevada mountain range.

A muscular man about five-foot-eleven walked up to the table where JP was waiting. It took a second before JP realized it was Tray. He was not the same little boy who was sent to DJJ three years ago.

JP stood up and shook his hand. "Hi, Tray. Remember me?"

"Yes, sir, you're the PI who worked with my attorney. Why are you here?" There was a slight edge in his voice. JP hoped his incarceration hadn't made him too bitter.

“There have been some new developments in your case."

Tray's face suddenly radiated hope. "Did they find who did it?"

"No, not yet, but we're working on it." JP sat down. "Let's sit and talk."

Tray followed suit. "So, what's going on?"

"Two more bodies have been found that have a similar M.O. to yours. They're both pedophiles and were involved in juvenile dependency cases. And the boys are, or were, at Wilson. I need to ask you a few questions about the residents and employees at the group home."

"Do you think someone there did it?"

"We're sure it's someone connected to the group home. We just don't know how." JP thought about how different it was talking to Tray now, like he was a different person—and in a way he was.

"Tray, do you remember anything new about the day that Irving was killed?"

"No. It's just like I told you all before. I've thought about it so much over the last couple of years. It made me angry that no one believed me. I realize now that if I'd said I killed him, I probably wouldn't have been convicted. Everyone was trying to tell me that I'd get off on self-defense, but I didn't kill him and I just wanted everyone to know that. And since I hadn't done anything wrong, I really thought I would go free."

"Sometimes the system just doesn't work."

"Then I hear all these other inmates saying how they got a raw deal, claiming they didn't do anything wrong, and I don't believe them. Why should anyone believe me? Then there's the other cocky kids who brag about their crimes to intimidate others."

"If it's any consolation, Sabre never stopped believing in you. To be truthful, I'd like to believe you, but I'm a little more skeptical. For your sake, I'd really like to prove that someone else killed Irving." JP paused. "Let's start with your telling me everything you know about Wilson Group Home. Do you remember Jesse Alder?"

"Sort of. I don't remember anything special about him."

"What about Callum Bridges?"

His mouth turned up slightly on one side in a quick half-smile. "Hagrid?"

"Yeah."

"He's a good guy. I always felt safe around him. I guess it was because he was so big. No one can hurt you when you have the jolly giant by your side." His face twisted slightly in anguish. "You don't think Hagrid killed them, do you?"

"He's pretty low on the list, but we have to check everyone."

"He was always so nice. There were many times I wished Hagrid was by my side when I was at DJJ. That place was horrible."

"How are things here?"

"Better. It's still a prison, but the guys are better here because most of them don't want to get sent somewhere else."

"Do you remember Cheryl Scobba? She worked in the office."

"She was a little scary."

"In what way?"

"She was loud and pretty much said whatever she wanted. The other kids claimed she had guns and you'd better do what she said. Hagrid said she was nice once you got to know her, but I guess I wasn't there long enough to know her that well."

"Do you remember a boy at the group home named Jacob Lowe? He's been at Wilson longer than anyone else."

"I kinda remember him. He always wanted to hang out with me and Mario," Tray said, and then paused. "But he was trouble."

"How do you mean?"

"He got into fights, talked back to the adults, and called kids names. I didn't really hang with him, so that's about all I can tell you."

"You mentioned Mario. I take it you remember him."

"He was my best friend. He made it a lot easier to be there."

"What about Isaac, the cook?"

He thought for a moment. "I remember the guy who ran the dining hall. I'm not sure if his name was Isaac. He was kinda grumpy."

"Did you know Antonio, the groundskeeper?"

Tray smiled. "He was cool. He always knew what we were up to, but he never told the others."

"You mean like when you and Mario built the fort?"

"I guess you know about that."

"Yeah, I even went inside it. You two did a good job. It's still standing."

"It wouldn't be if Antonio hadn't added a few extra two-by-fours. He never said anything to us, but we saw him carrying the wood in that direction. The next day we saw the braces he had added. Mario and I both felt bad about taking his wood to build the fort, but we didn't have any other way to get it and we didn't think he'd miss a few boards."

"Did you know that instead of saying anything, he just paid for those supplies out of his own pocket?"

"No, I didn't, but that sounds like Antonio. Now I feel even worse about taking them." He looked pensive. "Maybe I'll be able to pay him back someday."

"There wasn't much in the fort—just a couple of old blankets, a deck of cards, a notebook, and some pretty beat-up *Playboy* magazines."

Tray chuckled. "I can't believe those magazines are still there. Mario stole them from another kid and hid them in the fort so the kid wouldn't get caught with them and get into trouble. The other kid never knew who took them. They sure gave us hours of entertainment. Mario even read some of the articles. I just looked at the pictures."

"I'm glad you're doing better here than you did at DJJ. I know that was a horrible experience for you."

"I thought I was going to die, but I'm still here and a little stronger than I was before. I'm about to get my high school diploma."

"Sabre will be glad to hear that."

Tray gave JP an imploring look. "Do you think there's a chance you'll find who did this?"

"We're going to do everything we possibly can."

"If I ever get out of here, I want to be a firefighter. When I was at Wilson, Mario and I played war games, using sticks for guns. His dream was to join the service. We always said we would join together, but that's not going to happen."

"Mario's finally going to be able to do that. He turns eighteen soon and he's already set to join."

"I know. He told me to join when I get out, that he would still be there because he was making a career out of it."

JP tried not to show his surprise. "Have you had contact with Mario?"

"He writes to me sometimes. He sent me a letter not too long ago and told me he was joining the Marine Corps."

Chapter 56

Sabre sat at her desk in her office, preparing for the next morning's court cases. She was just about ready to leave when JP called.

"Where are you?" Sabre asked.

"I'm waiting for my plane. I'll board in about fifteen minutes."

"What time do you get in? I'll pick you up."

"No need. My car is at the airport."

"That's right. I forgot. Why don't you come by on your way home? We can grab a quick bite to eat."

"And miss out on good airplane food?"

"That would be a real loss. Even I cook better than what you get on a plane."

"I'll be there," JP said.

"How's Tray?"

"Happy to be out of San Bernardino. He likes the conservation camp, as much as anyone can like to be imprisoned, I guess. He's hopeful. Even talked about being a firefighter when he gets out."

"That's a good sign. With any luck, we'll get to the bottom of this mystery and get him released before he's too old to enjoy his life. He's already spent too much time there."

"There's something else you should know."

"What's that?" Sabre asked.

"He's had contact with Mario—just letters as far as I know."

"Mario?"

"Yes, he received a letter from him about a week ago."

"So after Oscar and Barlowe were arrested?"

"Yes, but Tray seemed genuinely surprised by the information about the bodies being found. When I told him, his reaction was that maybe we'd find the real killer. He still maintains that he knows nothing about it. I didn't give him too much information, but I assured him that we were investigating."

"Did Mario say anything when you talked to him about having contact with Tray?"

"No, but in all fairness I never came right out and asked him."

"How much contact have they had?"

"I don't know. Once Tray realized that we didn't know anything about it, he kind of clammed up. I got the impression that he was afraid he might say the wrong thing."

"Like maybe implicate Mario?"

"Maybe."

"I'm about done here at the office. I'll run by Wilson and see Mario."

"Why don't you wait until I get there?"

"I'll be fine. I'm going to see him. What could go wrong?"

***

Twilight was setting in as Sabre arrived at Wilson Group Home. She saw Cheryl walking to her car as Sabre got out of hers. They passed in the parking lot and greeted one another. Sabre wondered if she was the killer. She saw Antonio in the distance putting away tools in the shed. She wondered the same thing about him.

Jesse's kind face and friendly smile greeted Sabre when she went inside. "Hello, Ms. Brown, I thought you might be stopping by."

"I hope it's okay. I would actually like to talk to Mario if I could."

"He's in the dining hall, but they should be about

done. Let's go see."

Jesse Alder had been totally cooperative, which took away some of the suspicion from him. *Or did it? Maybe that was part of his game.*

Isaac was barking orders about cleanup when they entered the dining room. *He always seems so angry,* she thought, which made him a more likely candidate.

Mario picked up his tray and walked toward the trashcan by the kitchen. He scraped the leftovers off his plate and into the trash, placed his dishes and silverware in the appropriate bins, and stacked his tray. As he walked back toward the door where Sabre was standing, he patted a younger boy with a sad face on the shoulder and smiled at him.

"Ms. Brown would like to talk to you, if you don't mind," Jesse said to Mario. "She's investigating the murders that Oscar and Barlowe have been accused of and would like your cooperation. Just so you know, you're not obligated to talk to her and you don't need to give us any reason if you choose not to. What would you like to do?"

"I'd like to help if I can."

Jesse said to Sabre, "You know where the interview room is. Please let me know when you're ready to leave."

Sabre chatted with Mario about his plans to join the military as they walked. Once inside the room, they sat on the sofa.

"Mario, have you had any contact with Tray Copley since he left here?"

He looked puzzled for a second. "Yes, why?"

"I didn't realize you two had remained friends."

"Yes, we were pretty tight when he was here, even though it was for only a few months. He used to call me when he was in the foster home, but we started writing letters when he was sent to prison. I feel bad for him, especially now that I'm joining the service. We had planned to go together."

Sabre must not have hidden her concern because Mario said, "Did I do something wrong?"

"No, not at all. There's nothing wrong with keeping in touch with a friend. I just didn't know how close you were. Did Tray ever tell you anything about Glen Irving?"

"He never told me what happened exactly. He didn't have to. All of us here know what happens. Most of us don't feel the need to explain. When new kids come, they're either sad or angry at the chomo. We try to cut them some slack. For most of us it gets better with time and therapy. Some like Jacob and Oscar stay angry. I guess that's how they cope."

Sabre was impressed with this young man's insight and empathy. "You used the term *chomo*. Is that how Tray referred to Irving?"

"No, he called him a goof, but I think he learned that from Cheryl. She says it all the time."

"What term do the other kids here use?"

"Most of the others call them chomos, but sometimes you hear the word *goof*. Like I said, I think that's because Cheryl uses it."

"What do the other adults here call them?"

Mario thought for a second. "I don't recall any of the others calling them anything. They don't really talk about the molesters. Except for the therapists.— They usually say 'abuser' or 'perpetrator,' or they call them by name."

Sabre thanked him for talking to her and congratulated him on his new adventure. They both stood and walked toward the door.

"By the way," Sabre said. "How did you know where Tray was located?"

"Dr. Deb gave me the address."

Chapter 57

JP and Sabre swapped stories about their day as they sat entwined on the sofa. He was tired from his trip and she was glad to have him home. He had only been gone overnight, but she always felt safer when he was in town. She always tried to put up a brave front—something she would never admit to him.

"Tray looks good. When he went in there, he was about as big as the little end of nothin'. But he's all grown up, nearly six-foot tall I'd guess, and he's been working out."

"I expect fitness training is part of what they do there at the camp."

"He didn't get as fit as he is in a couple of months. He must've started at DJJ, probably to protect himself, but there's always someone bigger and badder in those places."

"I'm sure his size has helped him feel a little more secure."

"He's definitely no longer the runt of the litter."

Sabre didn't respond. They sat in silence for a few minutes until JP said, "Are you okay? You seem a little down."

"Do you know what's really frustrating about this whole thing?"

"Besides not being able to solve this case?"

"That's the thing. Even if we solve this case and we have new evidence, it may not be enough to free Tray."

"I don't understand. If we can prove that he didn't do it, we can't get him out?"

"In California, if you're given a fair trial and are found guilty, it's not enough to show there is new evidence that defines your innocence. There is a bill before the Assembly right now, *SB-1134,* which will allow the defense to submit a writ of habeas corpus on the basis of new evidence that is credible and would more likely than not change the verdict in the trial. It has already passed the Senate. Most of the other states already have such a law, but this is one where California is way behind."

"So what do you have to prove?"

"We have to prove some technical reason why Tray didn't get a fair trial."

"Such as?"

"Such as ineffective counsel."

"But you did all you could do."

"If Firmstone hadn't been on the case with me, it might fly because of my lack of experience. I don't care about how it looks on me; we'll do whatever it takes. We have to get him out of there." Sabre reached for her notepad on the coffee table and started making notes. "I need you to research Judge Palatini. I've heard some rumors, but I don't know how much is based in fact. Maybe we could show bias or something. I'm not even sure we could do anything with the information, but check his record for 707 hearings and see how many children he sent to adult court. There have been a lot of complaints about that from other delinquency attorneys. And while you're at it, see if you can find anything personal on him that might lead to something we can use somehow. I don't know what it might be, so find anything you can."

"You got it. Anything else?"

"See if you can find anything on DDA Marge Benson. I don't know what that might be either, but we need something to get a new trial for Tray."

"I'm just a dumb cowboy, but I don't understand. It's difficult to believe that Tray may have to remain incarcerated even if he's actually innocent. There is something wrong with a system where proof of innocence isn't enough to get you out of prison."

"It might help if we can prove that someone else killed Irving, but even that isn't always enough." Sabre leaned back in JP's arms again. "You know, if Tray did block everything out, I wonder if it would've helped him remember if we had had him hypnotized. Maybe he could have recovered his memories."

"You have to stop second-guessing yourself. You did all you could back then. Besides, hypnotism isn't all that reliable."

"That's what Dr. Bell said when I suggested we have Oscar hypnotized. He didn't trust anyone else doing it, but admitted he was not proficient in it himself. He was afraid it would be detrimental to Oscar's recovery."

"There you go. He's the man. Now tell me about your visit with Mario."

Sabre informed JP that Mario admitted, without any qualms, to his contact with Tray. "But the curious thing is that he got Tray's address from Dr. Deb."

"That sparks a few questions."

"Yeah, like how would she know where Tray was? Why would she give the address to Mario? And has she had contact with Tray herself?"

"I should have checked the visitors' log when I was there. I don't know how I missed doing that, except Tray said he had had no visitors at the camp. We should check the log at DJJ also."

"They wouldn't have given you the information anyway. I'll get that for us." Sabre sat forward out of JP's embrace and looked directly at him.

"What's the matter?" he asked.

"Nothing. It's just that when I went to Wilson today I saw all the 'suspects' on our list, and I saw them in a very suspicious light. Cheryl was just leaving as I came and I thought, 'It could be you.' And sweet Antonio was going into his shed and I thought, 'Are you the killer?' Same with Jesse, Isaac, and Mario. I even thought Callum, who walked me to my car because it was almost dark, might be the killer. Then I realized that it couldn't be all of them. We have to figure a way to narrow it down."

"Which we are trying to do," JP said.

"I know." Sabre fanned both hands out in front of her as if she had an Aha! moment. "What if we're wrong about that?"

"You mean, none of them did it? Because we've explored that too."

"No, I mean what if they are all involved? Isn't it odd that every clue and every person leads us back to the group home? That the group home is within six miles of all the bodies? And even though everyone has been cooperative, no one seems to have seen anything or heard anything that might help with the investigation."

JP looked at her with suspicious bewilderment.

"What?" she said.

"It's not like you to have conspiracy theories."

"I know, but think about it. How could there be three murders—"

"Maybe four," JP interjected. "If Carl Murray, Jacob's goof, is the other body."

"Maybe four, involving all those boys, and no one knows anything? How is that possible?"

Chapter 58

JP sat at his desk in front of his computer checking record after record of every person who had a connection to Mary Ellen Wilson Group Home. He ran background checks on every therapist, teacher, and volunteer who would've had contact with Tray, Oscar, or Barlowe, some for the second or third time. He even investigated the UPS man who delivered regularly to Wilson.

He called Sabre and left a message reminding her that he needed the visitor logs at DJJ and at Northern to see if Tray had had any visitors over the last three years. Then he continued with his research, this time concentrating on DDA Marge Benson and Judge Thomas Palatini.

Louie, JP's beagle, dashed up to him with a Frisbee in his mouth. JP stood up and stretched. He had been sitting longer than he should have without a break, so he took Louie outside. For the next ten minutes, he and Louie played catch with the Frisbee, but JP couldn't get his mind off of his investigation.

He went back inside, poured a cup of coffee, and positioned himself in front of his whiteboard. He had so many suspects he decided to approach his board differently than the one at Sabre's office. He made sticky notes for each of the residents who had lived at the group home since Tray's case began or for anyone who was directly involved with a murder victim. They included Jacob, Mario, Tray, Oscar, and Barlowe. He had sticky notes for all the group home staff for that same time period: Jesse, Callum, Cheryl, Isaac, and Antonio. There were more sticky notes for the three therapists. After investigating the rest of the adjunct staff, teachers, and volunteers, he couldn't find any reason to continue with any of them.

He created two categories. The first category he labeled "Dead Goofs." Even though these men had been murdered, JP couldn't get himself to call them victims. As far as he was concerned, the boys were the real victims. The second was "Goof-Killer Leader." The other possible scenarios were that the defendants did it themselves on their own and copied Tray or that an outside copycat had done it. JP had already investigated possible family members of Oscar and Barlowe and had come up dry, which didn't surprise him since it was highly unlikely that random people with no connection to the group home killed all three men.

Then he placed the sticky notes of the names of anyone who didn't have a good alibi for at least one of the murders into the first group. Since the exact time of death for Sammy Everton wasn't determined, that left only the time frame for when Glen Irving and Roy Harris were murdered. JP excluded the defendants for this round, which left Cheryl and Dr. Deb. Dr. Deb was home alone when both men were killed. Her husband traveled a lot with the ministry, and he was out of town on both occasions. And Cheryl, who lived by herself, was home alone with only her cats to vouch for her.

The next category, "Goof-Killer Leader," included Cheryl, Jesse, Callum, Mario, Antonio, Dr. Deb, and Dr. Bell. JP excluded Dr. Prasad because he had had very little contact with Tray. Isaac was unlikely because none of the boys liked him enough to follow him. Cheryl and Dr. Deb had risen on JP's "most likely suspect" list. They fit on both lists, so not only could they have led the goof-killer organization, but they were available to assist since it seemed unlikely any of these boys could've pulled off the murders alone.

The phone rang and JP picked it up. "Hi, Greg. Do

you have something new for me?"

"You're all business today."

"Sorry, I'm knee-deep in this investigation."

"Maybe the question should be: do you have anything for me?" Nelson said.

"No, just a lot of dead ends."

"I called to tell you that you were right."

"Of course I was right. What about?"

"The other body we found is Carl Murray. So spill. What exactly do you know?"

JP sighed. "Murray molested another resident of Mary Ellen Wilson Group Home."

"Are you kidding me? Who was Murray's victim?"

"He's a seventeen-year-old boy named Jacob Lowe. His dependency case is about five years old, so he would've been about twelve. He still lives at Wilson."

"Anything else?"

"There's something very wrong with this whole thing, Nelson. Too much doesn't add up."

"I know. We're looking beyond these boys, but we still think they were involved."

"There's definitely something beyond what these kids are capable of. By the way, have they narrowed the time of death on Murray yet?"

"Determining his identity helped with the time of death. Based on what the entomologists, the coroner, and the witnesses have reported as to when he was last seen, we've pinpointed the death on or around five years ago."

"He was definitely around the first part of April that year because the accusations on the petition are for April 2."

"Good to know."

"Thanks, Nelson, for the info. That's a big help."

"How's that? What else do you know?"

"Nothing for certain. I'll let you know when I get

something concrete."

"Don't hold out on me, Torn."

They hung up, and JP checked his notes and wrote out a quick timeline. Then he went to the board and removed four of the names—those who were not involved with the group home when Carl Murray, Jacob's goof, was killed. Then he went back on the computer and continued to research the remaining two suspects but was unsuccessful in finding anything that might help.

JP had reached a frustration point when Sabre called. He took a deep breath and smiled. Hearing from her was a welcomed break.

"Hey, kid," JP said.

"I only have a second, but I have the information you wanted on Tray's visitors. His mother was there three times while he was in San Bernardino and she has not been to Northern. Each time, June Longe, the foster mother, transported her. I'm sure it wasn't easy for the mother to get there on her own. Tray's sister, Shanisha, never came. On two other occasions the foster parents went without the mother. My guess is that his mother was probably in no shape to go. She's been in and out of rehab since he left. The only other visitor he had was his therapist, a Dr. J. Williams."

"Is that 'J' as in an initial or a name?"

"It's an initial."

"How many times did the doctor go?"

Sabre didn't answer right away, but JP could hear her counting. "Five times," she said. "Looks like every six months, probably some kind of evaluation or something. I'm not sure what they do there, but I'll check to see if there is some paperwork I should be reviewing since I'm still the attorney of record."

"Has the doctor been to Northern?"

"Just once."

"And Mario, or anyone else from Wilson, has not been to visit him?"

"No. No one else has visited. I'll email you the paperwork."

"Thanks, and if you get any reports from Dr. Williams, send those too, please."

"Will do, but it isn't likely it'll be today. It's already late. By the way, have you learned anything about Judge Palatini?"

"For what it's worth, Palatini had a minor grandson who was charged with armed robbery. He won his 707 hearing and was tried in juvenile court but lost. He maintains his innocence and the judge has been his biggest champion. The judge stated publicly that a jury would've found him innocent and the kid should've had a jury trial. He wasn't slamming the judge who made the ruling but rather the system."

"There's been a lot of scuttlebutt here at juvenile court that Palatini has never ruled for a minor to stay in juvenile on a 707, but I don't know if it's an exaggeration. I know he's conservative, but I don't know that he's unfair. I have a friend in the clerk's office who has agreed to get me that information, so we'll see. They're ready for me in court. I gotta go." She hung up.

JP returned to his computer and began searching for Dr. J. Williams. He found Joseph Williams, PhD in Staten Island, NY; Jaqueline in Roseville, California; Jessica in Woodland Hills, California; and another fifteen or so possibilities. He Googled the doctors who were local but quickly eliminated the majority of them for one reason or another. He had two left who were possibilities: Jessica of Woodland Hills and J.B. Williams of Los Angeles. He continued to dig and discovered that J.B. was educated at McGill University in Montreal and was an internationally famous, renowned expert in hypnotism and had served time in the Marine Corps. Jessica received her PhD from the University of California, San Diego. She was a member of the American Psychological Association and the Society for the Scientific Study of Sexuality. Her expertise was child abuse.

Next he researched Under the Same Sun, the program in Africa that worked with the albinos. Dr. John Bell was a regular, loyal participant of the program. There were photos of the good doctor working with children at the school.

JP picked up his phone and started making phone calls. What he found proved to be very informative.

Louie walked up and laid his head on JP's leg. JP reached down and petted him. "Hey, boy. Let's watch a movie."

JP retrieved the flash drive of the Albertsons' security video when Tray was in the store. He had probably watched it forty times when they were preparing for Tray's trial. He was hoping he might see something he had missed in light of all he had learned. Maybe one of the other "suspects" would show up on the video. He ran it through, stopping frequently to zero in on different people. When he saw Irving, he blew it up and looked at him from every possible angle, and then he saw something. "See that, Louie! How did I miss it before?"

He called and left Sabre a message as to where he was going.

Chapter 59

JP opened the door to Dr. Bell's office to find the doctor standing behind his desk, which was off to the right of the room. He had several stacks of files in front of him.

"Come on in," Bell said.

"Thanks for seeing me so late." JP stepped inside, leaving the door about three-quarters of the way open.

"No problem. You know I'm glad to help these boys."

JP found something uncomfortable about the stance the doctor had. He couldn't see his right hand. JP stopped. His first reaction was to reach for his shoulder holster, but before he could, Bell raised his right hand, exposing his FNS9 semi-automatic 9mm pistol. The doctor's hand was steady and he looked all too confident for JP not to take him seriously. "Keep your hands where I can see them. And don't underestimate me. I may be short, but I'm no slouch. I did my time in the U.S. Marine Corps in a special psychological ops unit that few people knew existed. We had extensive combat training as well as PsyOp training. I will kill you if I need to."

"Okay," JP said. "It's your rodeo."

"I want you to remove your gun very slowly with your left hand and lay it on the floor."

JP did as he was told.

"Kick it over there." He nodded to the side of the room farthest from the door.

JP kicked the gun, and it stopped as it slid into the wall about ten feet from him.

"Now, slowly sit down in that chair over there."

As JP sat down, Bell walked around to the front of

the desk and leaned against it, positioning himself about six feet from JP. The door was still open, but JP didn't look at it for fear Bell would close it.

"I know you've been looking into my past."

"I don't know that much," JP said.

"It would be only a matter of time before you do. You already know my name is 'Williams,' not 'Bell.'"

JP's phone rang.

"Don't answer that."

"Okay." When it stopped ringing, JP said, "Are you really a psychologist?"

"Yes. Dr. John Williams is a graduate of McGill University in Montreal. Dr. Bell had to fix a few documents, but he's just as much a psychologist."

"What is it that John Williams has done that John Bell doesn't want anyone to know?" JP thought that as long as the doctor was speaking in the third person, he may as well too.

"I was ridding Canada of child abusers."

"The way you have been here?"

Bell smiled. "I've been concerned about Ms. Brown. When she gets her teeth into something, she doesn't let go, does she?"

"No, she doesn't." JP watched for any clue that Bell wasn't fully focused so JP might catch him off guard, but so far he hadn't seen any. JP's phone rang again.

Bell shook his head.

"It's probably Sabre, and if I don't answer it soon, she'll call the cops. She knows I'm here."

"What else does she know?"

"Only that I had some suspicions. She doesn't have any specifics."

"Answer it and if you do anything funny, I'll have to shoot you, and then I'll go find her and shoot her. Put it on speaker."

JP caught the call on the last ring. "Hi, Sabre."

"Hi, are you okay?"

"Sure, I just finished up with the doctor and I'm going to stop on the way home for a beer, a good ol' Shiner Bock."

"Okay. Don't be too late."

He hung up.

"What kind of beer is Shiner Bock?"

"It's a Texas beer, the very best."

"Slide your phone across the floor over there by your gun."

JP slid his phone away, and asked, "Why did you do it?"

"They got what they deserved. They were walking around free to molest other children. I had to stop them."

"But you let Tray go to prison for it."

"I tried to stop it. I did everything I could."

"Except tell the truth. Were you going to let Oscar and Barlowe get convicted as well?"

"Only if I had to. It's for the greater good."

JP tried to come up with a plan, but the best idea he had was to keep Bell talking until Sabre found help. He just hoped she wouldn't try to come herself. All of a sudden he was concerned that she might, but the clues he gave her sent a pretty strong message. JP was sure that he could keep Bell talking. The doctor seemed to enjoy the interchange almost as if he were proud of what he had done and finally had the opportunity to talk about it.

"Did you kill the men or did you have the boys do it?"

Bell scowled at him. "I wouldn't do that. What kind of an animal do you think I am?"

JP still wasn't certain which question he had answered. He waited for Bell to explain.

"Don't you understand? These boys needed justice and closure. This way, they got both."

"How did you get them to do it?"

"Are you not listening to me?" His voice was louder. "I wouldn't let those boys take a life at their age and have to live with that forever. I know what that's like. I'm trying to stop their suffering, not add to it."

"But won't they suffer in prison? I know Tray is miserable."

"You don't get it. They're already in prison in their minds. There is no prison worse than that. The only thing that helps is to see their predator get his due. If the justice system works, the abusers go to prison. If it doesn't, the goofs must die."

"You said you knew what it was like. Were you young the first time you killed someone?" JP knew he had to keep him talking.

"I was fifteen, but that doesn't matter. After a while, it gets easier. But I have never killed anyone who didn't deserve it."

"Until now. We both know you're going to have to kill me to shut me up. Besides, you wouldn't tell me everything if you didn't already plan to get rid of me."

"Sometimes it's about survival. I learned that in Vietnam."

"Tell me, Dr. Bell, why did you write *GOOF* on their foreheads?"

"So the world would know who and what they were."

"Did you write it, or did the boys?"

"I did. I wanted them to do it, but then they would've had to see their abusers and I didn't want to put them through that. But if they had seen them dead, I think that might've been good for them. But I wasn't sure that I could control them enough to keep them quiet about it."

"And the notebooks with their handwriting? They were samples for you?"

"Yes, I traced them right onto the bodies."

"How did you get the boys to write in the notebooks and not tell? Did you hypnotize them?"

"You could say that. It actually took a little more mind control than your ordinary hypnotism, but I still didn't make them do anything they didn't want to. None of them wanted to kill them, except maybe Jacob. He might have been able to. Even Oscar, as angry as he is, didn't have it in him. But they all wanted to see them pay for what they did. The shame children suffer when they have been molested can be almost unbearable. It can affect every part of their lives. Some of them never get over the anger and the shame, and they end up hurting other children. It's a vicious cycle. I helped to cleanse some of that."

"It sounds like you know this from experience. Were you molested when you were young?"

"No."

"But someone you were close to was?"

"We had been living in Oregon when our mother died. We were nine years old. They sent my twin brother and me to live with my father in Canada. He was a horrible man who called my brother a freak because he was albino. He treated him like he wasn't even human. My father claimed the only thing my brother was good for was to satisfy his urges, and so he used him. I tried to stop him, but he would just knock me around."

"Until?" JP asked.

"One day my brother couldn't take it any longer and he hanged himself. My father just laughed, so I grabbed an iron skillet and hit him on the head. Then I buried him in the woods."

"That explains a lot."

"Don't try to placate me. It won't work."

JP was silent for a few minutes.

"There are some statistics to show that when a child's abuser is punished, the victim is less likely to offend himself. I believe if the abuser is dead, the numbers will be even better."

"Really?"

"The stats are from such a small test sample that it's not really a valid test, so I've been collecting data myself for over ten years now. My biggest concern is that I won't live long enough to prove my theory because we have to wait for the boys to grow up and go out into the world. And then I have to keep in touch with them so I can see how they end up. I have records stored away and I've written the study into my trust, so they'll be shared with the scientific world and eventually the public."

"Are you killing these men as a part of an experiment?"

"No. I'm killing them because they need to be stopped, so they can't hurt anyone else; because their victims need relief; and because they don't deserve to live. Having material for my study is just a bonus."

JP decided to try again to placate him. "I can see how the study would be an important tool."

"Don't try to play mind games with me. I know them all."

"I'm not saying you're going about this the right way. In fact, I think what you're doing is about a half a bubble off plumb, but that doesn't mean the results wouldn't be worthwhile. I can see how it would benefit those boys to see that justice was done. So how are you going to get out of this alive and not go to prison so you can finish what you started?"

Chapter 60

As soon as Sabre hung up the phone with JP, she called Deputy Sheriff Ernie Madrigal's cell phone.

"JP's in trouble," she said.

"Where is he?"

"He's at a Dr. Bell's office in El Cajon." She gave him the address.

"I'm on my way." She heard a car door open and close and the car engine start. "Does this have anything to do with a case you're working on?"

"Yes, the goof-killer cases," she said.

"What kind of trouble is he in?"

"I think he's being held hostage. I'm not one hundred percent certain, but I know there's something seriously wrong."

"Why?"

"He left me a message earlier saying he was going to Dr. Bell's office. I called him back and he didn't answer. When I called him the second time, he answered and said he was at the doctor's office, but he was going to stop and get a Shiner Bock on the way home. He would never drink a Shiner Bock or even joke about it. We had an old case once where I was held hostage by a gunman who drank Shiner Bock. I'm sure he was trying to tell me he was in the same predicament. Oh, and when he answered the phone he said, 'Hi, Sabre.' He never does that. He always says, 'Hey, kid.'"

"I'm about seven minutes away." Ernie asked Sabre a lot of questions about the layout of Bell's office. She told him everything she could remember about it. "Is this Greg Nelson's case?" he asked.

"Yes, it is."

"I'll call Nelson and let him know."

"I'll see you there," Sabre said.

"No! Do not come!"

"I won't go into the building, but I'm going." She hung up.

***

The sound of a door closing gave JP hope, but it didn't seem to deter the doctor. Bell glanced at his clock on the wall behind JP. Even though his glance was very quick, JP considered trying to take him out, but he was too far away. JP was sure Bell knew exactly how far to stay from him—just out of arm's reach.

"It's the custodian," Bell said, "always right on time, but don't get too excited. He won't come in here. He's been instructed to not enter when there's a light on. He understands the importance of privacy." Then, almost as if the doctor could read JP's mind, he said, "Don't bother to make noise because he's deaf. And if he were to see something, I'd have to kill him too. So, if you don't want an innocent man to die, you'll just ignore him."

JP thought he heard another sound, but Bell didn't react. He hoped it was because Bell's hearing wasn't that good either, or maybe it was nothing. He prepared himself just in case. He sat up a little straighter, ready to plunge forward if he needed to but without looking like he was about to attack. He had to keep him talking.

"I know you killed Carl Murphy. Was that your first?"

"My first in San Diego." His eyes took on a haunted look. "That was a tough one."

"Why's that?"

"Jacob wasn't an easy subject. He was all over the place and it was difficult to get him to concentrate. I was afraid he'd remember things, but he never did."

"You had good control over Tray, didn't you?"

"He was my easiest because he tried to do what he was told. He's a good kid. It's a shame he had to go to prison."

JP wanted to punch him, but he kept his cool. Instead he asked, "Did you kill them all where you buried them?"

"Yes, moving them would've been too risky."

"How did you get them there?" JP asked, observing that Dr. Bell seemed to be enjoying the conversation.

"I recorded all the sessions with the boys. I'd hypnotize them and then have them role play. I got a lot of good material to use. Then I pieced together the words I needed to lure the goofs to where I wanted them."

"Did you take the boys with you?"

"No."

"Not even Tray?"

"Irving was very suspicious, but I knew he couldn't resist if he saw Tray. Some of them are like that. They get real attached to their victims, telling themselves that they only do this because they love them. Irving was like that." Bell spoke in a very even tone as he explained. Then he spat out the words, "That guy was sick."

"So, that's why you took him to Albertsons? So Irving could see him? But you had messed with Tray's mind so he wouldn't remember anything."

"Of course. He could hardly even talk about Irving. I knew how devastating it would be if he had to face him. As far as Tray knew, we were at therapy."

"And Tray was in the store with you, not Irving."

"How did you figure that out?"

"You put on sunglasses, a baseball cap, and you

covered your 'Semper Fi' tattoo with makeup or something. But it was hot and some of the concealer was gone. On the security footage it looked like a dirt smudge, but when I magnified it, I could see the 'Fi' and I remembered seeing you with a tattoo that day in Sabre's office. It was unusual and it stuck in my mind."

"Good memory."

"You were very careful to never look at a camera. How did you know where the cameras were?"

"Reconnaissance. A good Marine always knows his surroundings. These things take careful planning."

"Where was Irving? I never saw him on the video."

"He didn't come inside the store, but we passed him when we came out. I made sure Tray didn't see him."

"And then after you killed Irving, you put the clothes on him that you were wearing just in case someone saw you."

"You're pretty good at your job, JP. Too bad you can't use the information you have." He glanced for just a split second at the clock. "It's been fun chatting with you, but it's time. The custodian will be gone soon and the building will be empty." Bell took a small step closer to JP, but he remained outside JP's reach.

Chapter 61

Detectives Nelson and DuBois, an old colleague of JP's, met Ernie outside of the doctor's office building. Ernie explained there was only one way into the doctor's office and there were no windows. They made a plan to reach the door without being heard. If the door was closed, Nelson and Ernie would go in guns-a-blazing. If the door was open and they could see what was happening, Ernie would be the designated shooter after they tried to distract Bell. Ernie had a flashlight on his belt to use if he needed it to get Bell's eye off his target. Plan B was to call in a swat team, depending on what they saw when they got to the office.

They walked up to the building and opened the door, guns in hands, in case Bell was not in his office. When they opened the door, they saw the custodian emptying a wastebasket into a large bin. He had his back to the door and didn't turn around when they entered. They circled and positioned themselves just as the custodian turned around. The man recoiled in fear, throwing his arms up in the air and then standing there speechless.

"Is anyone else here?" Ernie whispered.

The custodian shrugged and then pointed to his ears with his index fingers without lowering his hands. Then he waved his finger back and forth at the same time he shook his head from side to side.

"Can you hear me?" Ernie asked.

He shook his head again from side to side. Ernie asked him more questions, moving the fingers on his right hands in a poor attempt to spell in sign language. The man still did not understand.

DuBois stepped forward. "I'll take care of this."

"Don't tell me you sign, DuBois," Nelson said.

"Of course not." He took a pad of paper and a pen out of his pocket and wrote on the paper, *Are you deaf?*

The man nodded affirmatively.

He wrote, *Is Dr. Bell still in his office?*

He nodded again.

Is anyone else in the building?

He shook his head no.

Where is Dr. Bell's office?

He pointed straight down the hallway, then turned his hand sideways and pointed to the right. Then he held up his fingers until he had three fingers in the air.

Down the hallway to the end, turn right, third door?

He nodded again.

Is the door on the left or the right?

He raised his right hand.

Thank you. Go outside. Get away from the building.

Nelson opened the door for the custodian, held onto it while the man exited, and closed it softly behind him. Then they worked their way down the hallway with their guns in position. They sneaked up to the open door. Ernie and DuBois were on the right against the wall. Nelson was across the small hallway. He kept creeping forward until he could see inside the room. All he could see was JP sitting in a chair, but he could hear voices. He turned back, pointed, and mouthed the word, *JP*.

Ernie moved all the way up to the door and peeked in the crack. He could see Bell leaning against the desk with a gun in his hand. From his view the door was blocking JP. He listened to the conversation. He heard Bell say, "The custodian will be gone soon and the building will be empty."

***

JP hoped he could distract Bell in some way. Bell was talking about leaving, which meant he was either going to kill JP before he left or they would walk out together and he'd try to kill him somewhere else. JP thought he might have a chance to catch Bell off guard as they walked out. On the other hand, he would likely have his back to Bell, who'd have his gun fairly close to JP's head. Then JP saw movement in the hallway. He thought he saw a glimpse of Nelson out of the corner of his eye, but he didn't dare look to confirm it.

Just then a black flashlight flew across the room to the back wall. Bell instinctively turned in that direction. Ernie and Nelson burst into the room and Ernie fired a shot just as Bell aimed his gun towards him. JP dived to his left to avoid the gunfire and to retrieve his gun. Bell shot, but he was already going down and his bullet went over Nelson's head. Bell dropped to the floor. Nelson kicked his gun out of the way. By then, JP had picked up his own gun and DuBois was by his side. It was over. DuBois reached his hand down to help him up.

"Thanks," JP said, as he stood.

"You okay, Torn?" Nelson called out.

"I am now."

Ernie called 9-1-1. He and Nelson knelt at Bell's side and Nelson cuffed him. Blood was oozing out of his chest.

"Grab that towel on the file cabinet over there," Nelson said.

JP asked, "Is he alive?"

"So far, which means Madrigal needs to go back to the shooting range," Nelson said.

Ernie returned with the towel and applied pressure

to the wound. Within seconds, the blue towel was spotted with clouds of purple as it filled with blood. "I took him down with one shot. Saved your sorry ass," Ernie said, as he continued to render first aid.

"You were less than ten feet away," Nelson said. "You'd have looked pretty sorry if you had missed."

Bell groaned, his face contorted in agony. Nelson asked him a few questions, but he didn't respond.

"I hope he lives," JP said, looking directly at Detective Nelson. "It'll be a lot easier for all of us to prove what really happened in the goof-killer cases. Besides, I'd like to see him get a little taste of what Tray has suffered for the last three years for the crimes this idiot committed."

"He's our killer?"

"At least four that I know here in the U.S., maybe more, and his own father years ago. And I'm pretty sure there were some goofs in Canada he murdered."

Within minutes, sirens sounded. DuBois went out front to lead the police and paramedics inside.

Four firefighters entered and approached Bell. Nelson was explaining the situation when two paramedics entered with a gurney. Nelson, JP, and Ernie stepped out of their way and let them work.

The DA came in just as they loaded Bell onto the gurney. Nelson attached the handcuffs to the stretcher and then joined the DA and the lieutenant who had just arrived. JP came up and tapped Nelson on the arm, and said, "Thanks, bud."

"You can thank Sabre, Torn. You want to come to the station and give me your statement?"

Just then Ernie and DuBois approached. "Sure," JP said, "but I need to call Sabre first and let her know I'm okay."

"She's probably outside waiting for you," Ernie said. "I told her not to come, but she's pretty stubborn."

"I'd better get out there."

"You've been off the force for over ten years, McCloud, and we're still saving your ass," DuBois teased.

"No one has called me that since I've been off the force until I saw you the other day, DuBois. Let it go before you get others calling me that."

"Whatever you say, McCloud."

JP shook his head.

"Are you sure you're okay?" Ernie asked.

"I can't tell you how happy I was to see the cavalry show up. Thanks, guys."

"How happy are you, McCloud?" DuBois asked.

"Don't encourage him," Nelson said, raising his voice. "You know he's going to give us one of those hick JPisms."

JP grinned, pushed his hat up with his index finger, and said, "I'm as happy as a 'coon in a cornfield with the dogs all tied up."

Nelson smacked him on the back. "Get out of here, Torn."

JP walked out the front door and spotted Sabre almost immediately standing back on the sidewalk. He started toward her, but before he could get there, she ran toward him. She threw her arms around him and held on. "I heard the gunshot. Are you okay?"

"I'm finer than frog fur."

She let go of the embrace and stepped back. "You're not hurt, are you?"

"Not a bit."

Then she smacked him playfully, but with a little more force than she meant to, across his upper arm.

"What's that for?"

"For coming here without backup, and for scaring me half to death."

"I really didn't expect to encounter what I did. I

thought I might get a little information that backed up the lies I had uncovered." He met Sabre's gaze and he kissed her. "Thanks for figuring out my cryptic message and for calling Ernie."

"I'm just glad you're okay," she said. They walked toward their cars. "Want to go get that Shiner Bock now?"

Chapter 62

Oscar, looking a little nervous, sat next to Sabre at the defense table. Sabre reassured him. Judge Jon Charles Trapnell was on the bench. He had returned a week earlier after a three-year bout with cancer, which he managed to beat. Sabre was more than thrilled to see he had returned, not only because he was physically well, but because he was a reasonable, fair judge and she liked him.

Deputy District Attorney Benson requested that the charges be dropped without prejudice.

Sabre stood up. "Your Honor, please dismiss this case *with* prejudice. This young man has been through enough. He doesn't need this hanging over his head. He's been sitting in juvenile hall for weeks for something he did not do. While incarcerated, he was teased, threatened, and beaten up, and he feared for his life. The DA has a full confession from the perpetrator and is fully aware that Oscar had no involvement of any kind with the exception of writing some words in a notebook, which he was not even aware he was doing."

"Were the parents notified of this hearing?" the judge asked.

"Yes, they were, Your Honor," Benson said.

"As you know, Your Honor, Oscar was a dependent of the court when this case was filed. I've filed a motion with the court to reinstate his dependency if this case is dismissed. Department Four will hear the case this morning. The social worker is waiting outside as well as the director of Mary Ellen Wilson Group Home. The administrator from Wilson is willing to take Oscar back upon his release from the

Hall and after his dependency case has been heard."

"I'll see that the minor is delivered to the social worker," the bailiff said.

Judge Trapnell said, "This case is dismissed *with* prejudice."

Sabre turned to Oscar. "It's over."

"What did that mean about the prejudice?" Oscar asked.

"That means these charges cannot be filed against you again."

For just a second Oscar looked like a little boy as he smiled at Sabre. Then the smile turned more to a look of smugness. Teenage Oscar was back—always the tough guy.

"The bailiff will take you to the Hall and get you released, and then he'll bring you to the lobby so we can do your dependency hearing," Sabre said. "When that is done Jesse will transport you back to Wilson."

Sabre waited until the bailiff escorted Oscar out the back door and then she left the courtroom, passing Roberto on her way out. She gave Roberto the thumbs up. He smiled. Then Sabre whispered to him, "Ask for the dismissal 'with prejudice' on Barlowe's case. The judge just gave it to me. You should get it too."

Sabre met Bob and they walked down the hallway to Department Four. The social worker was there with County Counsel Canedy. Jesse Alder was present, but no parents were in court. Judge Hekman reinstated dependency and ordered Oscar placed in Wilson Group Home.

As soon as Roberto obtained Barlowe Carrasco's dismissal, he came to Department Four to inform Bob. Sabre and Roberto waited in the hallway for Bob to finish Barlowe's reinstatement.

"I think Barlowe learned a lesson from all this," Roberto said. "I don't think he'll ever wind up in juvie again."

"Sometimes it works that way," Sabre said. "Other times, being incarcerated gives them status and just makes them think they're tough. They often forget too quickly how much they hated being there. I worry that Oscar might fall into that second group."

"All done," Bob said, as he exited the courtroom. "Anyone for lunch?"

"You bet," Roberto said.

"Let's go to Pho's," Sabre said.

"Yes, let's Pho-Nicate," Bob said, as they walked out of the courthouse.

Chapter 63

Bob and Sabre were sitting in her office when Roberto stopped by.

"Can anyone join this party?" Roberto asked.

"You're always welcome, Q," Sabre said. "Have a seat."

Bob spoke. "I was just telling Sobs that I saw something on the news this morning about Ruben Parks, the guy who was buried by Glen Irving."

"I missed that," Roberto said. "Was he one of Bell's victims too?"

"No," Bob said, "his wife and her boyfriend killed him. They just had the bad luck of burying him too close to Glen Irving, or he might never have been found. They turned on each other in the end, and both are now going to prison. The boyfriend actually committed the act, but he couldn't have done it without her help. She lured her husband into a web like a spider."

"I'm glad Bell confessed so the boys won't be put through any more hell testifying at his trial."

"His biggest concern once he was caught was making sure his research was continued," Sabre said. "Sick man."

"There's something I don't understand," Roberto said. "I thought Bell was in Africa when two of the men were killed."

"Bell had his receptionist buy tickets for the flights under the name of Dr. John Bell, which were scheduled a day or two before each of the murders," Sabre said. "He even went so far as to have her drive him to the airport for a flight he never intended to take."

"But I thought Homeland Security said he was on

the flight."

"A Dr. John Bell was on the flight, but not the one we know. Apparently, he used that name because there was a Dr. John Bell from San Diego County who worked with the albino program. That way he had cover in Africa if anyone called about him. Dr. Williams even was kind enough to make the reservations for Dr. Bell."

"Pretty clever."

"Right after each murder he committed, he flew to Africa with a ticket under the name of Dr. John Williams."

"The guy is no dummy," Roberto said. "You've got to give him that. I'm just glad it's all over."

"Now if I can just get Tray's case dismissed," Sabre said. "I've filed every motion and writ available—mostly on the basis that we have new evidence that would change the outcome of the verdict. But if I'm granted a new trial, then I want the case back in juvenile court where it should've been heard in the first place, just in case we can't get it dismissed. We should have the ruling any day now."

"You've created quite a stir on the delinquency panel and with the public defenders. Everyone is rooting for your motion against Palatini."

"What motion was that?" Bob asked.

"She filed a motion accusing Palatini of misconduct, abusing judicial power, prejudice, and I don't know what all, but it was a great move," Roberto said. "She cited a public statement that he made when his grandson was tried in juvenile court, suggesting that the boy should've had a jury trial. That was brilliant."

"I don't get it," Bob said.

"You know how they have a 707 hearing in certain cases to determine if the minor should be tried as an adult?"

Bob nodded.

"In every single hearing, Palatini ruled against the minor and sent him or her downtown for trial."

"Every one?"

"Every one, and we're not talking a couple of cases. And he's on some committee where they're trying to make all juvenile delinquency cases jury trials. I only knew about the committee because Judge Trapnell happened to mention it to me one day, which I think he did intentionally to lead me in that direction."

"You're suggesting Palatini had an agenda?"

"Yes, which means he didn't really apply the law. I just hope his actions have been clear enough to get Tray's case moved all the way back here to juvenile court."

"And if you win," Roberto said, "every 707 hearing Palatini ruled on will be open to appeal. And that's a lot of cases in the last three years."

Elaine, Sabre's receptionist, carried in the mail. Her face wore a worried expression.

Sabre jumped up. "Is it here?"

Elaine nodded and handed her the mail.

Sabre's hand shook as she tore open the envelope. This was her last chance to get Tray out of prison. She was pretty sure he would get a new trial, although even that wasn't an absolute, but she was hoping for more than that. As she shuffled through the papers, her lips twitched. Then suddenly her eyes sparkled and a broad smile crossed her face.

"Yahoo," she shouted, and threw her fist in the air. "We got it! Tray's case is being remanded for a new trial *and* a new 707 hearing. We're going back to juvenile court."

Chapter 64

Two months later...

"In the case of Tray Copley, Judge Jon Charles Trapnell presiding," the court clerk called the case.

Tray's mother and his foster parents, June and George Longe, were in the courtroom. At the table were DDA Benson, Sabre, and Tray, who sat up straight with the dignity of an innocent man as he waited for the case to be heard. Although Sabre had briefly met with Tray earlier, she couldn't stop looking at him. He was no longer a little boy, but rather a handsome, smart, young man. He had lost his innocence and his youth, but his character was still intact. He didn't appear bitter. He just seemed anxious to start his new life. She was proud of him.

Sabre asked for a dismissal of the charges with prejudice and that the earlier conviction be set aside. As had already been agreed upon, Benson joined in her motion.

Judge Trapnell said, "Son, this was a long time coming. I am terribly disappointed in the way the system worked, or rather, didn't work for you. I hope you can put this behind you and go forward to make a better life for yourself. You have people in this courtroom who love you, people who never gave up on you, so please remember that when times get tough, and don't ever give up on yourself." The judge took a deep breath. "The motion is granted. The conviction for P.C. 187 is set aside, and the petition is dismissed. Since you are eighteen now, there's no need to re-open a dependency case. You're free to go."

Tray reached down and hugged Sabre. "Thank

you. Thank you," he said, his voice cracking. Then he ran to his mother and hugged her and his foster parents.

"Where's Shanisha?" Tray asked.

"She's outside waiting for you with JP. Come, we'll go see her."

When they got outside the courthouse Shanisha and JP were about twenty feet away. Shanisha was playing imaginary hopscotch. He called out to her, and she ran and jumped into his arms.

As he swung her around, he said, "I've missed you, Pooh Bear."

Dear Reader,

Would you like a FREE copy of a short story about JP when he was young? If so, please go to www.teresaburrell.com and sign up for my mailing list. You will automatically receive a code to retrieve the story.

What did you think of THE ADVOCATE'S HOMICIDES? I would love to hear from you. Please email me and let me know at Teresa@teresaburrell.com.

Thank you,

Teresa

ABOUT THE AUTHOR

Teresa Burrell has dedicated her life to helping children and their families. Her first career was spent teaching elementary school in the San Bernardino City School District. As an attorney, Ms. Burrell has spent countless hours working pro bono in the family court system. For twelve years she practiced law in San Diego Superior Court, Juvenile Division. She continues to advocate children's issues and write novels, many of which are inspired by actual legal cases.

Teresa Burrell is available at www.teresaburrell.com.
Like her page on Facebook at
www.facebook.com/theadvocateseries

CPSIA information can be obtained
at www.ICGtesting.com
Printed in the USA
LVHW031643060421
683591LV00001B/90

9 781938 680212